A Madcap Arrangement

COURTING *the* UNCONVENTIONAL

LAURA BEERS

1

England, 1814

Richard Kendall, Marquess of Wilton, was beginning to wonder if finding the man who had ruined his sister's life was a fool's errand. He scowled down at the crumpled scrap of paper in his hand—three names already slashed through in furious strokes. Only one remained: a final "Mr. Smith", as vague and common a name as the others. But what if this last lead was no different? What if this was just another dead end, another false hope?

With a sigh, he tossed the list onto the table and reached for his tankard of watered-down ale. The stuff was barely drinkable. He grimaced at the bitter swallow and longed for the comforts of home—his study, a crackling fire, and a glass of fine port, not this miserable excuse for ale in a dingy coaching inn on the edge of nowhere. His body ached from the journey, the jolting coach ride turning his muscles stiff and sore. When had he become so old? He was not yet thirty, yet the strain of this endless hunt weighed on him like an anvil strapped to his back.

He glanced around the hall, carefully avoiding the hopeful

glances of the barmaid weaving between the tables. Her bodice
was indecently low, her smile overly bright. It was a desperate
kind of bravado that made Richard's stomach twist with pity.
She wasn't much older than he was, but years of fending off
leering patrons had hollowed her gaze. She deserved better
than the lot she was dealt, but he had no kindness to spare
today.

The door swung open, and Mr. Crosby, the Bow Street
Runner he had hired, entered the hall. Tall, broad, and grim,
the man moved with purpose, his boots thudding against the
worn floorboards.

Without preamble, the Bow Street Runner pulled out a
chair and said, "I come bearing good news."

Richard was desperate for something—anything—that
would move this wretched search forward. "I could use some,"
he muttered.

Crosby leaned in, lowering his voice. "I spotted a man fitting
your sister's description leaving a manor on the edge of the
village this morning."

Every part of Richard snapped to attention. "Did you speak
to him?"

"I did not," Crosby replied. "I thought it would be best to
approach the manor together."

Richard shoved back his chair, the legs scraping harshly
against the floor. "We should go now," he said.

Crosby, however, remained seated, his hand tapping the
table. "Are you sure that's wise?"

"I am," Richard asserted. "I'll challenge him to a duel and
we'll be on the road before sunset."

"Or you'll be dead," Crosby pointed out.

Richard gave him a smug smile. "I am an excellent shot."

"And you think he isn't?"

"He's a coward," Richard replied. "He eloped with my sister
to Gretna Green, only to abandon her the moment he had her

dowry in his hands. He deserves a fate far worse than a bullet."

Crosby's eyes flicked towards the pistol tucked in Richard's waistband. "I agree he deserves punishment. But why not sue him for abandonment? You've found where he lives."

Richard's hand settled on the butt of his pistol, the gesture deliberate. "Because men like him slip through the cracks of the law. I would see him answer to me, not a distant judge."

"You are angry," Crosby said bluntly.

"Good gads, yes," Richard snapped, his voice rising enough to turn a few heads nearby.

Crosby stood and held up a placating hand. "All right. Let's go visit Mr. Smith, but keep your wits about you. Death's a poor remedy if you plan to save your sister's honor."

Without waiting for a response, Richard strode for the door.

Outside, they retrieved their horses and set off at a gallop. The wind tore at Richard's coat, but he relished the bite of the chill air against his skin. It wasn't long before they arrived at a modest stone manor nestled behind oak trees, with neat gardens blooming along the front and a slender creek weaving through the property.

Richard scowled. It was far too picturesque for the lair of a scoundrel. He dismounted, tying his reins to a hitching post with sharp, jerking motions. He stalked up the path without hesitation and hammered his fist against the door.

"Subtle," Crosby muttered under his breath.

The door creaked open, and a fair-haired maid peered out. Her apron was crisp, her expression wary. "May I help you, sir?"

Richard stepped forward, looming over her. "I demand to speak with Mr. Smith. Immediately."

The maid glanced nervously over her shoulder. "I regret to inform you that Mr. Smith passed away a little over a year ago."

"That is impossible!" Richard barked. "You are lying."

The maid shrank back. "I assure you that I am not."

Crosby stepped in swiftly, flashing the girl a reassuring smile. "Forgive my companion's rudeness, Miss. He is... overwrought. Did Mr. Smith leave behind a son we might speak to?"

"No, sir. Only two daughters," came the maid's soft reply.

Richard's hands curled into fists. Some trickery was at work —he could feel it. "Then fetch them. At once."

The maid bobbed a quick curtsy. "I shall see if the mistress is available for callers."

Richard added sharply, "Inform her that the Marquess of Wilton demands an audience and I will not be turned away."

The maid's eyes widened at the title, but she merely nodded and disappeared inside, shutting the door firmly behind her.

Crosby shot him a glare. "That was poorly done."

"I will not suffer lies," Richard growled.

"We are here to gather information, not frighten women out of their wits," Crosby remarked. "If you charge through this investigation half-cocked, you'll have nothing to show for it but a ruined house and a reputation in tatters."

Richard said nothing, his gaze locked on the door.

"I understand your anger," Crosby continued. "But justice requires patience, my lord. If you want to win, you must think."

Before Richard could retort, the door creaked open again. The maid reappeared, her cheeks flushed. "Miss Theodosia Smith will see you now, my lord."

Richard squared his shoulders. Of course she would. A country bumpkin with little status would not dare deny a marquess, especially not when he came demanding answers. He stepped forward, ready to confront whoever dared stand between him and the retribution his sister deserved.

He followed the maid down a dim, paneled corridor towards the rear of the manor. The house smelled faintly of lavender and beeswax polish, a humble but pleasant scent. At the end of the hallway, the maid paused before a heavy door, gave a small curtsy, and gestured for him to enter.

Richard strode inside, his mind braced for confrontation.

The room was surprisingly grand for such a modest manor: the walls lined with shelves of leather-bound books, a faded but elegant carpet underfoot, and a massive mahogany desk anchoring the space. Behind it sat a young woman, dressed in a simple blue gown that contrasted beautifully with her fair complexion. Her dark hair was gathered into a loose chignon at the nape of her neck, stray wisps framing her striking features —high cheekbones and a pair of disarmingly intelligent eyes.

He faltered for the briefest of moments, unsettled by her unexpected beauty, but steeled himself. He was not here for admiration. He was here for justice.

Straightening, he demanded, "Are you Miss Theodosia Smith?"

The woman lifted her gaze to his without the faintest flicker of fear. "I am. And I must assume you are the bad-mannered lord who so thoroughly frightened my maid."

Her tone was calm, almost amused, and it caught Richard off guard. Few women dared to speak to him so plainly.

"I am here to ask the questions," he snapped, recovering quickly.

Miss Theodosia's lips twitched, though whether from irritation or amusement he couldn't tell. "And I daresay I must wonder what I have done to earn your ire, my lord," she said, her words edged with a distinct sharpness.

He ignored the bait and pressed on. "I wish to speak to the master of the house."

She rose then, slow and deliberate, placing her slender hand firmly on the polished surface of the desk. "There is no master here. I am the mistress of this household."

He let out a short, incredulous laugh. "You? You can't possibly be old enough to run an estate."

Her chin tilted upward with defiance. "I am two and twenty years old. I can read ledgers, manage tenants, and balance accounts quite capably. But then, I suppose your mind cannot fathom a woman doing what a man might bungle."

Richard stepped forward, closing some of the space between them in a manner that made the maid by the door fidget nervously. "You are lying," he said.

Miss Theodosia's green eyes sparked with indignation. "And you, sir, have worn out your welcome." She resumed her seat, dismissing him with a regal grace. "You may see yourself out."

He remained rooted to the spot, his hand itching at his side. "I am not leaving until you answer my questions."

"Then we are at an impasse, for I have no desire to speak with you any further." Turning her gaze to Mr. Crosby, she asked, "Is your companion always so ill-tempered and tiresome?"

To Richard's annoyance, Crosby actually chuckled. "He is."

"How unfortunate," Miss Theodosia said, her lips curving into a faint, mocking smile. "Still, for your sake, I shall indulge a few inquiries. What would you like to know?"

Richard opened his mouth to demand answers, but she cut in sharply, "Not you, my lord. I've heard enough of your blustering. *You*," she said, looking at Crosby, "may ask."

Crosby, still grinning faintly, inclined his head. "My condolences, Miss Theodosia. I understand your father passed away?"

She sobered. "Yes. Over a year ago now."

"Did he leave behind a son?" Crosby asked.

"No. Only me and my elder sister."

Crosby nodded thoughtfully. "Earlier this morning, a man was seen leaving your property. Can you tell us who he was?"

A slight line formed between Miss Theodosia's brows. "You must be mistaken. No man departed from this house this morning."

Richard stiffened, his patience evaporating. "Stop lying," he ground out.

Miss Theodosia leaned back in her chair, regarding him as one might a particularly irksome insect. "You are a bothersome man, indeed. Pray tell—what offense did this mysterious figure commit against you that you are so determined to hunt him down?"

"I intend to kill him," Richard said, his voice unflinching.

In a calm, expectant voice, she asked, "And you expect me to assist you in your murderous intent?"

"I expect you to tell me where to find your brother," Richard demanded.

"I have no brother," she repeated. "Only an older sister."

"Then who," Richard began, "was the man who left your house this morning?"

She gave a delicate shrug. "Perhaps you saw our gardener or one of our tenants leaving for their day's work. We do keep early hours here in the country."

Her eyes danced with a hint of mischief, as if daring him to accuse her further. She was either the best liar he had ever encountered or she was telling the truth. And Richard hated the gnawing uncertainty clawing at his gut.

Theodosia wasn't entirely certain whether she ought to laugh at the absurdity of the situation or weep from sheer frustration. It took every ounce of restraint instilled by years of genteel breeding not to reach for the pistol discreetly hidden in the top drawer of her desk. Of course, brandishing a weapon at a marquess—even one as arrogant and insufferable as the one presently standing before her—would likely end poorly.

Still, the temptation lingered.

She regarded the lord with a critical eye. He was tall, broad-shouldered, with strikingly dark hair that curled just enough to suggest it defied control. He was impossibly handsome with his chiseled jaw and straight nose. However, all that physical perfection was marred by the thunderous scowl etched onto his face and the scorn in his voice. He radiated entitlement, as though the mere act of questioning him was an affront punishable by death.

Theodosia hadn't spoken a single untruth since he'd stormed into her study, but that didn't seem to matter to him.

"I know the difference between a gardener and a gentleman," he said with no small amount of derision, as if her refusal to tremble under his gaze somehow proved her guilt.

"How very clever of you," she said sweetly. "Do tell, my lord —can you also distinguish between a goat and a vicar? Or perhaps a duchess and a dairymaid?"

His eyes narrowed into dangerous slits. "You are an impertinent thing."

"And you seem to forget," she countered, "that you forced your way into my home and are now accusing me of harboring a brother I do not possess. As I've told you—twice now—I have only an elder sister."

The second man took a step forward, his demeanor less hostile than that of his companion. "Is your sister here?"

Theodosia gave a polite shake of her head. "I'm afraid not. She departed last night to visit friends in Essex. I seldom see her, to be frank."

Lord Wilton made a dismissive sound. "I have no interest in your sister. I came seeking your brother."

She sighed, exasperated. "And I keep telling you that I haven't one. Honestly, my lord, speaking to you is like shouting into the wind."

She returned her attention to the open ledger before her, as if that might prompt him to leave, and continued. "If you would be so kind as to remove yourself, I have accounts to balance, and your presence is most unhelpful."

He opened his mouth, clearly intent on launching another round of accusations, but his companion intervened before he could.

"Thank you for your time, Miss," the man said, offering her a short, respectful bow.

She dipped her head in return. "Good day to you, sir."

But Lord Wilton did not leave immediately. Instead, he stepped closer to her desk, his voice dropping to a low growl. "This is not over."

Their eyes locked briefly before he turned on his heel and stalked from the room. With a look that blended apology and faint amusement, the second man gave her one last glance before following after him.

Theodosia exhaled slowly as the door clicked shut and silence blanketed the room once more. Dear heavens, but Lord Wilton was the most arrogant man she had ever had the misfortune of meeting. She had heard whispers of him, of course—who in London hadn't? A marquess, wealthy, powerful, and, according to the Society pages, among the Season's most eligible bachelors. But none of that mattered to her.

She was the daughter of a baronet and had no desire to mingle with the *ton*. They would only judge her for her rustic upbringing and dismiss her as provincial. Let them. She was perfectly content with her life here in the village. And with her father gone, she had the estate to oversee, a duty she took most seriously.

Her thoughts were interrupted by her dearest friend's familiar, cheerful voice. "Did I just see two very handsome gentlemen leaving your front steps?"

Theodosia looked up to see Miss Penelope Worthing sweeping into the room, her golden curls bouncing beneath a wide-brimmed bonnet. "You did," she confirmed, folding her hands atop the ledger she had been reviewing.

Penelope's eyes sparkled as she sat, not bothering to conceal her curiosity. "They had the look of important men. Particularly the tall one."

"That," Theodosia said, "was Lord Wilton."

Penelope's brows shot up. "The Marquess of Wilton?"

"The very same."

Penelope leaned forward, eyes wide with disbelief. "And you let him leave without securing a proposal? Dosia, you must marry him!"

Theodosia gave an inelegant snort and shook her head. "I would sooner throw myself into the lake behind the stables. He was intolerable. He burst in here, demanded to see my brother, and would not take no for an answer."

"But... you haven't a brother," Penelope said, bewildered.

"Precisely," Theodosia responded. "Yet he insisted he had seen a gentleman leaving the manor earlier this morning."

Penelope frowned, her expression turning thoughtful. "Could it have been Lucinda with a caller?"

Theodosia shook her head, her voice tight. "No, because she left last night," she replied. "I hardly see her these days. She comes and goes as she pleases."

"That must grieve you," Penelope said. "Your father would have been saddened to see such distance between his daughters."

"It is what it is," Theodosia replied, her voice carefully composed, though her chest ached. "When Papa passed, Lucinda made it clear she had no intention of staying. She wanted more than this inconsequential village could offer."

"And left you to manage the estate alone."

Theodosia gestured towards the ledgers with a flick of her hand. "I don't mind. I rather enjoy it. There's a comfort in order, in knowing each task matters."

"Or perhaps you enjoy having something to fill the silence."

Theodosia didn't answer. Her friend wasn't wrong. She did feel rather lonely.

After a moment, Penelope said, "You could always marry Mr. Pritchett."

A shudder passed through Theodosia. "I think not. He deserves someone who can return his affections. And I... cannot."

As if summoned by the mere utterance of his name, the drawing room door creaked open, and a maid stepped inside. "Miss, Mr. Pritchett requests a moment of your time."

Penelope stifled a laugh. "Speak of the devil. He is nothing if not persistent."

"That he is," Theodosia agreed wearily before nodding to the maid. "You may show him in."

Penelope rose. "And that is my cue to leave."

"Must you?" Theodosia asked, only half-teasing.

Grinning, Penelope swept towards the door. "I wouldn't dream of interrupting a most intriguing social call." Her laughter echoed down the corridor as she departed.

Moments later, Mr. Pritchett was shown into the room by a maid. He was tall and lanky, with an earnest expression. His long face, narrow shoulders, and thinning hair were offset by an eagerness she had always found... tolerable, if nothing else.

"Mr. Pritchett," she greeted, rising.

He bowed low. "Miss Theodosia. Thank you for receiving me."

She dropped into a curtsy. "Of course."

He removed his hat and immediately began wringing it in his hands, the brim twisting beneath his fingers. "I won't waste your time with unnecessary pleasantries," he said abruptly. Then, before she could so much as blink, he dropped to one knee. "I've come to ask for your hand in marriage."

Theodosia's breath caught. *No, no, no... this cannot be happening.*

He pressed forward. "I've given this matter considerable thought. A union between us would be both logical and beneficial. Together, we would control the largest acreage in the county."

"Mr. Pritchett—" she began.

But he lifted a hand, stopping her. "Please, allow me to finish. I have admired you for years. I believe I could make you happy, if given the chance."

She opened her mouth to respond again, but he barreled on. "You've done an admirable job managing your father's estate, but I believe it would be best if I took over the responsibilities of both households. You could then devote yourself to more womanly pursuits—needlework, social visits... things of that nature."

Her lips parted in astonishment. She had endured many things in her life—loss, loneliness, even Lord Wilton's arrogant disdain—but this? This was beyond the pale. Not only had Mr. Pritchett proposed with hardly a word of affection, but he had somehow managed to insult her competence, erase her independence, and relegate her existence to embroidery hoops and tepid tea visits in the space of a single conversation.

Her voice, when it finally emerged, was calm and measured —far calmer than she felt. "Mr. Pritchett—"

"Adam," he interjected, as if that slight familiarity might sway her.

She gave him a weak smile. "Mr. Pritchett," she repeated, "I appreciate the offer... truly. But I must decline."

He blinked, confusion flashing across his face. Then again, more slowly. "I beg your pardon?"

"You and I have always maintained a cordial relationship," she said, carefully choosing each word, "and I value that. I do. But I do not believe marriage would suit either of us."

There was an awkward moment of silence.

"You are rejecting me?" he asked, still on one knee, as if the very idea was too foreign to be real.

"I propose," she continued with deliberate delicacy, "that we put this unfortunate moment behind us and continue on as friends. As we always have."

He did not rise immediately. Instead, his brow furrowed, and he stared up at her as if she had spoken in a foreign tongue. "But... it makes perfect sense," he said at last. "Our lands adjoin. We've known each other for years. And—" he hesitated, then pressed on, "you have no other prospects."

"That may be true, Mr. Pritchett. But even so, I must decline."

He huffed. "My mother said you were desperate to marry. That you were only waiting to be asked."

Theodosia stiffened, her smile now gone. "Did she?"

"I mean no insult," he said quickly, climbing to his feet at last, brushing off his knee with a stiff motion. "It's just that you are two and twenty years old. And alone. It is not unreasonable to assume..."

"That I ought to leap at the first proposal I receive?"

His mouth opened and closed again, as if trying to gather words that wouldn't make things worse.

"You are mistaken," she said, clasping her hands before her. "I may be unmarried, but I am not desperate."

He looked away, clearly uncomfortable. "Forgive me. I... I only meant to help."

"I am certain you did," she replied. "But I must live a life of my own choosing, not one arranged for convenience."

For a long moment, he said nothing. Then, with a tight nod, he replaced his hat and offered her a bow far less confident than the one he'd entered with. "Good day, Miss Theodosia."

She inclined her head. "Good day, Mr. Pritchett."

He turned and walked out, his steps brisk and uneven, leaving Theodosia standing in the silence of the study, her heart pounding—but not with regret. It was with steady certainty that she had made the right choice.

Penelope's voice drifted in through the open window, laced with amusement. "Poor Mr. Pritchett."

Startled, Theodosia turned towards the sound and spotted her friend leaning casually against the window frame. "Were you eavesdropping?"

"I was," Penelope said unrepentantly, resting her chin in her hand. "How could I not?" A glint of mischief danced in her eyes. "Though I must say, I nearly swooned when he invoked his mother during the proposal. That was a bold strategy."

Theodosia let out a weary sigh and sank into her chair. "Why must a woman be married to be considered of value?" she asked, not entirely expecting an answer.

"Do you not wish to marry?"

"I do want to marry. Truly. But not like that. I want to love the man I marry. I want to choose him."

A shadow passed over Penelope's expression, and her usual playfulness waned. "Some of us don't have the luxury of such lofty ideals," she said. "I would settle for a marriage built on admiration. Respect, at the very least."

Theodosia's gaze swept around the study. "And once I marry," she said, "all of this—my work, my independence—will be gone. I'll be relegated to the drawing room to pour tea and discuss floral arrangements until I die."

Penelope's lips twitched. "But you would be married," she replied with mock solemnity, her tone lightening once more.

Reaching for the nearest ledger, Theodosia flipped it open with a familiar sense of purpose. "I have work that must be done," she said.

Penelope sighed dramatically. "You are no fun at all."

Theodosia's fingers trailed down a column of estate expenditures. "I consider balancing ledgers to be fun."

"Then I shall leave you to your thrilling calculations," Penelope responded. "But before I go, Mother hoped you might join us for supper this evening. She insists, in fact."

Theodosia looked up, pleased by the invitation. "I'd be delighted."

"Excellent. I'll tell Cook to prepare an extra custard tart. You've earned it, what with the day you've had." Penelope backed away from the window. "Until tonight, then," she called, her voice trailing behind her as she strolled down the gardens' path.

Left alone once more, Theodosia stared at the open ledger but didn't immediately resume her work. Instead, her mind drifted to Lord Wilton. How could such a handsome man be so entirely disagreeable?

2

———

Richard paced the length of his modest room at the coaching inn, his boots scuffing the uneven wooden floorboards. The walls pressed in on him, the low ceiling and threadbare furnishings doing little to soothe the frustration that churned within. He was tired—tired of staying in this godforsaken village, tired of asking questions that yielded no answers, and most of all, tired of chasing shadows.

He needed the truth.

How had it come to this?

His sister, Olivia, had been preyed upon when she was most vulnerable, and she didn't deserve this public ruin. She had eloped with a man calling himself Mr. Smith, a man who had whispered vows of forever all the way to Gretna Green, only to abandon her once he had received her dowry. She had returned home heartbroken and humiliated, while the *ton* tore her apart one whisper at a time.

Their mother had taken to bed, inconsolable, alternating between fits of weeping and strained silence. It fell to Richard to restore the family's honor—to *fix* this. And yet, every step forward led him nowhere.

He clenched his fists. *I failed them.*

A sharp knock at the door dragged him from his spiraling thoughts. He strode over and opened it to find Mr. Crosby standing on the threshold, his expression grim.

Richard didn't need to ask. "Do come in," he said with a resigned sigh, stepping aside.

The Bow Street Runner entered, brushing road dust from his coat. "I've confirmed what we suspected," he revealed. "The late Sir Atticus Smith had no sons. Only two daughters—Miss Lucinda and Miss Theodosia."

Richard muttered a curse under his breath. "Wonderful. Another dead end."

"Not entirely," Crosby added, a glint in his eyes. "I made a few inquiries. Slipped a few coins into the right hands. One of Miss Theodosia's tenants was willing to talk."

Richard's head snapped up. "What did he say?"

"The man fitting your sister's description has been seen leaving Miss Theodosia's manor at strange hours. Early mornings, late at night. Always alone. Always cautious."

"And no one knows who he is?"

Crosby shrugged. "Only that he doesn't belong in the village. Keeps to himself. It wouldn't be unreasonable to suspect he is an illegitimate son or nephew. But from the description, he could very well be your sister's mysterious husband."

"Then I'll wait for him," Richard said at once, pacing again. "I'll stay near the manor. Watch. Eventually, he'll return."

"That could take weeks. Months, even," Crosby warned. "What if he's already gone? What if he never comes back?"

Richard ran a hand through his hair in frustration. "What choice do I have? We know my sister's dowry was deposited at the bank in this village. I do not doubt that Mr. Smith will return for the money."

Crosby hesitated, then said, "There may be another way. Though I doubt you'll like it."

Richard turned towards him. "At this point, I'll consider anything short of murder."

"We take Miss Theodosia," Crosby said plainly. "Escort her to London under guard. Leave a note for this 'Mr. Smith'—whoever he truly is—informing him that if he wants her back, he'll have to come and fetch her."

Richard stared at him. "You want me to abduct her?"

Crosby folded his arms. "It would be a means to an end. If she's truly innocent, no harm will come to her. And if she's hiding something—or someone—then this will draw him out. Or at the very least, it will draw out her secret."

"And if he doesn't come to collect Miss Theodosia?" Richard asked, skeptical.

"Then we let her go. No worse off than she was before. And you'll have your answer, one way or the other."

Richard shook his head. "It's madness. She's a baronet's daughter, not a common thief."

"Which makes it all the more likely she knows something. For all we know, she and this man are in it together. He might be hiding behind her skirts while she plays the innocent hostess."

"There has to be another way."

Crosby gave a short nod. "There is. We could ride to Essex to speak to the older sister, Lucinda. She might know more. But it'll cost us time."

Richard crossed the room and sat heavily on the edge of the narrow bed, the thin mattress creaking beneath his weight. He buried his face in his hands for a long moment, then looked up. "Even if I took Miss Theodosia to London, what would I do with her while we waited for this man to appear? Lock her in a cellar?"

Crosby gave him a thoughtful look. "What if you did it under the guise of hiring her as a companion for your sister?"

Richard shook his head. "My sister is newly married. She has no need of a companion."

"She might not," Crosby said with a shrug, "but it could only help your sister's tainted reputation."

Richard stood again, pacing towards the window. "Miss Theodosia will never agree. And I am not the sort of man who drags women from their homes under false pretenses."

"Then let's hope you find the strength to keep waiting," Crosby replied, his tone edged with irony, "because if the man you're after doesn't return, your sister's scandal will go unresolved and your family's reputation will only sink further."

Richard didn't answer at first. He knew perfectly well that Mr. Crosby spoke the truth and it grated on his last nerve. The worst part of it all was not Crosby's suggestion, but the fact that it was necessary. He was running out of options. Each day that passed was another day the scandal surrounding Olivia festered and spread.

He was the head of the family. He was supposed to protect them.

And now he found himself preparing to trick, or perhaps abduct, a woman who may or may not be complicit in the ruin of his sister.

No, he thought. Not yet.

He rose from the edge of the bed. "Before we consider anything drastic, I'll attempt to speak to Miss Theodosia once more. Perhaps she can be persuaded to come to London of her own accord."

Mr. Crosby lifted a skeptical brow. "Forgive me for the reminder, my lord, but your last encounter did not end well for you. Why would she give you the time of day now?"

Richard walked to the door. "Because I am a marquess and I

have the power to make her life very difficult," he responded. "Furthermore, if she comes willingly, it spares us both the unpleasantness. And it eases my conscience, if only marginally."

Crosby gave a short, humorless chuckle. "By all means, I wish you the best of luck."

Without another word, Richard descended the stairs, crossed the inn yard, and made for the stables. His horse was saddled within minutes, and he rode hard along the winding country road, the crisp wind biting at his face as he replayed every word he might say in his mind. None of them seemed adequate.

He arrived at the manor just as Miss Theodosia stepped out onto the front steps, a shawl draped around her shoulders and her dark hair pinned in a loose chignon that the breeze threatened to unravel.

Their eyes locked, and hers narrowed in unmistakable annoyance. "What, pray tell, are you doing here, my lord?" Her voice was clipped, her civility strained to its breaking point.

Richard dismounted and secured his horse. "I was hoping you might allow me a moment of your time."

"I believe you said quite enough the last time we spoke," she said, sweeping past him.

Matching her stride, he stepped in line with her. "I've come to offer an apology for my earlier behavior."

She paused, turning just slightly, a single brow arched. "Have you? What brought about this sudden burst of contrition?"

Richard hesitated, then gave the lie he had rehearsed. "I have since learned that you have no brother. The other villagers confirmed it."

She drew up, folding her arms as she turned to face him fully. "Very well," she said, "proceed with your apology."

He blinked, momentarily thrown. "Pardon?"

"You stated your intent to apologize," she said, tilting her head, "yet I have heard no such words from your mouth. I believe the phrase is, 'I'm sorry'?"

Richard's mouth tugged into an involuntary smirk. "It was implied."

A faint smile touched her lips, though it didn't warm her eyes. "I gather you don't apologize often, my lord."

"There's rarely a need," he replied with a shrug, then added quickly, "though I admit this may be one of those rare circumstances."

Her expression sharpened. "And yet your arrogance remains entirely intact. How convenient."

"I am not arrogant," he said, straightening instinctively.

She rolled her eyes. "Pompous, then."

He gave an exasperated sigh. "I apologized, didn't I?"

She stepped back. "If you'll excuse me, I have plans to dine with a friend this evening, and I have no desire to be late."

Before she could move past him again, he held up a hand. "Miss Theodosia—wait. I have a proposition for you."

She reared back. "I beg your pardon?"

Realizing the implication, Richard quickly clarified, both hands now raised. "Not that sort of proposition. I assure you that it is entirely respectable."

Eyeing him warily, she replied, "Go on."

He lowered his hands. "My sister, Olivia, is in need of a companion in London. I was wondering if you might consider accepting the position."

Theodosia didn't even hesitate. "No, thank you."

"You didn't even consider it."

"I didn't need to," she said. "I'm quite content here in the country, running my estate. But thank you for the generous offer."

He stepped closer, his voice softening slightly. "It would elevate your standing in Society. Being a companion to a lady of rank would open many doors."

"I have no interest in those doors," she replied. "I value my independence far more than the approval of a drawing room full of strangers."

"So you'd rather stay here forever?" he asked, incredulous. "Tending to ledgers and managing tenants until you grow old and forgotten?"

Her eyes flashed. "Yes, I'd rather that than be paraded through parlors as someone's ornament. I have work here. People who rely on me."

"Do you not have a man of business?"

"I do," she said slowly, clearly beginning to lose patience, "but I choose to oversee matters myself."

"Then delegate. Let him run it in your absence," Richard pressed. "Surely a few weeks in London would not bring your estate to ruin."

She drew herself up, hands clasped tightly in front of her. "Why, exactly, are you so invested in this?"

"Because..." Richard began, then met her gaze with something approaching sincerity. "Because I truly believe that you and my sister would get along rather well."

It wasn't a lie. If anything, it was the only truth he could safely admit aloud. Both women were obstinate, headstrong, and entirely unafraid to speak their minds.

He continued. "Olivia is opinionated. As are you," he added. "And she's in need of distraction, something... or someone to take her mind off her present difficulties."

Something flickered behind Miss Theodosia's eyes—curiosity, perhaps, or a quiet pang of empathy—but it passed so quickly, he couldn't be certain.

"I have never been to London," she admitted.

"Then come," Richard said, taking a small step closer. He kept his voice low, careful, less like a demand and more like an invitation. "See it for yourself. You needn't stay long. If you hate it, you may return to your estate. No obligation. No pressure."

He saw her weighing the offer, her fingers tightening slightly around the folds of her shawl. She was not a woman easily swayed, and he knew that now, more than ever, every word mattered.

"And I would be traveling," she said, "under your protection?"

"Yes," he replied, holding her gaze. "I would see to your safety personally. As any gentleman would."

Miss Theodosia tilted her head as she studied him. "How very curious," she said at last. "One moment, you burst into my home, accusing me of harboring a mysterious gentleman, and suggest I am lying to protect him. The next, you invite me to travel across the country with you, as though we are... friendly acquaintances."

Richard's jaw tensed. He had no ready answer—at least, none that wouldn't reveal the carefully concealed layers of manipulation behind his proposal. *Because I need you as bait. Because I don't trust you. Because I think you know more than you claim, and this is the only way I can keep you close.*

But he said none of that.

Instead, he gave a small shrug. "I may have misjudged you," he said. "Or perhaps I hoped I had."

Miss Theodosia's expression didn't change, but something in her posture shifted—just slightly, a subtle easing of the shoulders, a flicker of intrigue she tried to disguise. For the first time, the silence between them wasn't heavy with accusation, but something else entirely. Something not unlike the beginning of an uneasy alliance.

"I shall think on it," she said.

Richard inclined his head in a bow. "Then, with your permission, I will return tomorrow to receive your answer."

She gave the faintest nod before she started to walk down the path, not bothering to glance back at him.

As he mounted his horse, the weight of her guarded tone

stayed with him. She had not said yes, but she had not said no either.

And that, for now, was enough.

———————⟨～⟩———————

Theodosia resisted the nearly overwhelming urge to glance back over her shoulder at Lord Wilton. She could still feel the weight of his gaze lingering on her, and it irked her more than she cared to admit. What nerve of that man! He accused her of deception and then, without the least hint of humility, offered her employment.

As though she were in need of his charity.

She had no desire for his money—or his approval. She had an income, a modest one perhaps, but sufficient. She managed her family's estate with diligence and precision. She had no need of a marquess to rescue her.

And yet... some part of her—a quiet, wistful part she kept buried down—was tempted.

Not because of him. Heavens, no. He was infuriatingly arrogant. But the offer itself... to travel to London, to see with her own eyes the things she had only ever read about in newssheets and books. Vauxhall Gardens. Hyde Park. The glittering spectacle of carriages on Rotten Row. And the balls... so many wonderful things to see in Town.

To be a companion to the sister of a marquess was no small honor. It was, in fact, the sort of opportunity most village girls only dreamed of.

But dreams were dangerous things. She was the daughter of a baronet, yes—but one with a small dowry and no connections. The world of the *ton* would not embrace her; it would merely tolerate her presence with veiled smiles and cutting remarks.

No. It was foolish to even entertain the thought.

With that determined conclusion, she pressed forward along the well-worn path until Penelope's ancestral home came into view. The Worthing manor was a charming two-story stone house, nestled amongst climbing roses and framed by quaint gardens she had helped tend since childhood. Many a summer afternoon had been spent there—elbows deep in soil beside Penelope and her mother, gossiping and laughing until the light faded.

As Theodosia approached the steps, the front door flung open, and Penelope grinned from the threshold like an excited child. "Come quickly—I am *starving!*"

Theodosia arched a brow, but couldn't suppress a smile. "You are always starving."

Penelope stepped aside to let her in. "Yes, but I walk everywhere, so my figure remains unaffected."

Before Theodosia could respond, a warm voice floated through the corridor. "I thought I heard your voice, dear. Do come in."

The silver-haired Mrs. Worthing appeared from around the corner, her round face alight with welcome. Theodosia smiled and stepped inside. The scent of roast venison and stewed apples drifted from the kitchen, and her stomach gave a quiet rumble in response.

She followed Penelope into the dining room, where the table was already set with gleaming silverware and simple porcelain dishes. Everything about this house—the warmth, the laughter, the familiarity—felt like home.

A moment later, Mr. Worthing entered and pressed a kiss to his wife's cheek. "Sorry I'm late, my love. That blasted tenant of ours can't seem to distinguish a fence post from a gate."

Mrs. Worthing grinned. "You arrived just in time. And look who we convinced to dine with us tonight."

Turning to Theodosia, he smiled fondly. "Our Dosia is practically family. She's always welcome at our table."

Theodosia returned his smile. "Thank you, sir. You always make me feel like one of your own."

Mr. Worthing took his seat at the head of the table. "Now, Penelope tells me that Lord Wilton paid you a visit this morning."

Theodosia groaned. "That he did. He was positively dreadful."

Penelope, eyes twinkling with mischief, leaned her elbows on the table. "You should have married him. Then you could've been *Lady Dreadful*."

Theodosia laughed. "Alas, he did not propose. And if he had, I assure you he would be the last man I'd consider accepting."

"Not even before Mr. Pritchett?" Penelope teased.

Theodosia feigned a dramatic shudder. "Even Mr. Pritchett would be preferable. And that is saying something."

Mrs. Worthing tsked. "Now, now, I won't have you speaking ill of Mr. Pritchett. He's a good-hearted gentleman."

"He is," Mr. Worthing agreed. "Steady fellow, and he has a sound head on his shoulders."

"I don't disagree," Theodosia said, reaching for her napkin, "but you must admit that I could never make him happy. Nor he me."

There was a pause, then a soft, almost reluctant nod from Mrs. Worthing. "Perhaps you are right, my dear."

Just then, a maid entered carrying a large tray and began placing steaming dishes upon the table. Mr. Worthing rose and moved to carve the meat. As he sliced, Mrs. Worthing, ever the matchmaker, turned to Theodosia.

"Is there anyone else in the village who has caught your eye?"

Theodosia shook her head as a plate of food was placed before her. "I'm afraid not."

Mrs. Worthing shifted her attention to her daughter. "What about you, Penelope? Mr. Pritchett does seem rather fond of you."

Penelope gave a nonchalant shrug. "I'm not opposed to him. He's always been kind."

"There's more to marriage than kindness," Theodosia interjected.

"Don't say such things," Mr. Worthing protested. "If Penelope marries, she'll leave us. I forbid it."

"Now, George," his wife scolded playfully. "Penelope can't stay forever."

"I can if I like," Penelope declared. "Besides, I've no prospects at present, and I'm quite happy here."

"Good," Mr. Worthing declared. "Then it's settled."

Laughter danced around the table as the family began to eat, the warmth of the evening settled into Theodosia's bones. It was moments like these that made her wonder why she ever longed for more.

Still, as the silence stretched into contentment, she found herself speaking. "Something rather absurd happened on my walk over."

Penelope perked up instantly. "Let me guess—you were attacked by a werewolf and bravely fought him off."

Theodosia snorted. "No. There were no werewolves."

"One more guess!" Penelope raised a finger. "You fell into a hole and discovered a secret society of subterranean villagers."

Mrs. Worthing laughed. "Let the poor girl speak, Penelope."

Theodosia reached for a roll as she revealed, "Lord Wilton returned to speak to me."

Penelope sat upright. "Did you kick him?"

"No, I did not kick him."

"Pity."

Theodosia smiled faintly. "He... apologized. For his behavior."

The room fell silent.

"He did?" Mrs. Worthing asked at last.

"And then," Theodosia continued, "he offered me employment as a companion for his sister. In *London*."

Mrs. Worthing leaned forward, her eyes alight. "What did you say?"

"I told him I would think on it," Theodosia admitted, cutting into her meat.

"You must go," Mrs. Worthing said at once.

Theodosia winced. "I don't think that would be wise. I fully intend to turn him down."

"You mustn't," Mrs. Worthing pressed, her voice urgent. "Do you not realize what an opportunity this is? You could travel to London and mingle with the *ton*!"

"The *ton* wouldn't accept me," Theodosia said. "I'm only the daughter of a baronet."

Mrs. Worthing gave her a knowing look. "My dear girl, you will belong wherever you choose to stand."

Theodosia stared down at her plate, idly pushing a bit of meat to the edge with her fork. "It would be a terrible idea," she said. "I can hardly stand Lord Wilton."

"You wouldn't be working for him," Mrs. Worthing responded. "You'd be a companion to his sister. There's a world of difference."

"She's right," Penelope added. "And just think, if you marry some fabulously wealthy and handsome lord, you could host me during the next Season."

Theodosia huffed. "I am not going to marry a lord. Don't be absurd."

"It's not absurd," Penelope said, eyes twinkling. "It's wishful thinking. And I am excellent at it."

Mr. Worthing cleared his throat and folded his napkin with

deliberate care. "As much as I hate to agree with my wife and daughter on anything, I must say they're right. Your mother would have leapt at such a chance for you."

At the mention of her mother, Theodosia's mirth faded. Her fingers stilled around her fork. "I doubt that."

"No," Mrs. Worthing said, "it's true. She used to speak so fondly of her Seasons in London. Of the lights, the music, the people. She said it made the world feel larger and her place in it more exciting."

Theodosia lifted her gaze. "Yes, but I wouldn't be debuting. I wouldn't even be there as a guest. I'd be working. As a companion."

"And companions are often invited to attend events with their charges," Mrs. Worthing countered with a knowing smile. "You'd still see the ballrooms, the fine gowns, and the glittering chandeliers. You may not be at the center of attention, but you would be close enough to touch it."

Penelope leaned in, her excitement palpable. "And Vauxhall Gardens! Do you know they set off fireworks there? Fireworks! That's practically magic. Imagine standing beneath them in a gown of silk, the stars above and music playing…"

"You've been reading too many romantic novels," Theodosia said with a half-smile, though her heart tugged at the image.

"And you haven't read enough," Penelope shot back.

Theodosia reached for her glass and took a slow sip. "But what about the estate? What if something goes wrong while I'm away?"

"Mr. Thornton has managed things before. He's perfectly capable," Mr. Worthing assured her. "And if anything urgent arises, I'm happy to lend a hand in your absence."

"You're very kind, but—" Theodosia began.

Mr. Worthing gently cut her off. "What is truly stopping you, Dosia? Is it the estate? Or is it something else?"

The room quieted. Penelope's teasing expression softened, and Mrs. Worthing gave her a look of quiet encouragement.

Theodosia's fingers tightened around the stem of her glass. She didn't answer at first. Because she didn't know. Not exactly.

Was it fear?

Perhaps.

She had never left the village. Never gone farther than the neighboring town for the market or the occasional fair. Her world had always been contained within tidy hedgerows, quiet lanes, and familiar faces.

What if she stepped beyond those boundaries and found nothing but disappointment? What if she hated it? What if she didn't belong?

She opened her mouth, then closed it again. The words refused to form. "I suppose," she said finally, "I don't know who I would be... if I left."

Mrs. Worthing reached across the table and took her hand. "Sometimes, my dear, the only way to find out who you are is to get lost entirely."

"It is not that simple," Theodosia murmured, casting a glance down at her blue gown. Though it was finely made and fit her well enough, it was clearly the garment of a country lady —neat, serviceable, and entirely unremarkable. "I do not even possess the proper wardrobe for London."

Mrs. Worthing looked unconcerned as she sat back. "Then you shall commission one in London."

"That takes time."

"Of course it does. And you will have the time. There is no urgency that you must attend a ball the moment your boots touch cobblestone," Mrs. Worthing said.

"But what am I to do with all that time?" Theodosia countered. "I shall be dreadfully bored without my ledgers, my tenant accounts, and estate affairs to occupy me."

Before Mrs. Worthing could reply, Penelope interjected.

"I've read in the newssheets that Lord Wilton's townhouse is quite grand. Surely there will be enough paintings, statues, and ancient tapestries to keep you amused."

Theodosia chuckled despite herself, but then grew quiet. Her smile faded as the weight of the decision crept back in.

Could she go to London?

The question echoed in her mind. It felt foreign—ridiculous, even. Nonetheless, the pull was there. Subtle but persistent. She could walk the same streets that her mother once had. She could stand beneath the crystal chandeliers of grand ballrooms that her mother once spoke of in wistful tones. She could *see* the life her mother had known—not in fragments or memories, but with her own eyes.

But was she strong enough to go alone?

As if sensing her inner turmoil, Penelope gave her a soft, encouraging smile. "You are strong enough, Dosia."

Theodosia looked at her friend in surprise. "How did you know I was thinking that?"

"Because I've known you since we wore matching pinafores and chased geese through our gardens. I've watched you survive heartbreak, loss, and the pressure of managing your family's estate on your own. You carry the world on your shoulders and still manage to lift your chin. I know you. And more importantly—I believe in you."

A lump formed in Theodosia's throat, one she wasn't entirely prepared for. She gave Penelope a shaky smile.

"And if you don't go," Penelope continued, now grinning, "I shall simply dress up in one of your gowns, pin my hair back like yours, and go in your place. I've been practicing your stern eyebrow in the mirror."

Theodosia laughed, fully and freely, the tension in her chest easing for the first time that evening. Maybe... just maybe... it wasn't such a terrible idea, after all.

3

The sun had barely lifted above the horizon as Richard urged his horse along the winding road that led to Miss Theodosia's estate. The morning air was brisk, heavy with dew and the scent of damp earth, but he barely noticed. His eyes were fixed ahead, narrowed in contemplation.

As he crested the hill overlooking her land, the full breadth of the property stretched out before him. The fields were neatly cultivated, the fences recently mended, and the manor sat stately at the end of a tree-lined drive. Everything was orderly, efficient, thriving.

A flicker of reluctant admiration stirred within him.

She's done well, he admitted silently. Not many women, particularly one so young, could have taken on the burden of running an estate. She had shown resilience, competence... and cunning.

But Richard wasn't here to admire Miss Theodosia. She was, in his mind, a liar—a clever one, yes, and capable of disarming charm—but still, a deceiver. She was hiding something, and he meant to uncover the truth.

If all went according to plan, she would accompany him to

London, and Mr. Smith—whoever he truly was—would be drawn out. Then, and only then, could justice be served. He'd see them both exposed for the pain they had caused. *Let the law deal with them after that.*

As he drew nearer to the manor, he caught sight of Miss Theodosia seated on a stone bench tucked beneath an ancient elm in the gardens. A sketchbook was open in her lap, and she was wholly absorbed in the scene before her. Her pencil moved in measured strokes as she glanced up at a small bird perched on a low branch.

For a brief, jarring moment, she looked... peaceful. Almost lovely.

He reined in his horse, and the bird startled at the sound, taking flight with a sharp flutter of wings.

Miss Theodosia's head turned at once, and the serenity in her expression vanished. Her brows drew together in irritation. "Oh, wonderful. You've returned, my lord."

He ignored the bite in her tone as he dismounted. "I see you're an early riser."

"That I am," she replied. "Mornings are the only time of day when peace is assured and uninvited visitors are rare."

Unbothered, he secured his horse to the nearby hitching post and walked towards her. "Were you sketching that bird?"

"I was trying to," she replied, lifting the book slightly in demonstration. "Though it's difficult to capture a creature that won't sit still for more than a moment."

He stepped closer and glanced at the page. To his surprise, the sketch was striking—graceful lines, careful shading, and a precise rendering of the bird's posture and movement. "That's impressive," he admitted, almost grudgingly.

A faint smile curved her lips. "I enjoy drawing. My mother was quite gifted at it, and she encouraged me from an early age."

He caught the subtle shift in her voice, the hint of grief

hidden beneath composed words. It struck something in him, but he pushed it aside. *She's playing a part. That's all.*

He gestured towards the bench. "May I?"

She gave a slight incline of her head and shifted towards one end of the bench, allowing him space. There was a stiffness in her posture, a silent reminder that this was no friendly visit.

He sat, leaving a proper distance between them. "Have you given any further thought to my offer?"

"I have," she said evenly, folding her hands in her lap. "Though I remain puzzled. Why me, my lord? There must be dozens of young ladies more suited to the task."

"I explained my reasoning yesterday."

"You did," she allowed, "but it all still feels rather... surreal. Has your sister even expressed a desire for a companion?"

Richard hesitated. Truthfully, Olivia would balk at the very idea, particularly if it involved deception. But she would come around once he explained the necessity.

He summoned a practiced smile. "That needn't concern you."

Her brow furrowed. "Why do you insist on dismissing my concerns, as though my thoughts are mere trifles?"

"I wasn't—" he began, but she cut him off.

"It certainly feels that way. What happens if I travel to London and your sister refuses to take me on as her companion?"

"Then I'll see you safely home again," he said, a touch too quickly.

She studied him, her gaze sharp. "How old is your sister?"

"Five and twenty."

"And she's married?"

A muscle ticked in his jaw. "She is. Or rather—was. Her husband abandoned her not long ago."

Miss Theodosia drew in a sharp breath. "How awful. Your poor sister. To be so betrayed..."

Her reaction was sincere. He could see it in the way her eyes softened and her hand pressed lightly to her chest. It made him sick. She was the reason Olivia's life had unraveled. She must know something. But her sympathy sounded genuine. *She was a good actress.*

"She's... surviving," he said. "My mother, however, is not faring as well. The scandal has made her beside herself."

"And what became of your sister's husband?" Miss Theodosia asked.

Richard bristled at the question. Was she merely testing him, attempting to uncover some hidden guilt—or perhaps to see how much responsibility he would claim? He could not tell.

"I do not rightly know," he replied, voice clipped with restrained frustration. "Which is why I am doing everything in my power to find him—for my sister's sake."

"And for yours," she added simply.

He looked away, unable to meet her eyes. How easily she struck at the heart of it. He did need to find Mr. Smith for Olivia, of course. But also for himself. It was his duty to fix this. It was the only way he would be able to live with himself.

"Will you tell me about your family?" she asked.

He did not like talking about himself, but he knew that he must for the sake of this ruse. "My father died some years ago. I've been the head of the family since. It hasn't been easy. Especially lately."

"I understand more than you might think," she said. She set the sketchbook down between them. "When my father died, the estate was in terrible condition. My sister left shortly after, and I was left to manage everything alone."

"And now?" he asked.

"I've restored the estate. It's rather profitable now. I know it's uncommon for a woman to take on such responsibilities, but I've always had a head for numbers. I see patterns others miss."

"That's admirable," he said, before he could stop himself.

She met his gaze, unflinching. "Your sister may surprise you as well. People often do when they have no choice but to rise to the challenges before them."

Her words echoed in his mind. A warning—or a promise? He wasn't sure.

Richard stretched his legs out before him as he leaned back slightly. "My sister is the daughter of a marquess. Her days are spent in the drawing room, quietly embroidering handkerchiefs and waiting for callers who never arrive on time."

"How perfectly dull," Theodosia muttered under her breath, not even bothering to conceal her disdain.

"It is what's expected of her," he said with a shrug, as if that settled the matter.

A crease formed between her brows. "Expected, perhaps. But is it what she wants?"

"Does it matter? It's her duty."

Her eyes narrowed. "So you believe duty should always come before desire?"

The question struck a nerve. Richard stiffened, his shoulders tensing beneath his coat. "You forget yourself. You are being far too familiar."

"True," she replied without the slightest hint of apology. "But I'm not in the habit of holding my tongue, particularly when a conversation becomes interesting."

"Then perhaps you ought to reconsider that habit," he snapped. "Your standing in Society hardly grants you the freedom to speak so freely."

That did it.

With an indignant huff, Miss Theodosia rose from the bench, causing him to rise as well. "I daresay I've reached my threshold for stupid remarks today, my lord," she declared.

"Miss Theodosia—"

She held up a hand to silence him. "You're asking me to leave my home, my work, my freedom, and enter a world where

I must constantly bite my tongue and pretend to be someone I'm not."

"I never said that," he countered, irritation threading through his tone.

Lowering her hand, she stared at him. "You didn't need to. To think I nearly agreed to go with you. What a terrible mistake that would have been."

Richard clenched his jaw. This woman. She was the most maddening creature he'd ever met—and yet, somehow, she was exactly the person he needed. He had no desire to force her hand. But he would have her in London, one way or another.

He took a breath and did something that did not come easily to him.

He swallowed his pride.

"You're making a mistake," he stated, as she turned to leave.

She paused. "Am I?"

"Yes." He took a slow step towards her. "You asked why I chose you. It's because my sister needs a friend. Someone with strength. Wit. A sharp tongue. Someone unafraid to speak her mind. You may think I find your honesty intolerable, but the truth is, it's precisely why I believe you would suit."

She blinked, clearly surprised by the admission, but before she could speak, he continued. "And if I'm wrong—if you meet my sister and decide it isn't a fit—I will pay you two thousand pounds for your time."

"Two thousand pounds?" she repeated.

He nodded. "A fair sum, I think. Come to London. Spend a fortnight in my sister's company. If, at the end of that time, you believe the arrangement would never work, I will see you returned home safely with the money."

"And if I stay on as her companion?"

"Then you will receive the money after one full month of employment."

Theodosia bit her lower lip, clearly weighing the offer.

"That's... generous. It would allow me to buy new farm equipment and fill the coffers."

"I hope it's generous enough to earn your agreement," he said, trying to keep the eagerness from his voice.

She studied him for a long moment. "And will I be expected to bite my tongue in your presence?"

"No," he replied. "Inside the townhouse, you may speak as freely as you wish. But I would advise discretion when among the *ton*. They are not as forgiving as I am."

That earned a small laugh from her. "Forgiving? You, my lord?"

He gave her a crooked smile. "Shocking, I know."

Her eyes dropped to her simple green gown. "And my wardrobe? I have nothing appropriate for Town."

"Then we'll see to it that you have one. I don't want you drawing unnecessary attention."

Her gaze lingered on him, the silence between them charged and thoughtful. He didn't press her. Not yet. But he could feel her resolve weakening.

At last, she drew in a steady breath. "Very well. I will go with you."

Richard barely resisted the urge to let out a breath of relief. He clasped his hands together to mask his satisfaction. *Step one accomplished.* Now it was only a matter of luring Mr. Smith into the open.

Taking a step back, he said, "Wonderful. If you have no objections, we will depart at first light tomorrow. I'll arrange for the coach."

"Will you also ride in the coach?"

"No," he replied promptly. "I'll ride alongside on horseback."

She smiled, a real one this time—cool, composed, but with the faintest glimmer of satisfaction. "Good. I find that much more preferable."

"As do I."

"Until tomorrow, then, my lord," Miss Theodosia said with a slight curtsy.

He bowed. "Until tomorrow."

———————— ~ ————————

Theodosia sat on the floor of her bedchamber, the morning sun slanting through the tall windows and casting long, golden beams across the room. Before her sat two open trunks—half-filled, half-forgotten—and a scattering of neatly folded gowns, underthings, and shawls strewn across the carpet.

Her hands rested in her lap, still, unmoving.

What am I doing?

The question rang in her mind like a bell. Could she really travel to London with Lord Wilton—a man she was hardly acquainted with and barely tolerated? He was arrogant, over-bearing, and altogether too self-satisfied. And if his sister was anything like him? Theodosia couldn't bear the thought of spending days—weeks—in the company of people who would surely look down their noses at her.

She belonged here. In the village. With her ledgers and her fields and her tenants. With the wind in the trees and the sound of the church bells each Sunday morning. She had a purpose here.

What if her steward failed her in her absence? What if rents went uncollected, roofs leaked, or livestock fell ill? People depended on her. She couldn't abandon them just to go galli-vanting off to London for some foolish adventure that might end in disaster.

Her resolve hardened. Rising from the floor, she moved towards the nearest trunk and reached for the lid. *No. She would stay. It was the sensible thing to do.*

Before she could close it, the door swung open, and Penelope swept into the room. "Good morning," her friend sang cheerfully, pausing at the threshold.

Theodosia turned, managing a faint smile. "Good morning."

Penelope's sharp eyes scanned the trunks and the piles of carefully arranged garments. With an exaggerated gasp, she dropped to the floor beside Theodosia. "Well, if the great packing has commenced, I assume this means you've decided to go to Town?"

Theodosia hesitated. Then, with a sigh, she closed the lid and settled onto the trunk. "Actually... I've decided not to go."

"What? Whyever not?"

"I have an estate to run," Theodosia replied. "People who rely on me. I can't leave them in the hands of someone else—not for weeks."

Penelope raised a brow. "You have a man of business. And a very capable one, if I recall correctly. You chose him."

"What if he isn't as capable as I thought?" Theodosia asked. "What if something goes wrong and I'm not here to fix it?"

"You won't know unless you trust someone else to try," Penelope replied. "And you are careful. You don't make hasty decisions. If you believe he can do the job, then he likely can."

Theodosia stared down at her hands. "Maybe. But even if I do go, I know nothing about being a companion. What if I make a fool of myself? What if I'm simply... not enough?"

Penelope gave her a wry look. "Methinks you protest too much."

Theodosia arched a brow. "I'm serious. What if I'm a disaster? What if I'm dismissed the moment we arrive?"

"Then you come home. And at least you'll have the satisfaction of knowing you tried."

"I don't like uncertainty," Theodosia murmured. "Here, I know what to expect."

Penelope leaned forward, her tone shifting to something softer. "And that is exactly why you should go. You've spent your life doing what is expected of you. Running an estate, tending to others, and being utterly dependable. But when was the last time you did something just for yourself?"

Theodosia didn't reply. She wasn't sure she could.

Penelope continued. "You deserve to see more of the world than the borders of this village. You deserve ballrooms and fireworks and whispered secrets behind fans. You deserve to stand in a grand house and know that you belong there."

"But what if I fail?"

"And what if you marry a prince?" Penelope said brightly.

Theodosia rolled her eyes. "I'm not going to marry a prince."

"You could," Penelope said with a grin. "And you'd have a castle, and dozens of servants to do your bidding."

"You, my dear friend, are completely delusional."

"Perhaps," Penelope conceded with a shrug, "but I'm your delusional friend. And I need to share in these adventures with you. Which means you must go and you must write to me with every delicious detail."

Theodosia rose from the trunk and wandered to the window. She stared out at the familiar gardens, the same ones she had played in as a child, learned to prune roses in, and walked through alone after her father's funeral.

The thought of leaving everything behind terrified her.

However, the thought of never leaving it at all terrified her even more.

Penelope came to stand beside her. "You don't have to stay caged by the life you've always known, Dosia. It's time to be brave."

"I wish you could come with me," Theodosia said.

"And leave my parents?" Penelope scoffed. "Impossible.

They'd be lost without me. I'm the glue that keeps them from driving each other mad."

Theodosia laughed, and the tightness in her chest eased just a little. "I'll go," she said, turning towards her friend with a small, determined nod. "I'll go to London."

Penelope threw her arms in the air triumphantly. "Good! And when you do marry a prince, I had better be invited to the wedding."

Theodosia smiled. "I promise you that I will not be marrying a prince."

"That is a real shame since the queen is trying to marry her sons off. You would've had your pick," Penelope replied with mock solemnity as she looped her arm through Theodosia's. "Now, since we've made the most momentous decision of your life, I believe we've earned a biscuit."

"I do love biscuits," Theodosia said as they started towards the door together.

"Then let us go and pillage the kitchen like the scandalous adventuresses we are."

Laughter still echoed between them as Theodosia and Penelope stepped out of the bedchamber and descended the staircase. Though a knot of uncertainty remained curled in Theodosia's chest, she felt lighter somehow. Doubts lingered, yes—but when would such an opportunity come again? Life rarely offered second chances at adventure.

As they walked into the sun-warmed kitchen, the scent of butter, herbs, and freshly baked bread wrapped around them like a familiar embrace. A cheerful fire crackled in the hearth, and Mrs. Meng, the stout, dark-haired cook, stood over a large iron pot, stirring with practiced ease.

Upon hearing the door, she glanced over her shoulder, her round face lighting with amusement. "I know exactly what you two are looking for," she said, her voice rich with affection. "Go on, now. They're on the table."

Theodosia crossed the room, lifted a linen cloth, and revealed a generous plate of biscuits. She plucked one free and bit into it with a soft sigh of contentment. "I'm going to miss these when I'm in London."

Mrs. Meng set her spoon aside. "I've no doubt that handsome marquess keeps a proper French chef on his household staff. You'll be well fed."

"Lord Wilton? Handsome?" Theodosia took another bite and chewed deliberately. "I hadn't noticed."

Penelope let out a dramatic gasp and pressed a hand to her chest. "You hadn't noticed?" she echoed. "Have your eyes failed you, Dosia? He's precisely what I imagined when I used to dream about tall, brooding lords riding up to the manor gates."

With an indifferent shrug, Theodosia replied, "He is not unpleasant to look at, I suppose."

Penelope narrowed her eyes. "That's it? *Not unpleasant?* Honestly, I'm beginning to question our entire friendship. Who are you? Have you been replaced by a changeling?"

Theodosia smirked into her next bite. "Because I don't swoon over Lord Wilton?"

"Exactly!" Penelope declared, throwing her hands up. "He's got that dark hair, that chiseled jaw, and stormy eyes. Don't you think he might've been a pirate in a former life?"

"A pirate?"

Penelope nodded, eyes sparkling. "Oh, yes. I can just see it now—him in a long coat, sword at his hip, rescuing innocent maidens from terrible fates."

"But aren't pirates usually the ones causing the terrible fates?"

"Not in my story," Penelope said firmly. "In mine, he's the misunderstood hero, with a shadowed past and a ship named *The Tempest's Kiss.*"

Theodosia glanced pointedly at the biscuit in her friend's

hand. "I wonder if Mrs. Meng slipped something stronger than sugar into these."

Mrs. Meng snorted with laughter. "No spirits in the biscuits, I assure you, but perhaps Miss Penelope's imagination doesn't need any help."

Penelope took another bite before saying, "Just admit it—he's handsome."

"I will do no such thing," Theodosia said. "He is arrogant, intolerably rude, and endlessly condescending."

"He's a marquess," Penelope remarked.

"That's not a character trait," Theodosia countered, though her lips twitched despite herself.

Brushing the crumbs from her skirt, Penelope turned to her with a teasing gleam in her eyes. "Very well, if you won't admit it freely, let's make a game of it."

Theodosia groaned. "I already don't like this game."

Penelope ignored her, pressing forward. "The rules are simple. Say one kind thing about Lord Wilton."

"Whatever for?"

"Because," Penelope said sweetly, "I do believe you protest entirely too much."

Theodosia folded her arms. "This is absurd."

"It's character building."

"I've enough character."

Mrs. Meng spoke up from the hearth. "Let the girl be, Miss Penelope. It's far too early for teasing."

"Not when I smell scandal in the air," Penelope replied with exaggerated drama. "Come on, Dosia. One nice thing. One."

Theodosia considered for a moment, then replied, "Fine. He is... of adequate height. He is neither too tall nor too short."

"That's a start. See? Not so hard."

Theodosia gave a dramatic sigh. "I fear I may never recover."

"It wasn't so painful, was it?" Penelope teased, her grin stretching wide.

"You say that now, but next you'll have me calling him charming, and if that day comes, I shall have to be examined for a fever. Or perhaps head trauma."

Penelope leaned back against the wall. "Too late. I daresay we're already halfway down that slippery slope."

Theodosia gave her friend a withering look, though a smile tugged stubbornly at the corner of her mouth. "If I ever utter the words 'Lord Wilton is charming,' I give you full permission to lock me in the cellar and throw away the key."

"Duly noted," Penelope said, raising her biscuit in a toast.

4

Richard sat astride his horse as the rain poured from the heavens with relentless fury. What had begun as a light drizzle had swiftly transformed into a soaking downpour, and now, rivulets of water streamed from the brim of his riding hat and down the back of his greatcoat. His gloves were sodden, his boots squelched with every shift of weight, and he was quite certain he had not felt dry in hours. The chill crept beneath his collar and settled in his bones, but he remained stoic, his gaze fixed ahead.

He had been following the coach since shortly after breakfast, and though he'd never admit it aloud, he was weary of the saddle and aching in places he'd rather not name. Still, he found a measure of satisfaction in the fact that everything had gone according to plan, thus far. Miss Theodosia had agreed to accompany him to London, albeit reluctantly, and Mr. Crosby had remained behind to deliver word to the elusive Mr. Smith. Now all that remained was to keep Miss Theodosia occupied—and under watch—until Mr. Smith came to collect her.

The rain showed no sign of letting up. He estimated they

had at least another hour's ride before reaching the coaching inn, and the thought of a roaring fire and a strong glass of brandy had become something of an obsession.

Just then, the coach lurched to a halt. The door creaked open, and Miss Theodosia leaned out, her bonnet askew and her cheeks flushed pink from the chill. "It would ease my conscience if you would ride in the coach with me, my lord."

Richard hesitated, blinking rain from his lashes. He had promised her he would not share the coach, a courtesy to preserve appearances. But as the wind howled past his ears and thunder growled in the distance, he found himself reconsidering.

Before he could speak, Theodosia added, "Do come in before you catch a cold and die." And with that, she disappeared inside, the door closing behind her.

He didn't need to be asked again. Swinging down from the saddle, Richard secured his dripping horse to the back of the coach, then climbed aboard. The warmth of the interior hit him immediately, though the scent of damp wool and wet leather quickly followed.

He settled into the seat across from her and shrugged off his saturated greatcoat, folding it with care and placing it beside him. His hair dripped into his eyes, and he ran a hand through it, attempting in vain to tame it.

Miss Theodosia regarded him with a softness that surprised him. "I'm sorry you had to endure that."

"Don't be," he replied. "Thank you for offering me shelter."

She gave a modest nod. "It's the least I could do. I wouldn't want to be held responsible for the untimely death of a marquess."

That coaxed a reluctant smile from him. "How considerate." He noticed the small, green-bound book resting in her lap. "Were you reading?"

"I attempted to," she said, her expression wry. "But the jostling of the coach disagreed with my stomach."

"What is it?" he asked.

"It's about farming implements and crop rotation," she replied, holding it up as though it were a prized possession. "It's quite informative."

"You must be jesting."

"Not at all," she said. "I find it fascinating."

"It sounds abysmally dull."

"To you, perhaps. But I enjoy learning new methods to improve estate efficiency."

He shifted uncomfortably, suddenly aware of how close they were seated. "I hope I'm not getting you wet."

"Would you care for a blanket?"

"No, thank you," he said. "Though I appreciate the offer."

An awkward silence fell between them. She turned her face towards the rain-spattered window, her features cast in profile against the gloom. It gave Richard the opportunity to study her more closely. Her features were refined and delicate, her eyes intelligent, though guarded. She was, objectively, quite beautiful.

Not that it mattered. She was here for a purpose, and any personal intrigue was a distraction he could ill afford.

Still, he needed to keep her engaged.

Clearing his throat, he attempted a conversational gambit. "Do you like to... ride?"

She glanced at him briefly. "I do, my lord."

And then, maddeningly, she returned her attention to the window.

He blinked. That was it?

Richard scowled. He was the blasted Marquess of Wilton. Women generally hung on his every word, not dismissed him like a housemaid with no time for gossip.

Determined, he tried again. "What occupies your time, Miss Theodosia?"

She turned her gaze back to him. "I manage my estate. I also draw, as you know."

"Yes, I recall."

Another pause. And again, she looked away.

His temper flared—just a flicker—but it was enough to sting his pride. Was she truly so indifferent to him?

Before he could make a cutting remark, she surprised him by asking, "What about you, my lord? What fills your days?"

"I box," he answered, perhaps too abruptly.

She raised a brow. "How barbaric."

He smirked. "Only when done poorly."

"And is that all you do? Punch people?"

"I oversee my estate," he said defensively. "Though I rely heavily on my man of business."

She shook her head. "I think that's foolish. A man should know his accounts as well as his steward."

He narrowed his eyes. "I don't recall asking for your opinion."

"You did say I could speak freely," she countered.

"Yes, but perhaps consider the wisdom of what you say before you speak it."

"Why?" she asked. "Because you're a marquess and I'm a baronet's daughter?"

Richard sighed, dragging a hand over his face. "We got off on the wrong foot. Let us start again."

Her expression softened, just a touch. "I am willing, if you are."

"Good." He inclined his head slightly. "I am Lord Wilton."

She mimicked the gesture. "I am Miss Theodosia Smith."

"There," he said. "A full exchange without a single insult."

A small smile played on her lips. "Progress, indeed."

He leaned forward slightly. "Besides estate management, drawing, and riding—what else do you enjoy?"

"Gardening."

He winced. "How dreadfully dull."

"I thought we were being civil?"

"I smiled when I said it," he replied. "Surely that softens the blow."

"Not particularly," she said with a shrug, though there was a glimmer of humor in her voice. "But it is true that it is not an exciting pastime. Still, I enjoy it. I spent many hours in the soil with my dearest friend, Penelope, and her mother."

"You speak of her fondly."

"She has a bright spirit. You would like her—everyone does."

"Then it is a shame I did not meet her."

Miss Theodosia fingered the edges of the blanket on her lap. "She was the one who urged me to take this trip. She said it would be an adventure."

Richard allowed himself a chuckle. "On that count, I believe she was right."

"I have known Penelope my entire life," Theodosia shared. "She's more than a friend. She is the one person who's always been there when I've needed someone most."

"That sounds like the mark of a true friend."

"She is." The corners of Theodosia's mouth lifted in a faint smile, but it faltered as she looked down at her folded hands. "When my father died…"

She didn't finish the sentence. Her voice caught, and her breath hitched. The silence that followed was heavy with unsaid words.

Richard didn't press her. He remained quiet, sensing that to interrupt would be to intrude on something sacred. If she wanted to continue, she would.

She blinked rapidly, but the tears welled anyway. "I do apologize," she murmured, her voice tight with emotion. "Even now, it sometimes takes me by surprise just how easily the tears come when I think of him."

Wordlessly, Richard reached into the inner pocket of his coat, retrieving a thoroughly damp handkerchief. It was creased and damp from the rain, but he held it out to her. "It's wet, I'm afraid," he said, offering a sheepish smile. "But it's the best I can do under the circumstances."

Her smile trembled at the edges as she accepted it. "Thank you, my lord. It's kinder than most would think to offer."

"If it offers you any comfort," Richard said, leaning back in his seat, "my own eyes still sting when I think of my father. You're not alone in that."

Theodosia dabbed delicately at her cheeks. "It does help. Truly."

He studied her a moment longer, thoughtful. "Your father must have been a remarkable man, for you to grieve him so deeply."

She bobbed her head. "He was the very best of men. He taught me how to think and how to ask questions. He never spoke down to me, not once. Even near the end... as the cancer ravaged his body, his only concern was for me and my sister. Not for himself. Never himself."

"That must bring you some measure of comfort."

"It does." She lowered her gaze, her fingers still gripping the handkerchief. "Though I do wish he had stayed longer. He should have seen how far we've come. How hard we've worked."

Then, as if suddenly aware of herself, she exhaled and pressed the handkerchief against her lips. "Dear heavens, I must apologize again. I hadn't meant to fall apart in front of you."

"Don't think twice about it," Richard said with sincerity. "You've nothing to apologize for."

She looked up, her eyes rimmed in red but clear. "May I ask about your father?"

The question struck a chord he hadn't expected. His body stiffened, his posture no longer relaxed. "What about him?"

"You must miss him terribly."

The words were simple, yet they cut with unsettling precision.

Richard turned his gaze away, fixing it on the rivulets of rain running down the coach window. He didn't want to speak of this. Not with her. Not with anyone. The wound was still too fresh, and his grief too private.

"I suppose I do," he muttered, his tone clipped, hoping she would let it drop.

But he was not so lucky.

"May I ask how he died?" she asked.

His jaw clenched, a muscle ticking in his cheek. "Illness," he said flatly. "It took him before any of us were ready."

"I'm sorry."

Richard gave no reply. His gaze remained fixed on the rain-drenched countryside flashing by the window. He remembered that night vividly—the frantic ride home, the sound of his mother's sobs, the stillness in his father's bedchamber. He hadn't been ready. He still wasn't ready.

Thankfully, Miss Theodosia said nothing more, and the silence that followed was different. It was gentler, less uncomfortable. They sat together as the coach rumbled through the rain, two people mourning in their own quiet ways.

Theodosia jolted forward as the coach lurched to a halt, the sudden motion pulling her from the fog of her thoughts. She peered out the window and took in the sight of a weary-looking coaching inn, its once-white walls streaked with soot and age. It was far from inviting, but after being confined in the coach for hours, her legs ached to stretch, and she longed for fresh air.

Outside, she spotted Lord Wilton dismounting his horse with practiced ease. He had ridden beside her inside the coach only until the rain ceased, then returned to his saddle, claiming he preferred the view from there. In truth, their earlier conversation had been... pleasant. Surprisingly so. Until she had foolishly allowed her emotions to stir, making the air between them taut and awkward. She would not make that mistake again. Better to remain composed. Detached. She would not allow herself to be mistaken for a simpering miss.

The door to the coach swung open with a groan, and Lord Wilton stood just beyond, offering his hand.

"We've arrived for the evening," he said, his voice low and even, with only a hint of fatigue.

She hesitated only a moment before placing her gloved hand in his. The instant her boot touched the ground, it slid out from beneath her. The muddy cobblestones were slick from the earlier storm, and she gave a small yelp as she stumbled forward.

His grip tightened reflexively, steadying her with ease. "Careful," he said. "The stones can be rather treacherous when wet."

She bit back a pointed retort—yes, thank you, she'd noticed—and instead murmured a stiff "thank you" as she withdrew her hand from his.

He gestured towards the inn's crooked entrance. "Shall we? One of the footmen went ahead to secure lodging."

"Wonderful," she replied, wrapping her shawl more tightly around her shoulders as a sharp breeze teased her skirts.

As they neared the door, it flew open with a bang. A burly man barreled through without so much as a glance and shouldered into her with enough force to jostle her back a step.

"Watch where ye're going!" he barked, not bothering to pause as he stomped off into the dusk.

Theodosia turned, stunned. She stared after the man, appalled. What sort of establishment was this? She had heard rumors of lawlessness at rural coaching inns—rowdy drinkers, vulgar company—but she had assumed such tales were exaggerated. Now, she wasn't so certain. Was she even safe here?

Lord Wilton, appearing unbothered by such a scene, opened the door for her and waited. She stepped inside, and at once, warmth enveloped her. The scent of roasted meat and damp wool filled the air. For a moment, she allowed herself to believe it might not be so terrible, after all.

Until they rounded the corner.

The main hall was thick with noise and pipe smoke. Men lounged at mismatched tables, tankards in hand, laughter rising in raucous waves. Their gazes turned towards her—some curious, others appraising, far too many crude.

She instinctively moved closer to Lord Wilton, standing near enough that their arms nearly brushed. Not because she wanted to. Certainly not. But because being near him felt marginally safer than enduring those stares alone.

He must have sensed her discomfort, for he leaned towards her slightly. "You're safe with me," he assured her.

She nodded, uncertain whether she believed it, but grateful for the reassurance, nonetheless. She didn't fully trust him, but compared to the others, he seemed almost noble.

A footman approached, holding two keys on a brass ring. "I've secured two rooms and a private dining space, as requested, my lord."

"Excellent," Lord Wilton replied. He accepted the keys and turned to her. "Are you hungry?"

"I could eat," she said, her tone deliberately mild.

"Then let's remedy that." His voice dipped low with warning. "Stay close to me. And don't make eye contact with the men. Some will take it as an invitation."

She stiffened but gave a small nod. Clinging to her composure, she followed him through the hall, keeping her gaze low and her expression neutral.

They reached a modest room tucked at the rear of the inn. A fire roared in the hearth, and she moved straight to it, holding her hands out to soak in the warmth.

Lord Wilton shut the door behind them, blocking out the noise of the main hall. He joined her at the fire. "How was the remainder of your journey?"

"Quiet," she said without looking at him.

He let out a dry chuckle. "I imagine that was to your preference."

"It was. I managed a nap." She allowed the barest hint of a smile.

A knock at the door interrupted them. It creaked open, revealing a portly woman with silver hair pulled tightly into a bun. She bore a tray laden with food and smiled warmly.

"Good evening," she greeted. "I do hope you're hungry."

"Famished, actually," Lord Wilton said.

She set the tray on the table and adjusted her apron. "I'm Mrs. Hodgkins, the innkeeper's wife. If you need anything, all you need to do is ask."

With a polite nod, she departed, leaving the scent of fresh bread in her wake.

Theodosia eyed the tray—thick slices of brown bread, ribbons of ham, wedges of cheese. Her stomach growled, but she held back. It wouldn't do to appear ravenous.

Lord Wilton gave her a pointed look. "Not hungry, after all?"

"I am," she admitted. "But you should eat first."

He arched a brow. "What sort of gentleman would I be if I allowed that?"

"Not a very good one, I suppose."

"Indeed. Go on."

With his encouragement, she moved to the table, pulled out a chair, and began assembling a modest plate. A slice of bread. A thin portion of ham. A sliver of cheese.

He took the seat across from her and studied her choices. "Is that truly all you intend to eat?"

"I only wanted to ensure there was enough for you."

A crooked smile tugged at his mouth. "There's enough here to feed a small regiment. You won't deprive me."

"Well, in that case..." She reached for another helping of meat and added it to her plate. "Thank you."

He began serving himself, then asked, "Is this your first visit to a coaching inn?"

She winced. "Was it that obvious?"

"Only a little. You looked... uncertain in the main hall. Most of the men mean no harm."

She caught his phrasing. "Most?"

He didn't flinch. "Just stay near me. And lock your door tonight."

A chill passed through her. "I've never traveled far beyond my village before this."

"A pity," he said as he bit into a piece of cheese. "There's something thrilling about travel. New places. New experiences."

"Perhaps. I never saw the need."

"Now you have one," he said easily. "And I think you'll enjoy London."

She tilted her head, intrigued despite herself. "What do you think I'll like best?"

He considered her for a moment before saying, "Hard to say. My sister swears by the circulating libraries. And shopping, of course."

"I would imagine that shopping in London will be quite a different experience than shopping in my small village," Theodosia remarked as she tore off another piece of bread, the crust crisp beneath her fingers.

"I do believe so," he agreed.

A comfortable silence settled between them, broken only by the soft clink of cutlery and the occasional pop from the fire. She was not one to feel burdened by silence. In fact, she welcomed it. Not every conversation needed to be filled with polite discussion. Sometimes, a quiet meal shared between two people was more telling than a dozen exchanged pleasantries.

Still, she felt the weight of his gaze as he leaned forward, his elbows resting lightly on the table's edge. "Will your sister be worried when she returns home and finds you gone?" he asked.

The question caught her off guard, and her jaw tightened slightly. "If she returns home," she replied as a thread of bitterness wove through the words. "I never quite know what Lucinda will do next. One moment she's preparing for a dinner party, the next she's off to Brighton without so much as a note."

"I'm sorry," he said after a pause, his voice sincere. "I shouldn't have asked."

"No, it's quite all right," she replied, waving a hand dismissively. "I suppose I shouldn't resent her for her desire to see the world. I just—well, it's difficult to plan for anything when I don't know whether she'll be gone a week or a month."

Lord Wilton gave her a pointed look. "She did leave you to manage the estate on your own."

"And I much prefer it that way," she replied.

Before he could respond, the door creaked open, and Mrs. Hodgkins bustled in once more, a smile on her lined face and a tankard in each hand.

"I brought you both something to drink," she announced cheerfully as she placed the mugs on the table. "The kitchen fire's still warming cider, but I thought this would settle your bellies in the meantime."

Theodosia murmured her thanks as the innkeeper's wife

bobbed a curtsy and departed, the door shutting behind her with a soft click.

She stared down at the tankard, her brows pulling together. "What is that?"

Lord Wilton reached for his and lifted it slightly, eyeing the murky liquid inside. "Watered-down ale, I imagine. It's the common fare at places like this."

Her nose wrinkled. "I can't possibly drink that."

A smirk tugged at the corner of his mouth. "I'm afraid your options are rather limited. Welcome to the rustic joys of coaching inns."

With great reluctance, Theodosia wrapped her fingers around the handle and lifted it to her lips. The scent was earthy and bitter, like something that had been left too long in the sun. She took the smallest possible sip.

The taste was somehow worse than the smell. The ale burned down her throat like sharp vinegar, catching her by surprise and triggering an abrupt cough. She set the tankard down with a loud thud and reached for her napkin.

"That is purely awful," she gasped, dabbing at her lips. "Is this what people choose to drink?"

Lord Wilton chuckled. "It's an acquired taste."

"I cannot imagine acquiring it."

"You've been far too sheltered," he said, still grinning. "Though I suppose that's not entirely your fault."

She narrowed her eyes, though her tone was more curious than offended. "Would you let your sister drink this?"

"From a coaching inn? Absolutely. It's safer than the water, which likely comes from a questionable well—or worse, a river."

She made a small, indelicate noise of disgust and pushed the tankard farther away. "Perhaps I'll just wait for the cider."

Lord Wilton lifted his own drink and took a long, unperturbed sip. "Suit yourself. But I daresay if you're to survive London, you'll need to develop a stronger constitution."

"Do ladies in London drink ale?"

A wry smile tugged at his lips. "No, not typically. They are far more likely to indulge in wine or champagne."

"I have never tasted champagne before."

"Then I do hope I'll be present to witness the occasion," he said with mirth in his eyes.

She let out a faint scoff. "I thought you were meant to be a gentleman."

Setting down his tankard with exaggerated care, he gave a mock-solemn nod. "It depends greatly on the day. Today, I appear to be failing miserably."

She didn't quite smile, but the corner of her mouth curved with reluctant amusement. Her gaze drifted towards the window, now completely black with night. Rain tapped softly against the glass in a steady rhythm.

"When do you think we'll arrive in London?" she asked.

"If all goes as planned, we should be there by tomorrow afternoon," he said. "Plenty of time for you to rest up before supper."

She folded her hands in her lap. "And your sister doesn't know I'm accompanying you?"

His lips twitched. "No. I thought it might be best to surprise her."

Theodosia gave him a long look, unsure if she should admire or admonish such a choice. "Do you think that's wise?"

"I do," he replied without hesitation. "My sister is quite fond of surprises."

"And what if she is not fond of me?"

"Then you shall return home, two thousand pounds richer," Lord Wilton replied, his tone light and his expression maddeningly unconcerned—as if her entire future were nothing more than a minor detail, easily dismissed.

Theodosia picked up her fork and resumed eating, though her appetite had dimmed. She chewed slowly, thoughtfully, the flavors on her plate fading beneath the weight of her thoughts.

She hated not knowing what the next day would bring, what role she was meant to play, or whether she even wanted the opportunities being laid before her. Her fingers tightened around her fork.

For a woman who had always prided herself on being practical and prepared, the uncertainty gnawed at her more than she dared admit.

5

Things were most certainly *not* going according to plan.

Richard stood beside his halted coach with a wheel so thoroughly splintered it looked as though it had been attacked by a battering ram rather than struck by an unfortunate rock. With the sun already high in the sky and no clouds in sight, the heat pressed down on them with relentless determination. He glanced upward and let out a quiet sigh. There was no telling how long the delay would be, but given his luck, it would be several hours at least.

Beside him stood Miss Theodosia, looking utterly unbothered by their predicament. She was dressed in a blue traveling habit that suited her figure entirely too well, with her dark hair tucked neatly beneath a coordinating bonnet. She had her hands folded in front of her, as if she were standing in the drawing room rather than beside a broken carriage on a dusty road in the middle of nowhere. Her serene expression only served to irritate him further.

A footman approached, one end of a neatly folded blanket draped over his forearm. "It may take some time to replace the wheel, my lord," he reported. "Would you like me to lay out a blanket for you while you wait?"

Richard opened his mouth to reply, but Miss Theodosia stepped in without hesitation.

"There's no need. I can lay out the blanket for his lordship," she said brightly, reaching out her gloved hand.

The footman hesitated. "It's no trouble, Miss."

"I insist," she replied, tone polite but firm. "You'll be of far more use assisting with the wheel."

After another uncertain glance between them, the footman gave a small bow and handed over the blanket.

Miss Theodosia turned her head slightly and gestured towards a patch of shade beneath an enormous oak tree just a few yards off the road. "We can sit over there. It should be far more comfortable than standing in the sun."

Without waiting for his agreement—or perhaps anticipating his protest—she began walking towards the tree with the blanket tucked under one arm.

Richard followed, falling into step beside her with a long-suffering sigh. "Do you always take charge of situations that don't require your involvement?"

She gave him a wide-eyed look that could have passed for innocence if not for the glint of mischief in her gaze. "Whatever do you mean?"

"The footman could have easily laid the blanket down for us. It's his job."

"And are we so helpless that we cannot manage a blanket ourselves?" she asked, arching an eyebrow.

"That's not the point," he muttered.

"Then do enlighten me, my lord. What is the point?"

He huffed. "It's simply a matter of propriety. Of station."

She came to an abrupt halt and turned to face him. "Propriety? Forgive me, but I would rather the man attend to the broken wheel—something that actually requires strength—

than spend his time smoothing a blanket upon the ground. Don't you agree?"

He opened his mouth to argue but stopped. "You make a good point—"

She cut in, already walking again. "Why do I sense a 'but' is coming?"

"Because..." he said, catching up, "you deprived him of doing his job."

She laughed softly. "Laying down a blanket is hardly a task of national importance. I daresay even you could manage it."

"I'm sure I could," he said, only mildly affronted. "But that's not the—"

"We're here," she announced cheerfully, spreading the blanket on the grass in one graceful motion. She turned to him with a smug smile. "Look what I've accomplished. All on my own."

He eyed her with no small amount of exasperation and lowered himself onto the farthest corner of the blanket, as though keeping distance might preserve his sanity.

Despite himself, he relished the opportunity to be off his feet. His legs ached from hours in the saddle, and every muscle in his back protested the jostling of the coach. Still, he would have preferred a steaming bath in his townhouse to this road-side interlude with the most maddening woman he had ever met.

From the reticule dangling from her wrist, Miss Theodosia retrieved a small green book—the very same one she had been reading the day before. She opened it and looked over at him with a hopeful expression. "Would you care for me to read aloud?"

"Good gads, no. That book sounded intolerably dull yester-day, and I cannot imagine it's improved overnight."

Unperturbed, she offered sweetly, "I could retrieve another from my trunk, if you'd like a different selection."

"I would prefer silence."

She shrugged one shoulder, utterly unbothered. "As you wish." She opened her book and began to read silently, her gaze drifting over the pages.

Richard leaned back on his elbows and tried to ignore her, tried to enjoy the stillness of the shaded grove. The breeze was faint but cooling, and for a fleeting moment, he thought he might actually relax.

Then something wet and warm landed squarely on his cheek.

His eyes flew open, and he reached up instinctively, fingers brushing against something unpleasantly sticky. He pulled his hand back and grimaced.

Bird droppings. Of course.

Miss Theodosia choked back a laugh, her shoulders shaking. "You have... something on your cheek," she said, with far too much amusement in her voice.

"Thank you for that helpful observation," he remarked dryly.

Reaching into her reticule again, she pulled out the handkerchief he had lent her the previous day. She extended it with a smile that was far too cheerful for his liking. "Here. This might help."

Accepting it with a sigh of resignation, he wiped his cheek and wondered if this day could get any worse.

As she returned to her reading, he lay back and stared at the canopy above. The birds chirped merrily, as if mocking him.

"Perhaps we should move the blanket?" Richard suggested, brushing once more at his cheek, even though the offending mess had already been wiped away.

Miss Theodosia gave him a look of such dry amusement that it bordered on affectionate mockery. "It is nearly mathematically impossible for the same man to be defecated on twice in one sitting."

"Mathematics offers me little comfort in this instance."

"Suit yourself," she said, turning a page in her book with lazy elegance. "But I do believe the birds have had their fun."

Still feeling vaguely offended by the indignity of it all, Richard tried a different tack. "What if you were to get droppings on your gown? Wouldn't that distress you?"

She glanced down at her blue skirts, then back up with a shrug. "Not particularly. I can think of far worse things. My father, for instance, kept a parrot that used to screech constantly. Compared to that, this is a delight."

"What an awful pet."

"You are quite the complainer, my lord. One might even call you delicate."

He bristled. "I am not delicate."

"No?" she asked, eyes twinkling. "Then why the melodrama over a little bird droppings?"

"Because I value hygiene. And dignity."

"And yet here you are," she replied, waving a hand at their rustic setting, "sitting on a blanket in the grass like a disgruntled schoolboy."

He narrowed his eyes. "Must you always speak your mind?"

"Yes," she replied. "It's my most charming trait."

"I would not call it charming," he muttered.

She tilted her head, lips twitching. "Have you ever stepped in manure?"

"Who hasn't?"

"Well then," she said, as though concluding a formal argument, "that is unequivocally worse. And as such, bird droppings are hardly cause for such dramatics."

Richard let out a weary sigh and leaned back on his elbows. "For the love of all things sacred, can we return to silence?"

"You were the one who broke it," she said sweetly. "Not I."

Before he could formulate a suitably scathing reply, one of the footmen approached with a respectful bow. "My lord, Miss —the wheel has been replaced. We are ready to resume our journey."

"Thank the heavens," Richard muttered, springing to his feet as if the earth itself had become intolerable.

Miss Theodosia rose more gracefully and gathered the blanket into a neat fold. "Should I take offense at your eagerness to be gone from my company?" she asked lightly.

"I merely wish to get back on the road."

She arched an elegant brow, clearly unconvinced but unwilling to press. "Of course," she murmured, handing the blanket to the waiting footman. Without another word, she turned and began the walk back to the coach, her back straight, her stride unhurried, never once glancing behind to see if he would follow.

Richard watched her for a moment before falling into step. She didn't behave like any woman of his acquaintance. She was strong-willed to the point of aggravation, stubborn, entirely too independent—but something about her refused to be dismissed.

She was also hiding something. That much, he knew without question.

And he intended to find out what it was.

A footman stepped forward and opened the coach door, offering a gloved hand to assist Miss Theodosia inside. She gathered her skirts, placing one foot on the iron step, but before ascending, she turned her head back towards Richard, her expression laced with that familiar, infuriating amusement.

"I do hope your ride will put you in a more tolerable mood, my lord," she said sweetly, her tone hovering somewhere between jest and gentle rebuke.

Richard's jaw tightened, but he forced himself to bite back the retort that sprang to mind. *Yes, well, not being in your company is a balm in and of itself,* he thought. Instead, he forced a smile and replied, "And I hope you enjoy your nap, assuming you plan to take one or two, which seems likely."

Her eyes sparkled as her lips curved into a small smile. "You are beginning to know me rather well."

He stepped closer, lowering his voice just enough to let the meaning linger between them. "I am learning a great many things about you, whether you wish me to or not."

At that, the smile faltered. Only slightly, but enough for him to notice.

"That almost sounds like a threat," she remarked.

"Not a threat," he replied, his gaze holding hers. "Merely an observation."

For a moment, something unspoken passed between them, but what it was, he did not know. Then, without another word, she turned and stepped up into the carriage, disappearing into its shadowed interior.

Richard stood there a moment longer than was necessary, staring after her, frowning slightly as the door was closed behind her.

She was not at all what he'd expected when this journey began.

And he had a distinct feeling she would prove even more complicated before it was through.

As the coach rolled through the vibrant heart of London, Theodosia pressed her gloved hand to the windowpane, her breath fogging the glass as she gazed out in open wonder. The streets bustled with life—more people than she had ever seen in one place. Elegant ladies in their finery and feathered hats strolled arm-in-arm while their maids followed a few paces behind, burdened with hatboxes and parcels. Hawkers shouted their wares from every corner, and children darted between carriage wheels, heedless of the danger, their laughter mingling with the city's ever-present din.

The carriage turned onto a quieter, more refined street, where the townhouses became grander, their facades gleaming in pale stone or pristine whitewash. Gas lamps stood sentry on each corner, and gravel courtyards kept the soot-stained world at bay. At last, the coach drew to a halt before a stately residence, its entrance flanked by white columns and tall sash windows that glittered like polished gems.

Theodosia instinctively smoothed a hand down the front of her modest traveling habit, suddenly keenly aware of how provincial she must appear in such surroundings.

The coach door swung open, and a liveried footman extended a white-gloved hand. She took it, her boots crunching on the gravel as she descended. Her gaze drifted upward once more, trying to take in the full height of the townhouse, with its elegant lines and air of imposing permanence.

Lord Wilton joined her, hands clasped behind his back. "Shall we?" he asked, watching her with a faint gleam of amusement.

"This is your home?" she managed to say.

He nodded. "For as long as I can remember. It's been in the family for three generations."

"It's... quite extraordinary."

He glanced at the building and shrugged. "It serves its purpose. But I'd prefer not to remain standing out here like a man preparing to be judged. Come along."

He offered his arm, and she hesitated.

"Is it wise for me to walk in on your arm?" she asked in a hushed voice. "I am meant to be a companion—at least, I hope to be. I do not believe I ought to enter the home of a marquess in such a fashion."

"I am offering you my arm as a gentleman," he replied, his brow lifting. "And you, Miss Theodosia, are overthinking it."

"I always do," she said with a rueful smile, accepting the gesture. Her hand settled lightly on his forearm.

He leaned closer. "But surely you must admit—it's much more fun to break a rule or two now and then."

"I tend to abide by them."

"A pity," he muttered.

The main door opened just then, revealing a dark-haired man in his middle years, dressed in the somber attire of a senior household servant. He bowed deeply.

"Good evening, my lord," he said before stepping aside to allow them entry.

Lord Wilton dropped her arm as they crossed the threshold. "Sterling, allow me to introduce Miss Theodosia Smith. She will serve as Lady Olivia's companion for the foreseeable future."

If Sterling was surprised by this pronouncement, his expression revealed nothing. "Very good, my lord. I shall see that the necessary arrangements are made."

"Excellent. Where is my sister?"

"In the drawing room with her ladyship."

Lord Wilton turned to Theodosia. "Are you prepared?"

She drew in a breath and lifted her chin. "As ready as I shall ever be."

Something flickered in his gaze—hesitation, perhaps, or doubt—but he blinked, and it vanished behind his usual impassive expression. He gestured towards a set of doors just off the entry hall. "Let us get this over with."

"You make it sound so inviting," she muttered, following him.

He pushed open the door, and Theodosia stepped into a tastefully appointed drawing room. A blonde-haired woman lounged on a settee near the window, idly twisting a strand of hair between her fingers. Beside her sat an older woman with distinguished white-streaked hair, bent over her embroidery frame with quiet focus.

Lord Wilton cleared his throat. "Olivia. Mother."

The younger woman's head snapped around. "Brother, you're finally—" She broke off, her eyes landing on Theodosia. "Who is this?"

"This is Miss Theodosia Smith," he replied.

Olivia's eyes narrowed with suspicion. "Is she—"

"She is to be your companion," he said firmly, cutting her off.

Olivia blinked. "Surely you are not serious."

"I am."

"I don't need a companion," she objected.

"Well, you now have one," Lord Wilton asserted. He turned to his mother. "I also promised Miss Theodosia a new wardrobe. Could you see to it that the dressmaker is summoned?"

Lady Wilton stood and approached with a kind smile. "Of course. I am Lady Wilton—Richard's mother."

Theodosia dipped into a curtsy. "It is an honor to meet you, my lady."

"And this," Lord Wilton continued, gesturing to his sister, "is Lady Olivia."

Theodosia offered a polite smile. "A pleasure, Lady Olivia. I have heard much about you."

Olivia arched a brow. "Then you have the advantage, Miss Smith, for I know nothing about you."

"Sister... be nice," Richard warned.

Olivia pressed her lips together and rose. "If you will excuse me, I need a moment to think this through."

As she swept from the room, Lord Wilton turned to Theodosia. "She will come around."

"And if she does not?" Theodosia asked.

"Then our arrangement remains as agreed." He turned to his mother. "I'll leave her in your capable hands. There is business I must attend to."

Without another word, he left, leaving Theodosia alone with a woman she had just met.

"You have a beautiful home," Theodosia offered, not knowing what else she should say.

"Thank you, my dear. You must be famished."

"I am a bit."

"Well, dinner isn't until eight," Lady Wilton said, glancing at the long clock in the corner. "I shall request a tray be sent to your room in the meantime. Come—I'll show you where you'll be staying. Will you tell me about yourself?"

As they ascended the stairs, Theodosia offered, "I fear there's not much to tell about me."

"Nonsense," Lady Wilton said with a smile. "My son has never brought a woman home before. Naturally, I am intrigued."

"I am the daughter of a baronet, from a small village in Sussex," Theodosia explained. "Both of my parents have passed."

"I'm sorry to hear that. And how old are you?"

"Two and twenty, my lady."

"Have you ever had a Season?"

"No. I remained home to manage our estate. I'm rather good at it."

"I believe you."

They turned down a richly carpeted corridor.

"I do have a sister," Theodosia added. "But she rarely stays in one place."

Lady Wilton stopped at a door and opened it. "This will be your room."

Theodosia stepped inside and her feet faltered. A grand four-poster bed stood before the hearth, its coverlet a shimmering pale blue. Plush lavender drapes framed tall windows, and the thick rug beneath her feet muffled her steps.

"This... this is lovely," she whispered, running her hand over the silk bedspread.

"I'm glad you think so. Olivia and I redecorated it for visiting guests."

"Oh, but I am not a guest. I'm a companion. Perhaps something smaller would be more appropriate."

"Nonsense. This will do perfectly. Dinner is promptly at eight—you'll hear the bell."

Her brow furrowed. "Am I to dine with the family?"

"I believe it is most appropriate, don't you?"

"I honestly don't know," Theodosia admitted. "I have never served as a companion before."

"Then we shall figure it out together. But first, you should rest. I'll have a maid sent up to help you dress."

"That won't be necessary. I can manage on my own."

"I've no doubt," Lady Wilton replied. "But this is London, my dear. Appearances matter. We all have our parts to play."

Theodosia glanced down at her traveling habit. "In that case, I should tell you that my gowns are quite plain. They will look terribly out of place in your dining hall."

Lady Wilton waved a dismissive hand. "Then you shall borrow one of Olivia's for tonight. You're about the same size."

"Would Lady Olivia mind?"

"I won't give her the chance," she said with a wink. "Now, is there anything else?"

Theodosia had a dozen reasons to refuse the offer, to protest the formality, to remind them all that she was only meant to serve—but Lady Wilton's warmth and determination were not easily refused.

"No, my lady," she said. "Thank you for your kindness."

Lady Wilton reached for the door but paused with her hand resting lightly on the handle. She turned back to Theodosia with a thoughtful expression. "If you would like, I can have a maid escort you to the dining room this evening. The layout of this townhouse can be rather bewildering until one grows accustomed to it."

"I would be most grateful," Theodosia replied, relief evident in her voice. "I fear I might end up in the kitchens or someone's bedchamber if left to my own devices."

A soft laugh escaped Lady Wilton's lips. "An understandable concern. Some of the corridors lead in peculiar directions and my late husband always swore the architect must have been drunk when he drew up the plans."

Theodosia smiled faintly, her nerves soothed somewhat by the older woman's humor.

"You are very welcome here," Lady Wilton said. "Do not give a second thought to Olivia's reaction. She has never taken kindly to surprises, especially those involving change."

"I hope I haven't caused her too much distress."

Lady Wilton's eyes softened. "You've done no such thing. Olivia has a flair for dramatics, but she is not unkind at heart. Give her a little time."

"Thank you, my lady."

"Now," Lady Wilton continued gently, "rest while you can. A tray will be brought up shortly, and I expect you to eat every bite of it. You've a long evening ahead."

With that, she slipped from the room, the quiet click of the door closing behind her.

Left alone, Theodosia drifted towards the tall windows. She pulled back the drape and gazed out at the expansive gardens. The scene was breathtaking—carefully trimmed hedges shaped into spirals, gravel paths meandering like rivers through patches of color, and rose bushes heavy with bloom. She spotted a marble fountain tucked beneath a linden tree.

It was a world so far removed from her modest home in Sussex that she could scarcely believe she now stood within it.

Her eyes followed a movement along the path—Lady Olivia. She was pacing briskly, arms crossed tightly over her chest, her expression stormy even at a distance. Theodosia's heart pinched. It was not her wish to unsettle anyone, least of all the woman she had been brought here to befriend and assist. If only there were a way to soothe her, to explain that she came not as a threat, but in good faith.

But for now, Olivia looked as if she would not welcome conversation.

A sudden yawn broke through her thoughts, catching her by surprise. The long hours of travel had finally taken their toll. Perhaps Lady Wilton was right. What she needed now more than anything was rest. A nap, even a brief one, might help her face the evening ahead with greater composure.

She turned from the window, crossed the room to the grand four-poster bed, and lay back against the cool silk coverlet. As her eyes fluttered closed, she could still see the image of Olivia pacing the gardens' path etched in her mind.

She hoped—desperately—that this arrangement might yet become something more than a strained obligation.

Something like belonging.

6

Richard searched through the townhouse with growing frustration, flinging open door after door and finding no sign of his sister. The morning room? Empty. The music salon? Silent. Olivia was nowhere to be found, and his patience—never abundant—was fast unraveling. Where in the blazes had she gone?

He came to a halt near the tall window in the corridor, bracing a hand on the sill. The moment his eyes fell on the gardens below, he spotted her. Olivia was pacing furiously along the gravel path that wound between the rose beds, her skirts swishing with each agitated turn. Her posture was rigid, and her hands were clenched at her sides.

He couldn't blame her. He had upended her world with little warning, presenting her with a new companion she neither expected nor welcomed. But he hadn't the luxury of easing her into the plan. Time was not on their side—and Olivia, unpredictable as ever, was capable of sabotaging the entire scheme if he didn't speak with her at once.

Without delay, he descended the stairs and strode out into the gardens, his boots crunching over the gravel. The sun had begun its slow descent, casting a golden hue across the blossoms, but the beauty of the setting was entirely lost on him.

The moment Olivia caught sight of him, she spun on her heel and advanced towards him.

"What were you thinking?" she demanded.

He lifted a hand in an attempt to calm her. "I know you're upset, but—"

"I'm not upset, I'm furious!" she snapped. "You brought that woman into our home—without so much as a word of warning!"

"She's part of a larger plan," he said carefully.

Olivia gave a humorless laugh. "If that's true, then it's a terrible one."

"Would you calm down and come sit with me?" he said, gesturing to a wrought iron bench tucked beneath the shade of a lilac tree.

"I've never listened to you before. Why start now?"

"Five minutes," he bargained. "Give me that, and I swear it will all begin to make sense."

With a dramatic exhale, she marched past him and sat, crossing her arms tightly. "Three minutes. Starting now."

"Very well," he said. "I went to the village where you claimed Mr. Smith was from. He wasn't there, but Miss Theodosia Smith was."

Olivia narrowed her eyes. "And how is she connected to him?"

"I don't know the exact relationship, but they are linked," Richard said. "According to the locals, a man matching Mr. Smith's description was seen leaving her estate. At night. Frequently."

Olivia arched a skeptical brow. "That still doesn't explain why you brought her here."

"Because I'm using her as bait."

Her head jerked back. "Bait?"

He nodded. "I brought her under the pretense of serving as your companion. If Mr. Smith truly cares for her, he'll come for her. And when he does, he won't slip away again."

"You've gone mad," she declared, standing abruptly.

"Mad or not, it's the best strategy we have."

"And you expect me to just... smile and play hostess to the woman connected to the man who humiliated me? Who married me for my dowry and then vanished without a trace?"

"You don't have to smile," Richard said. "But you will cooperate."

"And what happens when Luke shows up?" she asked bitterly. "You can't force him to return to me. You can't make him stay."

"No," Richard agreed. "But I can challenge him to a duel."

Olivia looked unimpressed. "A duel? That's your plan?"

"It may not solve the problem," he admitted. "But I assure you, it would be most satisfying."

She shook her head in disbelief. "You don't need to defend my honor, Brother."

Richard took a step towards her, his tone turning tight. "I refuse to let him win. I refuse to let him vanish into the shadows and leave you broken."

A new voice broke through the tension. "Good heavens, what are you two arguing about now?"

They both turned to see their mother standing at the edge of the gardens, her hands clasped loosely in front of her.

Olivia stormed past Richard. "Miss Theodosia is connected to Luke," she stated. "And Richard tricked her into coming here so he could use her to lure him back."

Their mother's brows lifted, but her voice remained calm. "I see. And is Miss Theodosia complicit in all this?"

Richard folded his arms. "She's no innocent. She's protecting him, I'm sure of it."

"And what proof have you?" his mother asked.

"A Bow Street Runner confirmed that Mr. Smith was seen leaving her estate on multiple occasions," Richard replied. "That is enough for me."

Their mother considered this in silence, her gaze steady. "Until we know the full extent of her involvement, she is to be treated with dignity and respect while she is under this roof."

"That is more than she deserves," Richard muttered.

"Nevertheless," their mother said, "if you expect me to go along with this absurd plan of yours, I won't have her treated poorly in my house."

Olivia threw up her hands. "And I'm simply meant to pretend that everything is perfectly fine?"

"Yes," Richard said.

"Yes," their mother echoed, in perfect harmony.

Richard turned back to his sister. "Spend time with her. Speak with her. Earn her trust. She knows more than she's letting on."

Olivia crossed her arms again. "That's distasteful."

"Perhaps," he said with a shrug. "But so was Luke's betrayal. If this is how we get answers, then so be it."

Olivia turned her face towards the towering façade of the townhouse. "I don't need a companion," she said. "And I certainly don't want one."

"I know," Richard replied. "But ask yourself—do you want Mr. Smith to win?"

She drew in a slow, shuddering breath and let it out in a sigh. "No," she said at last. "I do not."

Richard stepped closer and gently laid a hand on her shoulder. "You didn't deserve what he did to you, Olivia. None of it."

She shrugged off his hand as though the contact stung. "I need to be alone until dinner."

Without another word, she turned and strode back towards the house, her back rigid.

Richard watched her go, a frown creasing his brow. A

moment later, their mother's voice broke the silence beside him. "She's hurting, Richard."

"I know," he said. "That's exactly why this plan has to work."

His mother's gaze settled on her son. "And if it doesn't?"

"It has to," he declared. "And when it does, Mr. Smith will be dealt with harshly. Swiftly. No one humiliates my sister and walks away untouched."

She reached out and placed a hand on his arm. "You're angry."

He let out a short, bitter laugh. "Of course I'm angry! Olivia eloped to Gretna Green with a man completely beneath her. A liar. A coward. And the moment he pocketed her dowry, he disappeared."

His mother tilted her head slightly, her expression contemplative. "And tell me, who exactly are you more angry with—Mr. Smith, or yourself?"

Richard didn't answer right away. He stared past her, jaw grinding, until finally he muttered, "I should have stopped her. I should have seen what was happening."

"No one could have known what she would do," she said. "She's always followed her own mind, even when it led her into trouble."

"I should have known," he said again, quieter this time, as if the words tasted of guilt.

Her hand fell away from his arm. "Perhaps," she allowed. "But what's done is done. Now we must move forward together, as a family."

He looked away, towards the rose gardens where his sister had paced only moments ago. "And the scandal?"

His mother's voice was tinged with weariness. "It's been relentless. The gossip columns, the whispers at every gathering. But it will fade, in time. They always do."

"But our family's name..." Richard looked down, a bitter taste on his tongue. "It's been dragged through the mud."

"It has," she admitted. "But hiding away hasn't helped. We've spent long enough in the shadows. It's time to hold our heads high again, no matter how heavy the burden."

Richard lifted his gaze to the sky, as though hoping for strength from the heavens. "It isn't so simple."

"I never said it was simple," she replied with a faint, sad smile. "Only necessary."

They walked in silence towards the house, the crunch of gravel underfoot the only sound for a moment.

"I've asked Miss Theodosia to join us for dinner," his mother informed him.

Richard stopped short. "Why would you do that?"

She offered him a knowing look. "Because if we want her to feel welcome—truly welcome—we must make the effort to embrace her."

He snorted. "Very clever. Keep your enemies close, is that it?"

"And what if she's not the enemy? What if Miss Theodosia is entirely innocent in this?"

Richard gave her a sharp look. "Impossible. She knows something. I can see it in her eyes. She's involved in Mr. Smith's lies. I'm sure of it."

"She seems rather sweet to me."

"Sweet?" Richard repeated. "That is not a word I would ever use to describe Miss Theodosia. Stubborn, perhaps. Aggravating, absolutely. Obstinate beyond measure. Those are far more accurate descriptions."

His mother gave him a sidelong glance, entirely unbothered by his vehemence. "Regardless, she is a beautiful young woman."

"Her beauty has nothing to do with this," he stated, as though the very suggestion was offensive. "You mustn't let that fool you. She's wearing a mask. Women like her always are."

"Not always," his mother murmured, a note of gentle

rebuke in her voice. "But even if she is, isn't it our task to see what lies beneath?"

Richard didn't respond. His mind was already working—assessing, running through every interaction he'd had with Miss Theodosia Smith since he'd first appeared on her doorstep. There was something about her he couldn't quite pin down. Something guarded. Controlled. And yet...

Doubt gnawed at the edge of his certainty.

He had no doubt that she was hiding something. But what exactly that was, he could not yet say.

His mother's voice interrupted his thoughts. "Just remember to be kind to her," she urged. "She's far from home, surrounded by strangers, and likely feels terribly out of place."

"I don't think she's capable of feeling anything."

Even as the words left his mouth, an image flickered unbidden through his mind: Miss Theodosia, sitting in the coach, her eyes shimmering with tears as she spoke of her late parents. The rawness in her voice and the way she had tried to smile through it. For the briefest moment, she had seemed heartbreakingly human.

He pushed the memory aside, hardening his expression.

She would get no sympathy from him. Not until he knew exactly what part she played in Mr. Smith's betrayal.

Not until she proved she wasn't just another beautifully constructed lie.

———————— ～ ————————

Theodosia stirred as the quiet click of the bedchamber door roused her from sleep. Blinking against the fading daylight spilling in through the tall windows, she sat upright just as a young blonde maid stepped inside, a pale green gown draped neatly over her arm.

"Good evening, Miss," the maid greeted with a brightness that bordered on overenthusiasm. "I've been sent to help you dress for dinner."

Theodosia rubbed the sleep from her eyes and swung her feet over the edge of the bed. "But I haven't anything appropriate to wear."

The maid lifted the gown slightly. "You'll be wearing this," she said with a little flourish. "Lady Olivia chose it herself."

Rising to her feet, Theodosia padded across the room, her stockinged feet silent against the thick carpet. She reached out to touch the gown and felt her breath hitch. The dress was exquisite. It was soft green muslin with a white net overlay delicately embroidered along the hem and sleeves.

"This is lovely," she murmured. It was far lovelier than anything she'd ever owned.

The maid beamed with satisfaction. "Lady Olivia thought it would suit your complexion, and I must agree. The green sets off your eyes beautifully."

Theodosia glanced down at her travel-worn habit, suddenly conscious of how coarse the fabric felt against her skin compared to the fine gown.

If the maid noticed her unease, she gave no sign of it. She crossed to the bed and laid the gown out with care. "Now, shall we begin with your hair?"

"I can manage it on my own," Theodosia said.

"I don't doubt it," the maid replied. "But I'm rather skilled at more elaborate styles, and I'd rather not be scolded for ignoring Lady Wilton's instructions."

Reluctantly, Theodosia relented and made her way to the dressing table, settling into the cushioned chair. "I would hate for you to get into trouble on my account."

"Thank you," the maid said, retrieving a silver-handled brush from the vanity and beginning to work it gently through her hair.

As the first strokes smoothed over her scalp, Theodosia caught the maid's reflection in the looking glass. "May I ask your name?"

"It's Mary, Miss."

The curt reply hinted that Mary wasn't fond of idle chatter, but Theodosia's curiosity refused to be quelled. She had far too many questions swirling in her mind.

"What is dinner like here?" she asked.

"Formal," Mary replied, her focus never wavering. "Though I imagine you're quite used to that."

Theodosia gave a soft laugh. "Not exactly. At home, I usually ate in the kitchen with our cook and housekeeper."

Mary paused, clearly surprised. "But aren't you the daughter of a baronet?"

"I am," she admitted. "But dining alone seemed... needlessly grand. I preferred the company."

Mary gave a cautious hum of acknowledgment. "That's... rather unusual."

Theodosia tilted her head. "What is Lady Olivia like?"

Mary set the brush aside and began deftly pinning her hair. "She's spirited," she said carefully. "Lively, intelligent... and accustomed to her independence."

"Does she even want a companion?"

There was a long pause before Mary answered. "It's not my place to say."

"I promise, anything you share will stay between us," Theodosia offered.

Mary shook her head. "That's kind, but I've no wish to be known as a gossip." Then, after a moment, she added in a low voice, "But I will say this—Lady Olivia was rather surprised by her brother's decision."

"I can imagine," Theodosia murmured.

With one last pin tucked securely into place, Mary stepped

back and surveyed her work. "She retired to her chambers shortly after you were introduced," she shared.

"That doesn't bode well," Theodosia said, trying to mask her anxiety.

Mary busied herself with tidying the dressing table. "That's all I should say on the matter."

Theodosia turned in her seat, facing the maid directly. "Thank you, truly. I've never been in a house this grand before. It's quite overwhelming."

Mary's lips curved into something like a knowing smile. "It is grand. But grandeur comes with shadows. This house has its share of secrets."

"What sort of secrets?"

Mary raised her brows but said nothing more. Instead, she walked to the bed and picked up the gown. "You'll find out in time. Now then, let's get you dressed."

Theodosia removed her habit and stepped into the gown, feeling the cool whisper of the muslin as Mary slid it over her shoulders. As the maid began fastening the row of pearl buttons along the back, Theodosia asked, "What do you know of Lord Wilton?"

"What do you wish to know?"

"He seems..." She trailed off, searching for a word that wouldn't reveal too much. Brooding came to mind. Handsome, guarded, vexing. "Tolerable," she said at last.

A soft laugh escaped the maid. "I rarely see him, but the other staff speak well of him. He's fair and exacting. He expects things to be done his way, but he's not unkind."

"That does sound like him," Theodosia admitted.

Before Mary could respond, the door opened, and Lady Olivia stepped into the room. She wore a deep maroon gown that set off her pale complexion, and her hair was arranged with elegant precision. Her expression, however, revealed nothing.

"I thought it best," Olivia said, "if I escorted you to the dining room myself."

"Thank you," Theodosia replied carefully, uncertain whether this was a peace offering or a calculated move.

Olivia's eyes flicked over her, pausing briefly at her face. "The gown suits you."

"Lady Olivia, thank you. It's beautiful."

Olivia gave the barest nod, then gestured towards the door. "Shall we?"

With a final glance at Mary, who offered a discreet, encouraging nod, Theodosia followed Olivia out of the room and into the unknown.

They stepped into the corridor, their slippers muffled against the thick carpeting, and a heavy silence quickly settled between them. Theodosia folded her hands in front of her, unsure of what to say or whether anything she said would make a difference. The tension in the air was palpable. Would she ever feel at ease in Olivia's presence?

She stole a glance at the other woman and noted the rigidity in her posture, the sharp set of her jaw. Olivia's expression was a mask of composure, but the flicker of tightness around her eyes revealed something less controlled. Oh, dear. This was not going well at all.

Theodosia decided to break the silence. "Do you enjoy reading, my lady?"

"I do," Olivia replied without looking at her.

Encouraged by the reply, Theodosia pressed on. "So do I. I heard you frequent the circulating libraries when you are in Town."

"That is correct."

The conversation was stilted, but Theodosia refused to give up. "My father had a small collection of books that I devoured many times over. Of course, our modest library cannot compare to yours."

Olivia's lips pressed into a thin line. "We do have a rather extensive collection here. You are welcome to explore it... on your own."

They walked a few more steps before Theodosia halted, her patience thinning. "Have I done something to offend you, Lady Olivia?"

Olivia stopped but did not immediately turn. "My brother was wrong to hire you," she said, her tone clipped. "I do not need a companion."

"If that's truly how you feel, then dismiss me," Theodosia said simply. "I'll return home, and you need never suffer my presence again."

That got Olivia's attention. She turned slowly, brow arched in disbelief. "I beg your pardon?"

"If you're adamant that you don't want a companion, send me home," Theodosia repeated. "I don't need the income, and I would happily return to managing my estate."

Olivia studied her, as though trying to determine whether she was bluffing. "You cannot be serious."

"I assure you, I am. Your brother offered me two thousand pounds to come to Town with him to be your companion," she explained. "If you send me away, I go home two thousand pounds richer, and none the worse for the experience."

"That is what he offered you to come?"

"He did," Theodosia confirmed. "But truth be told, I accepted because I've never been to London. My mother used to speak so fondly of her time here. I suppose I wanted to see it for myself, just once."

"And you would walk away without complaint?"

"I would," Theodosia replied, unwavering.

A long pause followed, and the only sound was the soft ticking of the longcase clock at the end of the hallway.

"You're not afraid to speak your mind, are you?" Olivia finally asked, sounding half-amused.

"It's one of the many traits your brother finds aggravating," Theodosia quipped.

To her great surprise, a smile ghosted across Olivia's lips— small but genuine. "I do so enjoy vexing my brother. It's one of life's simpler pleasures."

Olivia stepped back, her expression softening, and continued. "I think I might have underestimated you, Miss Theodosia. Perhaps we ought to start over."

"I would like that very much."

They resumed walking, the atmosphere between them noticeably lighter.

"I still don't need a companion," Olivia said. "But I might... benefit from a friend."

"That's good," Theodosia replied with a smile, matching her stride. "Because I have no idea how to be a proper companion."

Olivia laughed under her breath. "So tell me—what do you think of London so far?"

She perked up. "It's unlike anything I've ever seen. So many people, so much movement. The buildings seem to stretch forever, and the townhouses... they're breathtaking."

Olivia's smile grew. "Then I must take you to the *Minerva Press Circulating Library*. It is the largest circulating library in London, with over twenty thousand titles. You might even find a few scandalous French romances if you know where to look."

"I'd enjoy that very much. And if we are to be friends, you must call me Dosia. It's far easier to say than Theodosia, and I've never forgiven my parents for giving me such a long name."

Olivia gave a genuine laugh at that. "It's not that bad."

"When I was younger," Theodosia said wistfully, "I would have given anything to be named something simple. I used to pretend I was an Olivia, in fact."

A faraway look entered Olivia's eyes, her expression shadowed by something more vulnerable than before. "And I wished I could be anyone else."

"Truly? But... you were the daughter of a marquess. A lady of rank, wealth, and influence."

Olivia huffed. "And all the more isolated for it," she said. "Everyone assumed I had everything. But it is lonely being where I am. You never truly know who's sincere. Every smile might conceal a motive. Every compliment could be a calculation. And the expectations, they don't just weigh on you, they smother you."

"I suppose I hadn't thought of it that way," Theodosia responded.

They reached the top of the grand staircase, and Olivia came to a stop, turning to face her with a solemn expression. "You have more freedom than you realize, living in the countryside. There's a kind of peace in being overlooked. In London, everything is a spectacle. You're on display—like a specimen under glass. A single misstep, and the whispers begin. And once they do... they never really stop."

"That sounds awful," Theodosia murmured.

Olivia bobbed her head. "Trust me. It is."

Before Theodosia could reply, a voice echoed from below. "The dinner bell has rung. Shall we adjourn to the dining room?"

They looked down the staircase to find Lady Wilton standing at the foot of the steps, one hand resting lightly on the banister. Beside her stood Lord Wilton, his gaze flicking upward. His expression bore the usual glint of restrained impatience—likely directed at her, Theodosia suspected.

"We're coming," Olivia called down.

Theodosia followed a few steps behind and eventually entered the dining room. The room was bathed in candlelight from a wrought iron chandelier overhead. Gilt-framed paintings adorned the dark paneled walls, and the long mahogany table gleamed beneath crystal decanters and sparkling silverware. Footmen stepped forward to pull out chairs as the ladies approached.

Theodosia murmured a quiet "thank you" as she sat down and unfolded her white linen napkin. The temptation to shrink into the upholstery was stronger than she cared to admit.

Lord Wilton and Lady Wilton took their seats at opposite ends of the table, and Olivia settled directly across from her.

Trying to fill the silence before it thickened, Theodosia said, a little louder than usual, "This is a beautiful table."

Lady Wilton smiled. "Thank you, my dear. It was commissioned by my father when I was a child. I insisted we bring it here when David inherited the house. It holds memories," she said, not looking up as the footmen began placing steaming bowls of creamy soup in front of each guest.

Theodosia reached for her spoon as the scent of leek and potato drifted upward. It was a familiar scent. Still, her appetite waned with nerves. Everything felt too rich, too grand—like slipping into a world she admired but didn't quite belong to.

7

Richard glared at Miss Theodosia over the rim of his spoon as she lifted hers with measured grace. Now that she was seated at his family's table, in his house, he no longer felt the need to offer even the barest illusion of civility. The time for politeness had passed. She was here, ensnared in his world, and she could not simply leave. Not without his permission. She may have walked in with her head high and her chin set, but he knew that she was effectively cornered.

Across the table, his mother caught his eye and gave a discreet clearing of her throat. A warning. A reminder.

"Do you intend to go to the House of Lords tomorrow, Richard?" she asked.

He was pulled from his thoughts and straightened. "I do," he said, adjusting his grip on his spoon. "Lord Warwicke and I are drafting a bill that would raise the minimum age for children in workhouses."

Olivia's eyes snapped up. "It's about time," she stated. "Children are being worked to death in those places. If they survive the labor, they don't survive the neglect."

"Warwicke is quite passionate about the matter," Richard said with a nod. "And I've decided to lend my support."

"Well, if you're in the mood to lend your support," Olivia began, arching a brow, "have you considered championing women's rights? It's positively barbaric how few rights we have."

Richard set his spoon down with a faint clink. "That's a lost cause."

"Says the *lord*," Olivia muttered under her breath, but not quietly enough to go unnoticed.

"Women's minds are too fickle for politics. They would vote based on sentiment, not reason."

Olivia's mouth dropped open. "That is the most backward thing I've heard this week. I am perfectly capable of forming an educated opinion."

"You may be," Richard conceded, "but most women are content to concern themselves with fashions and gossip, not matters of state."

With a fierce glare, Olivia asked, "Were you dropped on your head as a child?"

Their mother laughed softly. "Olivia, really. Play fair."

"That is me playing fair," she replied. "The only thing idiotic in this room is that opinion."

Richard leaned back in his chair, folding his arms. "This is precisely what I mean. You go straight to insult instead of debate. Emotion over logic."

"I only insult idiotic arguments," she shot back. "Don't confuse passion with irrationality." She turned to Miss Theodosia with a dramatic flourish of her hand. "Dosia agrees with me, don't you?"

Miss Theodosia set her spoon aside and dabbed the corners of her mouth with her napkin. Her tone was calm, but her eyes gleamed with quiet conviction. "I do, in fact. I believe women are just as capable as men of making informed political decisions. And I suspect that frightens some men."

Richard's jaw tensed. "And what, pray tell, do we have to be frightened of?"

Miss Theodosia met his gaze evenly. "Loss of control. For centuries, men have held the reins of power. Granting women a voice challenges that authority."

He shook his head. "It's not fear. It's pragmatism."

"No, my lord," she said, "it's denial. You deny women their rights not because they are incapable, but because they threaten the comfortable order you've grown used to."

Olivia raised her spoon triumphantly. "Hear, hear!"

Richard gave a theatrical shudder. "Heaven help us all if women ever gain control of the government."

"We've had queens," Olivia reminded him. "And I don't recall England descending into chaos under Elizabeth."

Their mother interjected. "Perhaps we can find a topic less likely to start a rebellion at the table."

Taking the cue with a smile, Olivia said, "I've decided to take Dosia to the circulating library tomorrow."

"A lovely idea," their mother replied. "And of course, our library is always at her disposal. We've a few first editions you might enjoy."

"Thank you, my lady," Miss Theodosia replied. "I've always loved reading. Books have a way of making the world feel both larger and more intimate at the same time."

Olivia's expression brightened. "Did you know Catherine Parr wrote books and had them published under her own name?"

"I didn't," Miss Theodosia said. "It's rare. Most women still write under pseudonyms to avoid prejudice."

"I once considered writing a novel," Olivia shared, swirling her spoon in her soup.

Richard groaned. "I'm not sure the world is ready for that."

She ignored him. "It was going to be a romance, naturally. But I abandoned it. I've decided love is dead."

"Love is not dead, my dear," their mother responded. "Your father and I loved each other very deeply."

Olivia's gaze dropped to her bowl. "Well, it's dead for me."

A silence followed—longer than it ought to have been.

Richard felt something shift in his chest. A pang. His sister had always believed in love. She used to sneak novels into her governess's lessons, daydreaming about gallant heroes and moonlit proposals. Mr. Smith had destroyed that part of her, and Richard didn't know how to bring it back.

Before he could speak, Miss Theodosia's voice broke through the silence. "Love never truly dies," she said. "Even when it's lost... it lingers. It stays with you."

Olivia snorted. "Love is a useless emotion. All it ever does is leave you with pain." But her voice cracked at the edges, and her eyes shimmered a little too brightly in the candlelight.

"I'm sorry for what happened to you," Miss Theodosia said, her voice barely above a whisper. "Lord Wilton told me only a little, just enough to understand—"

The chair scraped sharply against the floor as Olivia shoved it back and shot to her feet. "Excuse me," she said. "I can't do this. Not right now."

Without another word, she turned and swept from the room, her skirts rustling with haste, leaving an uneasy silence in her wake.

Miss Theodosia watched her go, her body half-turned in her chair. "I shouldn't have said anything," she murmured, her voice filled with remorse.

"No," Richard said curtly, not bothering to mask his irritation. "You shouldn't have."

She turned back to him slowly. "Should I go after her?"

"No," he snapped. "That will only make it worse."

Miss Theodosia lowered her gaze to the table, her fingers curled slightly against the edge of her napkin. The slump of her shoulders and the quiet way her chest rose and fell made it clear that she wasn't skilled at hiding her emotions—not yet, at least. The guilt she carried was written clearly across her face.

He picked up his spoon again and resumed eating his soup, determined to ignore the knot in his stomach. The silence that followed felt oppressive. He could feel his mother's disapproval radiating from her end of the table.

Still, he said nothing.

After what felt like an eternity, Miss Theodosia pushed her chair back with slow deliberation. "I believe it would be best if I retired for the evening," she said, rising with dignity despite the tremor in her voice.

Finally. That was the first sensible thing she'd said all night. He opened his mouth to agree—

"Nonsense," his mother interjected. "You will remain right where you are."

Miss Theodosia paused, caught off guard. "But, my lady—"

His mother leaned forward slightly. "You did nothing wrong. You offered kindness. That is not a crime. You have no reason to punish yourself for Olivia's pain."

Then she turned her gaze sharply towards her son. "Isn't that right, Richard?"

The words were there, poised on the edge of his tongue. He wanted to argue. Wanted to protest that Miss Theodosia had overstepped, that she didn't belong, that she should have known better. But something in his mother's stare stopped him. There was a challenge in it, and disappointment.

He swallowed his retort. "Yes," he said grudgingly. "That's right."

His mother gave a satisfied nod. "Good. Now, let us enjoy the next course, shall we?"

She lifted her hand in a subtle, graceful gesture, and the footmen moved forward at once, collecting the soup bowls with silent efficiency. Another servant appeared, bearing a silver tray upon which rested a beautifully roasted haunch of venison, its scent filling the room with rich notes of rosemary and wine.

As the platter was placed at the center of the table, Miss Theodosia slowly sat back down. She straightened her posture, smoothing her napkin once more across her lap. Though her face remained composed, there was a flicker of sadness in her eyes that even Richard couldn't ignore.

Blast it.

Richard clenched his jaw and shoved a piece of venison across his plate. He didn't give a whit what Miss Theodosia was feeling. She was the deceiver in all of this, not him. So why was he noticing the shadow in her eyes or the way her hands lingered on her napkin as if it were an anchor?

He scowled into his wine, annoyed with himself.

Across the table, his mother took a sip from her glass, then turned to Theodosia. "Tell me, Miss Theodosia," she said, "what usually occupies your time in the countryside?"

Miss Theodosia lifted her chin with quiet poise. "As I mentioned earlier, I manage a small estate, my lady."

"That is rather unusual," Lady Wilton said.

Miss Theodosia squared her shoulders with subtle pride. "Yes. My father passed away without any sons, and as I had a head for figures and a familiarity with the land, the responsibility fell to me. I've been managing the estate for nearly a year now."

"That's quite remarkable," Lady Wilton said, clearly intrigued. "Not many ladies would claim such a task—or succeed in it."

"It may be unconventional," Miss Theodosia allowed, "but I find it suits me. I've little time for more traditional pursuits, and I prefer it that way."

Despite himself, Richard spoke. "Miss Theodosia is also quite skilled at drawing."

"Lord Wilton flatters me," Miss Theodosia said with a modest smile. "I'm merely proficient."

"Nonsense. My son is many things, but a flatterer is not one of them. If he says you're talented, I have no reason to doubt it," his mother stated, placing her napkin beside her plate. "I shall ensure you are given proper supplies."

"That is most generous, my lady," Miss Theodosia replied.

Before anyone could say more, the door to the dining room opened again and Olivia swept in. Her gown was still perfectly in place, her posture poised, but her eyes were red-rimmed and her smile a little too tight.

"I apologize for leaving so suddenly," she said as she reclaimed her chair. "But I'm back now, and I'd rather not dwell on the why."

Richard stood without hesitation and reached for the platter of venison. "We're glad you returned," he said as he served her a generous portion.

"Was anything of note discussed while I was gone?" Olivia asked, stabbing at her food more than slicing it.

His mother gestured lightly towards Miss Theodosia. "We were just speaking about Miss Theodosia's artistic talents. It seems she has quite the talent for drawing."

Olivia glanced up. "Is that so? That's a talent I never had. My horses always looked like unfortunate cows."

Miss Theodosia laughed. "I doubt that to be true."

"Perhaps you'll show me sometime. I might yet learn to draw something more dignified than a misshapen goat," Olivia joked.

"I would be happy to," Miss Theodosia replied.

Richard's fork moved with measured deliberation as he focused on the task of cutting his venison into even bites. Fortunately, the attention had shifted away from him, and he was grateful for the reprieve.

He chewed slowly but was glad for the silence inside his

own head. He didn't have to defend, argue, or explain himself, especially to the infuriating Miss Theodosia.

And that, he decided, was enough.

———————

Theodosia lay on her back, staring up at the shadowy canopy of her four-poster bed. The moonlight filtering through the parted curtains painted silver lines across the ceiling, but offered no comfort. It was late—well past midnight, surely—but her mind refused to rest.

Her thoughts lingered on Olivia's stricken face, the abrupt scrape of her chair against the polished floor, the echo of her retreating footsteps. Theodosia winced inwardly. She had meant only to offer sympathy, not wound her. But she'd overstepped. Spoken as though she had any true understanding of heartbreak, when in truth, she had only ever brushed its edges.

And now, to make matters worse, she was starving. She had barely touched her supper, and her stomach protested with persistent grumbles that refused to be ignored.

Perhaps Cook left out some bread, she mused. *Something simple. Anything at all.*

She hesitated, then pushed back the heavy covers and swung her legs over the side of the bed. The floor was cool beneath her feet as she reached for her wrapper, a white muslin garment she tied snugly around her waist before stepping quietly into the corridor.

The house was hushed and dim, the sconces along the walls darkened for the night. Shadows danced along the edges of the gilded wallpaper, and the silence stretched with every tentative footstep she took.

Where is the kitchen? she thought. *And do I even know how to get there?*

She wandered through the corridor with cautious steps until a faint flicker of candlelight caught her attention. A thin ribbon of gold spilled out from beneath a partially open door just ahead.

Curiosity nudged her forward.

She padded towards the door and peered inside.

Lord Wilton sat at an ornate desk surrounded by strewn ledgers and papers. His dinner jacket had been discarded, and the candlelight cast long shadows over his face, accentuating the stern line of his jaw. But he wasn't working. He sat utterly still, staring out the window, lost in thought.

Something in his expression—so far from the arrogance she was accustomed to—gave her pause. There was weariness there. And solitude.

She began to quietly step back, hoping to retreat unnoticed, but her heel pressed against a loose floorboard with an unfortunate creak.

He turned sharply.

"Who's there?" he barked.

She froze, inwardly cursing her luck. Then, seeing no escape, she stepped fully into the room.

"It's just me, my lord," she said, her voice calm despite her flustered heart.

His gaze narrowed. "Miss Theodosia? What exactly are you doing sneaking about the house at this hour?"

"I wasn't sneaking," she replied, though her smile was sheepish. "I was looking for the kitchen."

"The kitchen," he echoed dryly. "Which happens to be on the opposite end of the house."

"Well... now I know," she said with a curtsy. "Good evening."

He shoved back his chair and stood. "You can drop the act. If you're here to entrap me into marriage, you'll be sorely disappointed."

Her eyes widened. "I beg your pardon?"

"You appear in my study, after midnight, wearing nothing but your wrapper," he said, folding his arms. "What impression am I meant to take from that?"

She squared her shoulders, her pride flaring to life. "No offense, my lord, but you are quite literally the last man I would ever wish to entrap."

He gave a scoffing laugh. "I doubt that."

"Oh, do you?" She took a step forward, chin lifted. "You're arrogant, condescending, and far too pleased with yourself. None of those are qualities I seek in a husband."

"I'm a marquess."

"That's a *title,* not a virtue," she snapped. "And it does not impress me."

He looked genuinely baffled. "My title impresses everyone."

She threw her hands up. "And we're back to arrogant. Do you even hear yourself speak?"

"If you're truly on a mission to find the kitchen, I won't keep you."

"I would appreciate that."

He gave a mockingly courtly bow. "Good evening, Miss Theodosia."

Rolling her eyes, she turned and exited the study.

"Wrong way," he called from behind her.

"I do believe any distance between us is a good thing," she retorted without stopping.

"Yes," he agreed, "but that direction leads to the gardens. Unless you intend to go for a moonlit stroll in your wrapper, I suggest otherwise."

She halted and turned back to find him leaning against the doorframe, smirking like the devil himself.

Grinding her teeth, she asked, "Would you kindly point me in the direction of the kitchen?"

He gestured smoothly down the corridor. "That way. Straight on until the long clock, then left."

Theodosia lifted her chin and marched past him, ignoring the way his gaze lingered as she passed.

When she reached the grand entry hall, she hesitated again. There were too many doors, and none of them felt particularly promising.

Lord Wilton reappeared beside her, maddeningly composed. "Allow me," he said. "The servants' staircase is this way."

"I can manage," she muttered, but followed him, nonetheless.

He led her to an unadorned door tucked behind a curtain, opened it, and gestured to the steep wooden staircase beyond. "This will take you down to the kitchens. Do mind the steps since they are narrow and worn."

"I think I can handle a staircase."

She brushed past him and descended—but misjudged the first step. Her foot slipped.

In a flash, his hand shot out, catching her arm firmly and steadying her.

"Careful, Miss Theodosia," he said, voice low, close to her ear.

She immediately pulled away. "I will be," she said stiffly.

"Perhaps I should follow you the rest of the way. Just in case."

She paused, turned her head slightly, and gave him a narrow look. "You must think yourself terribly gallant."

"No," he replied with a slow smile. "Merely observant. You do have a tendency to miscalculate."

With a dramatic sigh, she resumed her descent. "And you have a tendency to be insufferable."

His voice drifted down after her, amused. "So I've been told."

As Theodosia carefully descended the narrow staircase, the soft scuff of leather shoes behind her announced that Lord Wilton had, predictably, decided to follow.

She didn't turn around. "You needn't accompany me. Don't feel obliged to stay on my account."

"Careful, Miss Theodosia," came his smooth reply from above. "That almost sounds as if you don't relish my company."

She tossed a glance over her shoulder. "Trust me—I do not."

He gave a theatrical *tsk* of mock disappointment. "Pity. I was beginning to think we were becoming friends."

She muttered a curse word under her breath and took the last step with a little more force than was strictly necessary. The corridor at the base of the staircase was dim, and the stone floor cool beneath her feet as she made her way towards the darkened kitchen.

She moved cautiously, her hands brushing across the counters as she fumbled for something—anything—resembling food.

She had just lifted a linen-draped basket when warm light spilled across the room, the soft glow of a candle stretching long shadows over the walls. She turned to see Lord Wilton standing in the doorway with a candleholder in one hand.

"I thought this might help," he said, lifting the flame slightly. "A little light to aid in your noble quest."

"That... does help," she admitted reluctantly.

With the added illumination, her search was more fruitful. She found a loaf of crusty bread nestled beneath the cloth, along with a crock of butter that still held its chill from the stone pantry. Locating a knife, she began slicing carefully.

"Would you care for a piece, my lord?" she asked, her tone far too polite to be sincere. She hoped, prayed even, that he would decline.

To her great annoyance, he smiled. "A slice of bread sounds delightful, thank you."

Of course it does, she thought, barely refraining from rolling her eyes.

She cut two slices and placed them on the plates he had helpfully retrieved from a nearby cupboard. He accepted his with a small nod of thanks and walked over to the long kitchen table, settling himself with all the ease of a man entirely comfortable in any room he entered.

Theodosia remained where she was for a moment, debating whether to simply snatch her plate and flee back upstairs. But that would look childish. Worse, it would look like he'd won some invisible battle. So she crossed the room and took the seat opposite him.

That didn't mean she intended to engage in conversation.

She broke off a piece of bread and chewed slowly, hoping he'd take the hint.

He didn't.

"I take it you've not yet memorized the configuration of the house," he said after a moment.

She swallowed and replied, "No. Your townhouse is... expansive. My entire manor could likely fit inside your servants' quarters."

He glanced around the kitchen, then leaned back with a self-satisfied air. "It is a magnificent house," he said, his tone bordering on smug. "My father made several improvements, and I've added a few of my own."

"It is quite impressive."

Lord Wilton cast her a sideways glance. "Is that a rare compliment I hear from you?"

"I am more than willing to offer praise when the situation warrants it."

"And I do not warrant it?" he asked, his tone half-teasing, half-genuine in its challenge.

A bark of laughter escaped her. "Heavens, no. You are insufferable, my lord."

Rather than appearing wounded by the insult, he leaned back in his chair, his lips curling into that maddening smirk of his. "If that is your way of flirting—"

"Flirting?" she interrupted, nearly choking on the word. "I would never flirt with you."

His grin only deepened, as if he were perfectly confident that her denial meant quite the opposite. "There will come a day when you will. Willingly and without shame."

"I assure you," she said, "that day will never come to pass."

"We shall see," he murmured.

Theodosia leaned back in her seat, exhaling slowly as she regarded him. The man was so smug—so entirely full of himself—it was astonishing that there was any place left for air in the room. And yet, despite herself, she couldn't help but notice the way the candlelight played along his angular jaw, or how his eyes seemed to hold secrets too heavy to name. What, precisely, was wrong with her?

Lord Wilton brushed the last crumbs from his fingertips and placed his empty plate aside. "That was delicious."

Theodosia hesitated, curiosity nudging at her. "Earlier," she began slowly, "in your office... you appeared rather preoccupied."

At once, the warmth drained from his features. The playfulness vanished as if it had never been there. "I was merely thinking," he said curtly.

She chose her next words with care. "Is it something you wish to speak of?"

He pushed his chair back. "You would do well to remember your place," he said, his voice now edged in warning.

"We agreed, did we not, that I might speak my mind?"

Lord Wilton stood to his full height, towering above her.

"What I think about is my own business," he asserted. "And none of your concern."

"I was only trying to help."

"I don't need your help," he snapped, stepping away from the table. His tone had hardened, and his retreat was swift. "I trust you can find your way back upstairs?"

Theodosia gave a stiff nod. "Yes, my lord."

He looked at her for a heartbeat longer, his expression unreadable—then, without another word, he turned and strode from the room.

She remained seated, staring at the space he had occupied only moments before. She should not have pressed him. He had made it clear that he guarded his thoughts closely, as though revealing them might unravel something he could not afford to lose. But she had seen the softer edges of him—the flickers of kindness, the glint of sorrow he tried so desperately to hide.

Perhaps that was what unsettled her most.

Because she, too, knew how it felt to keep the world at bay. To hide behind walls of sharp wit and cold indifference. To protect what remained of one's heart by never offering it.

She ought to leave well enough alone.

But part of her wanted to understand the man behind the mask.

And that, she suspected, was the true danger.

8

R ichard emerged from his bedchamber and strode down the dim corridor. Sleep had eluded him last night. His thoughts had churned relentlessly throughout the night, circling back to one frustrating, utterly maddening subject: Miss Theodosia Smith.

Why did she persist in asking questions he had no desire— no intention—of answering?

She could not possibly understand the weight that came with being a marquess. The constant obligations and the expectations that pressed down like a lead cloak. He had been thrust into the role far too soon, with little preparation and no time to grieve the man whose legacy he was meant to uphold. His father had been a pillar of strength, a man of unshakable integrity and presence. And now that pillar was gone, leaving Richard to build a life from the rubble of duty and doubt.

He should feel grateful—honored, even. But gratitude had no power against the creeping fear that whispered: *What if I am not enough? What if I fail?*

It was a relentless fear, one that throbbed in time with his very heartbeat. And it was not something he would ever confess aloud. Not to his mother, or even to his closest friends. Certainly not to Miss Theodosia, who had a knack for asking the wrong questions with infuriating persistence.

She was vexing.

And the most irritating part was that he noticed her at all.

As if summoned by the very force of his thoughts, she appeared at the top of the staircase, her pale blue gown catching a shaft of morning light. She offered him a polite smile.

"Good morning, my lord."

He paused and gave her a shallow bow. "Miss Theodosia."

"Are you on your way to breakfast?"

"I am."

"Well then," she said, falling into step beside him, "as we are bound for the same destination, shall we walk together?"

Richard resisted the urge to groan. "If we must."

Her smile widened, as if she found his reluctance endlessly amusing. She fluttered her lashes in exaggerated coquetry. "You certainly know how to make a lady feel special."

"You wish me to flatter you?" he asked dryly.

"I should hope not. I have no need for empty praise," she replied breezily. "I prefer honesty. Always."

They descended the stairs side by side, and he glanced her way. "Ah, yes. Honesty—the most elusive of virtues. Not for the faint of heart."

"Perhaps not," she allowed, her tone thoughtful, "but surely it is better to be honest with oneself, if nothing else."

Richard nearly scoffed. How easily she spoke of truth, when she had lied to him—boldly, unapologetically. She had deceived him about Mr. Smith, misled him with her charm and calm demeanor, all while pretending to be the very embodiment of integrity. Her hypocrisy was laughable.

He opened his mouth, prepared to remind her of it in no uncertain terms, when a familiar voice called from behind.

"Good heavens," his mother declared, her tone touched with surprise. "There are two of you up at this hour?"

Richard halted at the base of the stairs and turned to see his mother approaching. "Pardon?"

"You and Miss Theodosia," she said with a wave of her hand. "You're both early risers. They must keep earlier hours in the countryside."

Miss Theodosia spoke up. "Indeed. I find the mornings quite peaceful. There is a certain quietude to them I rather like."

His mother made a dismissive noise. "There is never any quiet in this house. Shall we adjourn to the dining room?"

Richard offered his arm to his mother. "Allow me."

"Thank you, dear," she said, resting her gloved hand on his sleeve.

As they walked, Miss Theodosia fell into step on his other side.

"And how did you sleep, Miss Theodosia?" his mother asked lightly.

She smiled, a glimmer of warmth softening her features. "Please, you must call me Dosia. It is far less cumbersome."

"How very gracious," his mother replied. "Isn't she gracious, Richard?"

He wasn't sure why he was suddenly involved in the conversation, but he offered a half-hearted shrug. "Yes, I suppose."

His mother patted his arm with a knowing look. "That wasn't so difficult to admit, was it?"

Richard grumbled under his breath. "Why must you ask so many questions before breakfast?"

"I take it you didn't sleep well," she said, undeterred.

"I rarely do."

Her expression softened. "Were you up late again?"

He hesitated before glancing briefly at Miss Theodosia. "I was."

They reached the dining room, where the table was laid with silver, porcelain, and trays of warm rolls and preserved fruits. He pulled out his mother's chair and waited for her to settle before taking his place at the head of the table.

To his right, Miss Theodosia sat down and immediately gasped with delight.

"Is this chocolate?" she asked, lifting a delicate porcelain cup to her lips. Her eyes widened in appreciation after a sip. "It's delicious."

"You've never had chocolate before?" he asked, raising a brow.

She nodded her head. "Only when my father visited Town and returned with it as a special treat. It was rare, but always memorable."

"Well," Richard replied, leaning back in his seat, "in this household, it is served every morning."

She met his gaze over the rim of her cup. "Then I do believe I could grow accustomed to mornings in your household."

He allowed himself a small smile—until he remembered who he was smiling at and quickly composed his expression. "My sister often requests a breakfast tray be sent to her bedchamber," he said, tone returning to its usual clipped civility.

As if summoned by his very mention of her, Olivia swept into the dining room, her presence as theatrical as ever. "But not today, Brother," she announced with a bright smile. "I have decided to grace you all with my company."

"How wonderful," Richard muttered under his breath, rising politely from his seat.

She waved a dismissive hand. "Do sit down. No need to rise on my account. I hope Dosia is as delighted as I am to visit the circulating library today. I've been looking forward to it all morning."

"I am rather excited," Miss Theodosia said with a smile.

"Thank you again for allowing me to borrow your gown for the outing."

Olivia waved the thanks away as she seated herself. "Think nothing of it. Now that I'm married, I am free of those pasty pale gowns meant to signify innocence and modesty. I have resolved to begin wearing crimson gowns."

Richard arched a brow. "Perhaps you might begin with shades that do not attract quite so much attention."

"Nonsense," Olivia replied. "It's one of the few freedoms that marriage affords me. If I must submit to the rest of it, I shall at least wear whatever color I please."

Before he could retort, the butler appeared silently in the doorway and approached with the morning newssheets balanced neatly on a silver tray. He placed them beside Richard with a slight bow. "Will there be anything further, my lord?"

"Not at this time, thank you," Richard replied with a nod of dismissal.

He had just reached for the topmost paper when Olivia snatched it up with a triumphant grin. "You must be faster next time, Brother."

"Need I remind you that reading the newssheets is not considered particularly ladylike?"

She did not even glance up from the page as she flipped it open. "Ah, but I am married now," she replied, as though that single fact rendered all previous expectations obsolete.

"Being married does not mean you must abandon all decorum," he responded.

Olivia peered over the newssheet at him with a smug look. "Oh, I think it rather means I can do exactly that."

Beside him, Miss Theodosia bit her lip to keep from smiling, though her eyes sparkled with amusement. Richard sighed, pressing his fingertips to his temple. He found he couldn't wait until these two departed for the circulating library.

For a few blissful moments, the only sound in the breakfast

room was the soft rustling of paper as Olivia perused the newssheets, her tea momentarily forgotten. Then without warning, she let out a sharp gasp.

"How extraordinary," she exclaimed. "It appears that Mr. Haverleigh's trial is moving forward. He is to be tried for attempting to murder his sister, Lady Warwicke!"

Lowering the newssheets, Olivia met Miss Theodosia's gaze and continued. "They claim he used an age-old poison that is so potent, it can kill with just four drops."

"That is awful," Miss Theodosia murmured.

Olivia gave a solemn nod, though a touch of mischief crept into her tone. "Yes, dreadful indeed. Still, one must admit, it is quite the scandal. Perhaps it will distract Society just long enough to forget I eloped to Gretna Green."

She had barely finished speaking when a flash of white fur and fluttering silk ribbons streaked into the dining room like a miniature whirlwind. Miss Theodosia shrieked and scrambled backward in her chair, clutching at the table edge.

"What is that?" she cried.

Unperturbed, Olivia bent down with a delighted laugh and scooped up the tiny bundle of fur. "That is a Pomeranian puppy. His name is Finnegan. Isn't he the dearest little thing you've ever seen?"

"I thought it was a rat," Miss Theodosia admitted.

Richard chuckled. "Frankly, I wouldn't be surprised if my sister did try to keep a rat as a pet."

"Hush," Olivia murmured as she brought the puppy close to her cheek. "Don't listen to them, Finnegan. You are nothing like a rat. You are perfection in a puffball."

"I meant no offense," Miss Theodosia said quickly, still eyeing the animal with uncertainty.

With a graceful shrug, Olivia placed Finnegan in her lap and reached for a slice of ham from the serving dish. "None taken. But I should remind you that Her Majesty herself keeps Pomeranians. They are very fashionable."

Richard's brow furrowed. "That may be, but you are not the queen. And more importantly, you are not to feed your dog from the breakfast table."

Olivia turned wide, innocent eyes upon her brother. "And where, pray tell, should I feed him?"

"In the kitchen, where his food dish is," Richard replied.

"But that's so far away," Olivia protested. "And Finnegan is simply famished. Besides, he's so very small. He eats hardly anything at all."

"Olivia—" Richard began, his voice edged with warning.

"Richard is right," their mother interjected. "You will not feed that dog at the table."

Olivia sighed with theatrical resignation. "Very well," she said, giving Finnegan a final nuzzle before placing him gently on the floor. The puppy gave a tiny sneeze, then scampered off, his little paws tapping a lively rhythm across the polished wood floor.

Miss Theodosia watched the dog warily before turning back towards her plate.

The long clock chimed in the corner and Olivia stood up. "Well, *Minerva Press Circulating Library* should be open by now," she announced. "Shall we be off, Dosia?"

"Yes, please do," Richard muttered.

Unbothered, Olivia grinned and cast him a knowing glance. "You say that now, Brother, but you'll miss us the moment we're gone."

"Highly unlikely, especially since I intend to go to the club the moment I finish breakfast," he replied.

Olivia placed a hand to her heart in mock offense. "What a cold farewell. One would think you were eager to be rid of us."

"I am," he replied evenly, lifting his cup in a mock toast.

"Now off you go—before I change my mind and accompany you, just to make the outing miserable."

Laughing, Olivia gestured towards the doorway with an elegant sweep of her arm. "Come along, Dosia. Let us leave my brother to his grumpiness and brandy-soaked solitude."

Once they had departed, Richard reached for the newssheets and started reading. He had barely read a paragraph when his mother's voice drifted across the table.

"You ought to be kinder to Miss Theodosia."

He didn't look up. "I won't throw rocks at her, if that's what you're worried about."

"That is a relief," his mother replied. "But there's a wide gulf between refraining from assault and exercising basic courtesy. Kindness often goes much further than you think."

He lowered the newssheets and met her gaze. "You forget that Miss Theodosia is not some innocent young miss in need of my civility. She is a liar. A clever, calculating one. She knows far more than she admits about Olivia's husband."

"Be that as it may..." his mother began.

"I've no time for a lecture," he interrupted, rising from his seat.

His mother's expression remained composed, though her eyes held a familiar glint of disapproval. "I raised you to be a gentleman. You'd do well to remember it."

"I am a gentleman," he replied. "I manage the estate, protect our name, and keep this family from collapsing under scandal. I know my duty."

"There is more to life than ledgers and accounts," she said. "One day, perhaps sooner than you think, you will want to start a family."

"But that day is not today," he stated before he departed from the room, having no desire to talk about such things.

Theodosia sat across from Olivia in the swaying coach, her gaze fixed on the passing scenery beyond the window. It was all so strange and thrilling—the crush of people bustling along the pavement, the elegant carriages weaving through narrow lanes, and the towering buildings rising side by side like sentinels of a world she had never known. She couldn't decide what fascinated her more: the ever-changing press of fashionable pedestrians or the architectural splendor that surrounded them. Both seemed to demand her attention at once.

Her thoughts were interrupted by Olivia's voice. "You must think I'm intolerably stupid for marrying a man I scarcely knew."

Theodosia turned her head and met Olivia's gaze. "I've thought no such thing."

A rueful smile played at Olivia's lips. "Well, that's precisely how I feel. Foolish." She shifted slightly in her seat, pulling her pelisse tighter around her. "I didn't even kiss Luke—not once, not even after the wedding. We barely even touched. It was as though he couldn't bear to be near me."

Theodosia felt a dozen questions spring to mind, but she hesitated, wary of prying too deeply into wounds that were clearly still raw. Yet Olivia didn't seem to need prompting.

"Luke promised me everything—security, affection, even adventure. He said he wanted to build a life with me. But none of it was true." Her voice grew tight, her hands clenched in her lap. "Why didn't I see it? Why didn't I know he was lying?"

"Because he deceived you," Theodosia said gently. "You placed your trust in him, and he exploited it. That's not your fault."

Olivia exhaled sharply through her nose. "I ran off to Gretna Green like some besotted fool. I destroyed my reputation, gave up any semblance of a respectable future—and for what? The moment he collected the dowry from the solicitor, he vanished."

"The man has no shame," Theodosia remarked.

There was a pause, and then Olivia studied her more intently. "You wouldn't do that, would you?"

"Do what?"

"Lie to me. Pretend to be someone you're not."

Theodosia furrowed her brow. "No. I've no reason to deceive you."

"None at all?" Olivia pressed, her tone sharp with suspicion.

"What would I even lie about?"

Olivia gave a weary sigh and looked away. "I suppose I have no choice but to trust you."

Before Theodosia could respond, the coach jerked to a halt in front of a whitewashed brick building nestled between taller establishments. A wrought iron sign swung overhead, proclaiming in elegant script: *Minerva Press Circulating Library*.

A footman appeared, swiftly opening the coach door and offering a gloved hand. Theodosia waited for Olivia to descend first before accepting the assistance herself, withdrawing her hand as soon as her boots touched the cobbled pavement.

"I can't wait for you to see this," Olivia said with genuine excitement, motioning towards the door. "You're going to adore it."

With a curious smile, Theodosia followed her inside and immediately came to a halt just beyond the threshold. The air was filled with the warm scent of aged paper and wood polish. Towering shelves crammed with books lined the walls in every direction. A wide, arched ceiling gave the room an almost cathedral-like sense of reverence.

Olivia beamed at her reaction. "Is it not spectacular?"

Theodosia's voice was hushed in awe. "I've never seen anything like it. Not even close."

Olivia pointed towards a doorway on their left. "That leads to the salon. Ladies gather there to play card games, gossip, and engage in what they call serious conversation." She grinned. "Come—I want to show you the books written by women."

She led Theodosia to a long shelf tucked along the back wall. With great reverence, Olivia ran her fingers along the spines as though greeting old friends. "Every book here was written by a woman," she explained.

"I had no idea so many women had written books."

"Oh, many more than you think. But these women"—she tapped one of the covers—"were brave enough to claim their words."

Theodosia plucked a small volume from the shelf, its cloth cover faded but the title embossed in gold. "Can anyone borrow these?"

"You must have a subscription," Olivia explained. "But the annual fee is less than two pounds, which is entirely manageable for a single reader."

"A fair price, considering what's available to us," Theodosia replied.

"My mother is a patron here," Olivia said with a note of pride. She opened a nearby volume and inhaled its scent. "She always believed in supporting women's education."

"That is most generous of her."

Olivia lowered her voice to a conspiratorial whisper. "Would you care to see the scandalous French romances?"

Theodosia laughed. "I doubt I have a choice in the matter."

With a gleam in her eye, Olivia guided her to another section, whispering as they walked, "Some critics claim these libraries encourage laziness and corrupt young ladies with fantastical ideas."

"I disagree."

"As do I," Olivia said firmly. "It's not as though I confuse Gothic horrors with everyday life."

"I should hope not," Theodosia responded, giggling.

They reached another row of shelves, and Olivia immediately began selecting books. "This one you must read," she said, thrusting a volume into Theodosia's hands. "And this one. Oh! You'll absolutely love this."

Before long, Theodosia was cradling an ever-growing stack of books, each one insisted upon with the same enthusiasm. She looked down at the pile and laughed. "I think I have enough to last me a fortnight—at the very least."

Olivia smiled with satisfaction. "That's the spirit."

Theodosia crossed the room and made her way to an empty reading table tucked near a tall window. The sunlight filtered through the glass panes. With a slight huff, she set her burden down. "They were becoming rather heavy," she shared.

Olivia joined her a moment later, brushing a few errant curls from her brow before plucking the top book from the stack. She turned it over in her hands, her expression thoughtful. "Dosia," she asked, "have you ever been in love?"

Caught off guard by the question, Theodosia straightened the spine of one of the books before replying, "No. I haven't."

Olivia's brow arched, curiosity still flickering in her gaze. "Any offers of marriage?"

Theodosia gave a small nod. "A gentleman from my village recently offered for me."

Olivia carefully returned the book to the top of the pile. "And you refused him?"

"I did," Theodosia confirmed, glancing down at her hands. "He was kind, respectable and a landowner. Everyone said I ought to be pleased, but... I didn't love him."

"You want love, then?"

Theodosia paused before admitting, "I do. I know some might think that naïve or even reckless. But I would rather be alone than marry without affection."

Olivia reached out and laid a hand over Theodosia's sleeve. "I think that's brave of you."

"Brave?"

"Yes. So many women accept what is offered to them—security, position, a name. But love? That is rarely promised. And even more rarely insisted upon."

There was something in Olivia's tone—wistful and shaded with regret—that gave Theodosia pause. "Were you in love with Mr. Smith?" she asked.

A laugh escaped Olivia, short and bitter. She gave a firm shake of her head. "Heavens, no. Whatever I felt for Luke, it was most certainly not love."

"But you have loved before, haven't you?" Theodosia pressed.

Olivia's posture stiffened slightly, and she turned her face away. "Yes. I loved someone once. And for a little while, I thought he loved me in return."

Theodosia said nothing, sensing this was a confession long kept buried.

"He made me believe there was a future for us," Olivia continued. "He gave me every reason to hope... and then he married someone else."

Silence fell between them for a long moment. The only sound was the faint rustle of pages turning somewhere across the room.

"I'm sorry," Theodosia murmured, unsure of what else she could say.

Olivia gave a small shrug, but her eyes shimmered. "It was a long time ago. And I've made my peace with it." She forced a faint smile. "But it does leave you wondering whether love is worth the ache."

Theodosia reached for Olivia's hand and gave it a gentle squeeze. "I think it is."

"That is why I so foolishly ran off to Gretna Green with

Luke," Olivia said, her voice barely above a whisper. "I wasn't thinking clearly, and I just wanted the pain to go away. But all I've done is make everything worse. I've only deepened the ache I was trying to escape."

Theodosia gave her a sympathetic look. "There's no simple remedy for a broken heart. I watched my father wrestle with his grief after my mother died. He went about his days as if nothing had changed, kept up appearances for my sake, but the sadness in his eyes never truly faded."

Olivia reached into the delicate reticule hanging from her wrist and pulled out a lace-trimmed handkerchief. She dabbed at the corners of her eyes. "My brother doesn't understand. How could he? I sometimes think his heart is partially made from stone."

"Have you tried talking to him about all this?" Theodosia asked.

Olivia looked horrified at the mere suggestion. "Good heavens, no. Richard values duty above all else. He would never understand why I acted the way I did. I know he resents me for dragging our family's name through the mud."

"Has he said as much to you?"

"No. But I see it in his eyes when he looks at me. That particular look of silent judgment."

Theodosia's lips twitched. "Would you describe it as something between profound disappointment and barely restrained annoyance?"

Olivia's brows lifted slightly. "That is... oddly precise."

"Well, then I wouldn't take it too personally," Theodosia said. "Because that is exactly how he looks at me most of the time."

Olivia laughed softly. "My brother plays the brooding lord role far too convincingly."

"It is rather fun to tease him," Theodosia admitted. "It is almost like poking a bear just to see its reaction."

Olivia tucked her handkerchief away. "I won't tell him you said that."

"Thank you," Theodosia replied, reaching for the stack of books she had earlier collected. "Now, where does one go to check these out?"

"Allow me," Olivia said, taking half the stack from Theodosia's arms. "This way."

They made their way across the circulating library, weaving between tall shelves and small clusters of women deep in conversation. In the center of the room, behind a wide wooden counter, stood a thin man with silver spectacles perched precariously on his nose. A large leather-bound ledger lay open in front of him, his quill poised in hand as if caught mid-thought.

Olivia set her portion of books down beside the ledger with a decisive thump. "We would like to take these books home with us."

The man looked up slowly, adjusting his spectacles and peering at the pile with wide eyes. "All of these?"

"Yes," Olivia replied. "That won't be a problem, will it?"

"No, my lady. Not at all," he said quickly. "I will simply need a moment to record the titles."

He reached for the first book, squinting slightly as he copied its information into the ledger with slow, precise strokes.

Olivia turned towards Theodosia and asked, "Have you ever been to Gunter's Tea Shop for some lemon ice?"

"No, but I have been dying to try some," she replied.

"We should go after this," Olivia suggested.

Theodosia felt her lips curl into a smile. "I would like that."

9

Richard sat in the far corner of White's, holding a drink in his hand. The gentlemen's club was unusually subdued for the afternoon, the soft murmur of conversation and the occasional rustle of a turning newssheet providing the only interruption to his thoughts. He had arrived early—deliberately so—and now found himself alone with his brooding.

He told himself he didn't mind the quiet. In truth, he welcomed it. The stillness allowed him to think, though his thoughts inevitably turned where he didn't want them to go: Miss Theodosia.

He had spent the better part of the last few days convincing himself that she was complicit in Mr. Smith's deceit. A woman of secrets. A liar by association, if not in action. However, whenever he recalled her expression when she spoke of books she loved, or how her eyes lit with quiet fire when she challenged him, something inside him faltered.

It should not matter that she was beautiful. That she was clever. That she had been, at times, genuinely kind. None of it should matter.

He was here to right a wrong. To force justice on the man who had married his sister and vanished. Mr. Smith would answer for what he had done. And if Miss Theodosia was a casualty of that justice, then so be it.

Still... there was that irritating prick of guilt. Guilt he had no business entertaining.

A familiar voice broke through his reverie.

"Why the long face, Wilton?" Lord Bedford asked. "Has being a marquess finally worn you down?"

Richard looked up to find Bedford standing beside Lord Westcott, both of them eyeing him with interest.

"I see the pair of you finally decided to grace me with your presence," Richard said dryly.

Westcott checked his timepiece with a flourish. "On the contrary, we are precisely on time. You, as usual, are early."

Richard gestured towards the empty wingback chairs at his table. "Sit down. I've no idea when Alcott or Addington will appear."

The two lords took their seats, their gazes settling on him with barely concealed curiosity.

"Well?" Westcott prompted. "Did you find this mysterious Mr. Smith?"

"I tracked him to a village, but he was already gone by the time I arrived," Richard said, leaning forward. "But I've devised a solution. A plan."

Bedford quirked a brow. "Do tell. Is it a good plan, or the kind that ends with us reading about you in the scandal sheets?"

"I think it's rather inspired," Richard replied. "While I was in the village, I discovered a young woman—Miss Theodosia Smith—who appears to be closely connected to him. I persuaded her to come to London under the pretense of acting as a companion to my sister."

"You persuaded her?" Westcott repeated, voice sharp with skepticism.

"I left a note for Mr. Smith," Richard continued, ignoring the tone. "Told him that if he ever wanted to see her again, he would have to come to London. He will come. He must."

There was a long pause.

Bedford blinked. "You abducted a woman?"

"Not exactly," Richard said, though his tone lacked conviction. "She came willingly, just not with all the facts. The important thing is that Mr. Smith will have no choice but to act."

Westcott leaned back in his chair, his expression unreadable. "And this young woman, Miss Theodosia... she's nothing more than a pawn to you?"

Richard exhaled. "Yes."

Bedford and Westcott exchanged a pointed glance.

"And what do you intend to do with her once your scheme succeeds?" Westcott asked at last.

Richard shrugged. "I will return her to her village. Or allow the law to determine her fate if she proves to be as deceitful as I suspect."

Bedford's brow furrowed. "You truly see nothing amiss in what you're doing?"

"She harbored Mr. Smith. She lied about knowing him. She deserves to be held accountable," Richard explained.

"And you have proof of this?" Bedford asked.

"I hired a Bow Street Runner," Richard said defensively. "He confirmed Mr. Smith was seen coming and going from her estate at all hours. She may deny knowing him, but she certainly acted like an accomplice."

Bedford opened his mouth, then closed it again. After a long moment, he shook his head. "I honestly don't know what to say."

"Me, either," Westcott muttered. "The worst part is that you don't seem to care that you've involved an innocent woman in your vendetta."

"She is not innocent," Richard said, his voice rising before he lowered it once more. "You would not say that if you had spent five minutes in her company. She is proud, secretive, and thoroughly maddening."

"None of which justifies what you've done," Bedford argued. "You've taken her freedom. Lied to her. Manipulated her. If the situation were reversed—if someone had done this to Olivia—you'd be demanding a comeuppance."

That struck deeper than Richard wanted to admit. He looked away, jaw tight. "I am doing this for Olivia," he said through clenched teeth. "To make sure no other woman is treated the way she was."

Westcott huffed. "You're punishing one woman to avenge another."

Richard's hands curled around the arms of his chair. "This is justice."

"No," Bedford said. "It's vengeance. And it's beneath you."

"You don't understand. None of you do." Richard's voice was low. "This isn't something I *want* to do. It's something I *must* do."

Westcott tilted his head, studying him. "And what precisely do you intend to do when Mr. Smith finally comes to London to retrieve Miss Theodosia?"

Richard met his gaze unflinchingly. "I will challenge him to a duel for what he did to Olivia. For abandoning her. For destroying her future and shaming our family name."

Before either of his friends could respond, a new voice cut through the tension.

"Did someone die?" Viscount Alcott approached the table, glancing around at the grim expressions with a note of confusion. "Or are you all merely contemplating your own mortality over brandy?"

"No," Bedford muttered under his breath, "but Wilton is determined to get himself killed."

Alcott turned to Richard. "Dare I ask what is going on?"

Bedford stood and motioned for Alcott to follow him a few steps away. Their conversation was low, but Richard could catch snippets—"abduction," "duel," "revenge."

When they returned to the table, Alcott's expression had shifted from curiosity to incredulity. He crossed his arms over his chest and leveled Richard with a hard stare. "Are you completely mad?"

"I am no such thing," Richard said, lifting a hand to ward off the accusation. "It's not madness. It's justice."

"It's idiocy," Alcott retorted, pulling out a chair and dropping into it. "You honestly believe you're going to duel this man and avenge your sister's honor?"

"That is the plan."

"I've seen you shoot," Alcott said. "You couldn't hit a barn door with a blunderbuss at five paces."

"That is an exaggeration," Richard muttered.

Westcott grinned. "Is it? Because the last time we went shooting at Eversham's estate, you didn't hit a single target."

"I was having an off day," Richard insisted.

"And what if you have another 'off day' when facing Mr. Smith?" Alcott challenged. "What happens then? You die? And what of your mother and Olivia? You'll leave them behind to bury you and carry on without a protector or provider?"

The words struck their mark. Richard's bravado flickered, and for a brief moment, doubt crept into his mind.

"What choice do I have?" he asked, his voice quieter now. "This man has to answer for what he's done."

"You do have a choice," Westcott responded firmly. "Return Miss Theodosia to her home. Let this go before it spirals even further out of your control."

"I can't," Richard said, shaking his head. "It's too late. The plan is already in motion. If I release her now, it will all be for nothing."

Bedford furrowed his brow. "And what does Olivia say about this plan of yours?"

Richard winced. "She... disagrees."

Alcott let out an exaggerated sigh. "At last, someone in your household still has their wits."

Richard reached for his glass and took a long sip, the brandy burning his throat but doing nothing to soothe the ache in his chest. After a heavy pause, he asked, "Can we please talk about something else?"

The others exchanged glances, but no one replied immediately. The air was thick with unspoken words, the camaraderie between them strained beneath the weight of Richard's decisions. Still, they were friends—loyal, exasperated, and perhaps the only ones who could still hope to sway him.

For now, he hoped they would let it rest.

Thankfully, Alcott broke the tension by saying, "If it's any consolation, I am on the verge of losing my mind. Charlotte is determined to drag me to an early grave."

"What has she done now?" Richard asked.

Exasperation etched every line in Alcott's face. "She insists upon going out nearly every night. Last evening, she pestered me into escorting her to Vauxhall Gardens, and we didn't return home until the sun had begun to rise."

"That sounds positively wretched," Westcott said, grimacing. "I can think of few things more exhausting than chaperoning a debutante through Vauxhall Gardens until dawn."

Alcott rubbed a hand down his face. "At least when I was at war, I had a purpose. I was respected. I gave orders and people listened. Now, I have a younger sister who treats me like a glorified footman and refuses to be reasoned with."

"We appreciate you," Bedford offered.

Alcott gave him a withering look. "Yes, and it's so

comforting to be appreciated while dealing with a debutante obsessed with Almack's and scandalous gossip."

Richard chuckled despite himself, grateful for the shift in conversation.

"The real problem," Alcott continued, his tone growing more serious, "is that my father all but ignored Charlotte after my mother passed. She was left to do as she pleased—spoiled by every indulgence, and never denied a thing."

"And no one stepped in? No governess or aunt to curb her behavior?" Bedford asked.

Alcott waved a hand. "Oh, there were governesses. Dozens of them. But Charlotte ran them off one by one with a sort of ruthless charm I've never seen before in someone so small and fashionably dressed. By the time she was presented to Court, she was practically feral."

"Feral?" Westcott repeated.

"Yes," Alcott said with a solemn expression. "Feral. Utterly unmanageable, full of opinions, and with an uncanny ability to feign innocence."

Bedford gave a low whistle. "Sounds like you've got your hands full."

"You have no idea," Alcott replied grimly. "If I survive this Season with my sanity intact, I'll consider it a miracle."

Richard allowed a small smile to tug at the corner of his mouth. The chaos of Alcott's domestic life, while unfortunate, was a welcome distraction from the moral mire he had dragged himself into. For now, at least, the conversation had turned away from Miss Theodosia and the consequences of his actions.

If only it could stay that way.

Theodosia scooped the last bit of lemon ice from her bowl and let it melt on her tongue, eyes fluttering shut in delight. The treat was cold and tart, with just enough sweetness to make her sigh in contentment. She scraped her spoon along the bottom of the glass bowl, hoping for one last taste. For a moment, she contemplated braving the long line again for a second serving but thought against it.

Across the dainty wrought iron table, Olivia watched her with an amused expression. "I told you that you would enjoy it," she said with a knowing smile, tilting her parasol ever so slightly to shield her face from the afternoon sun.

"Enjoy is an understatement," Theodosia replied, setting down her spoon with reluctant finality. "Do you think anyone would notice if I licked the bowl clean?"

Olivia laughed. "Yes, I do. And so would the rest of the *ton*."

With a dramatic sigh, Theodosia slid the empty dish away. "Then I suppose I must at least pretend to have some semblance of decorum."

But even as they shared their lighthearted banter, Theodosia's eyes caught the subtle movements around them—the way a pair of matrons whispered behind their fans, their gazes darting towards Olivia with ill-concealed curiosity.

Olivia's smile faltered, and she exhaled a weary breath. "I should have known better than to come to Gunter's. What was I thinking? I might as well have painted a sign and worn it around my neck."

"Ignore them," Theodosia encouraged.

"That is easy for you to say," Olivia murmured, lowering her eyes. "You weren't the one foolish enough to elope to Gretna Green only to be discarded like yesterday's gossip."

"True," Theodosia acknowledged, "but you are not defined by one mistake."

Olivia shook her head. "Not according to Society. To them, I am the cautionary tale whispered over teacups. We should leave."

"No," Theodosia said firmly. "We will stay as long as you like. We will not be chased away by gossiping busybodies."

Olivia looked up, surprised. "You do not mind being associated with me?"

"Of course I do," Theodosia said with mock severity. "But alas, that is the solemn duty of a loyal companion."

A smile tugged at Olivia's lips. "You're my first, you know. I haven't the faintest idea what a proper companion should be."

"Nor I," Theodosia replied with a grin. "But I suspect enduring slander and defending your lemon ice is part of the role."

"I daresay you're doing admirably."

Before Theodosia could respond, a familiar voice reached her ears.

"Miss Theodosia, what a pleasant surprise."

She looked up—and blinked. "Mr. Pritchett?"

He offered a genial smile as he approached their table. "I had business to attend to in Town and decided to indulge in a little treat. I had no idea I'd find such pleasant company here."

"You certainly won't be disappointed by the lemon ice," Theodosia said, gesturing towards Olivia. "May I present Lady Olivia?"

Mr. Pritchett bowed politely. "It is a pleasure, my lady."

Olivia dipped her head in return. "Likewise. May I ask how you are acquainted with Miss Theodosia?"

Mr. Pritchett gave a quick glance at Theodosia before answering. "We grew up in the same village and our families have long been acquainted."

"Then you must join us," Olivia said, gesturing to the empty space beside Theodosia.

Trying to mask her dismay, Theodosia gave a tight smile. "Yes, do join us."

Clearly pleased, Mr. Pritchett went to fetch a nearby chair as Theodosia leaned towards Olivia and whispered quickly, "He's the man who offered for me."

Olivia's brows shot up, but she schooled her expression into polite neutrality.

"I must say," Mr. Pritchett said as he sat down, "it's a marvel running into you here. I had planned to seek you out during my stay."

That was the last thing that she wanted. "I've been rather occupied as of late with my new position."

"Yes," Olivia added. "Miss Theodosia has been a most attentive companion. I truly do not know what I would do without her."

Theodosia gave her a grateful look. "You'd be just fine, my lady."

"Perhaps," Olivia replied, "but why tempt fate?"

Mr. Pritchett turned his attention back to Theodosia. "Might I call upon you while I am in Town?"

"Oh—um..." Theodosia hesitated, scrambling for a polite excuse. "That would be... lovely. But I fear our schedule is quite full for the foreseeable future."

Olivia nodded quickly. "Yes, terribly full. Errands, fittings, social calls—it's a whirlwind."

Mr. Pritchett's face fell ever so slightly. "A shame. I had hoped..."

"It is, isn't it?" Theodosia rose, brushing her hands against her skirts. "But we must be going now. So much to do, and the day is slipping away."

He stood as well. "Good day, Miss Theodosia. Lady Olivia."

Olivia looped her arm through Theodosia's as they walked away from the table. Once they were out of earshot, she whispered, "I'm sorry. I didn't realize who he was or else I wouldn't have invited him to join us."

"It's quite all right," Theodosia said with a shrug. "He is a good man. But I'd rather not encourage him."

"Nor should you," Olivia agreed as they resumed their walk down the bustling pavement. "Kindness is no excuse to be misleading."

They strolled in comfortable silence for a few paces, the hum of carriages and the chatter of passing pedestrians all around them. As they passed a milliner's shop with lace and silk bonnets on display in the window, the door swung open with a faint jingle of bells, and a slender young woman with blonde hair stepped out. Her eyes widened as they met Olivia's.

"Lady Olivia," she said in surprise.

Olivia came to an abrupt halt. "Lady Jane," she responded.

Jane's expression shifted, the formality in her posture fading as something softer and more sincere took its place. "How are you faring?" she asked quietly.

"I've been better."

Jane glanced around as if to be sure they weren't observed. Then, lowering her voice, she added, "I've thought about writing, but my father forbade me from contacting you. He said I was to keep my distance."

"I understand," Olivia murmured.

Jane cast another quick glance over her shoulder. "But what my father doesn't know won't hurt him," she said with sudden resolve. "Come inside. We can speak freely there."

She gestured to the shop, and the trio stepped inside the narrow space, the bell above the door jingling softly. The walls were lined with hats, bonnets, and rows of silk ribbons in every shade imaginable.

They wandered among the displays, their fingers drifting over the spools of ribbon, pretending to shop as they spoke in lowered tones.

"Miss Theodosia is my companion now," Olivia offered after a moment, breaking the silence.

Jane looked up in surprise. "You have a companion?"

"My brother insisted," Olivia replied, casting a glance towards Theodosia with a smile. "But Dosia and I are managing quite well."

Jane's expression softened with warmth. "It's a pleasure to meet you," she said, turning towards Theodosia. "I'm Lady Jane."

Theodosia offered a small curtsy. "It's lovely to make your acquaintance."

Jane idly picked up a ribbon and ran her fingers over its edge. Her voice dropped as she turned her attention back to Olivia. "I must confess, I was rather stunned when I read you had married Mr. Smith. I thought... well, I thought your affections were elsewhere."

Olivia's face tightened slightly, but her tone remained composed. "It was a rash decision," she said. "One I regret more than I can say."

Jane set the ribbon down with care. "You may regret it, but in some ways... you're fortunate."

Olivia raised an eyebrow. "I wouldn't say that."

"I would," Jane insisted. "He left you, yes—but you still have the legal standing of a married woman. That gives you more freedom than most of us can even dream of."

Olivia turned to look out the shop's large front window, her reflection faintly visible in the glass. "Freedom comes at a price. And mine was a scandal."

Jane gave a wistful smile. "I still think you were brave. I envy that. I live beneath the constant gaze of my father and brother. I suspect they're plotting my marriage this very moment."

Olivia reached out and gently rested a hand on Jane's shoulder. "You don't have to marry the first man they parade before you."

Jane looked at her with weary eyes. "Don't I?" she whispered.

Theodosia, who had been silently watching the exchange, picked up a ribbon of deep emerald green and studied it, though her attention was on the pain threaded through Jane's voice. Something about her tone—about the way she avoided eye contact—made Theodosia wonder what cruelty, subtle or otherwise, Jane had endured behind the walls of her family's home.

Olivia dropped her hand to her side. "It's illegal to force someone into marriage."

Jane looked down at the floor, her expression bleak. "Legalities mean little when your choices are taken from you," she murmured.

The door opened behind them, and two finely dressed women entered, engaged in conversation. Jane's posture straightened instantly, and her voice returned to polite brightness.

"Well, I should be off before my brother comes looking for me," she said. "It was lovely to meet you, Miss Theodosia."

"And you, my lady," Theodosia replied.

With a final smile that didn't quite reach her eyes, Jane slipped through the door and disappeared into the crowd beyond.

Olivia watched the door for a long moment, her expression somber. "I feel awful for her," she said. "Her father and brother are so overbearing. She's never had a chance to live for herself."

"Is there anything we can do to help her?"

Olivia shook her head. "Even speaking to me today was a risk. Her father loathes scandal and controls everything—his house, his name, and sadly, his daughter."

Theodosia gave a sad smile. "At the expense of her happiness."

"It's always been that way," Olivia said. "Even when we were girls."

Just then, a stout, matronly woman approached in a crisp

white apron, her hands folded in front of her. "May I help you find something, my lady?"

Olivia lifted a spool of pale blue and held it up. "I'd like to purchase these, please."

"Of course, it would be my pleasure to assist you," the woman said, taking the ribbons from her with a practiced smile. "I'll place them on your account."

As the woman bustled away, Theodosia looked again to the front window, her thoughts still with Jane. She wondered how many other young women were trapped in gilded cages, their futures dictated by duty and pride.

And how many would ever escape?

As they waited for the ribbon to be boxed up, Theodosia couldn't help but reflect on how fortunate she was. Unlike so many young women of her station, she possessed something rare: independence. The modest estate her late father had left her was not only profitable but also a source of quiet pride. She genuinely enjoyed managing it. It gave her purpose and, more importantly, choices. Choices that women like Jane could only dream of.

The shop assistant returned with a neat parcel wrapped in brown paper and tied with a ribbon. "Here is your ribbon, my lady. All boxed up and ready to go."

Olivia accepted the bundle. "Thank you."

They stepped outside onto the pavement, and a footman appeared by their side, having maintained a discreet distance throughout their outing. Olivia handed off the parcel without breaking stride.

As they made their way down the pavement towards the waiting coach, Olivia asked, "What shall we do now?"

A mischievous smile came to Theodosia's lips. "We could return home and read one of those scandalous French romance novels you were telling me about."

Olivia's eyes sparkled with amusement as she picked up her pace. "Now that is a truly brilliant idea."

Feeling bold, Theodosia added, "And with any luck, your brother won't be home to scowl disapprovingly from the doorway."

Olivia laughed loudly. "I must say, your disdain for Richard is one of my favorite things."

"Trust me, the feeling is entirely mutual," Theodosia said dryly.

"That," Olivia replied, casting her a sidelong grin, "only makes it more entertaining for me."

An image of Lord Wilton came to her mind as she climbed into the coach across from Olivia, and she quickly banished it. Why did it matter if he disapproved of what she read? His opinion had no bearing on her life. He was merely a vexing marquess with an overdeveloped sense of propriety and a talent for provoking her at every turn.

Still, the memory of his piercing blue eyes lingered longer than she liked, unsettling her more than she cared to admit. She straightened her spine, forcing herself to focus on the present. *He doesn't matter. You don't answer to him*, she reminded herself firmly.

So why did a small, traitorous part of her long to see him truly smile at her?

10

Richard sat at his desk, quill in hand, trying for the third time to make sense of the estate ledgers spread before him. Figures blurred together, and the column he had been attempting to tally slipped from his concentration once more—thanks to the persistent sound of female laughter drifting down the corridor. It was high-pitched, incessant, and thoroughly maddening.

He gritted his teeth, pressing the nib of his quill harder than necessary against the parchment. What could possibly be so amusing? With a muttered oath, he shoved back his chair, the legs scraping against the hardwood floor as he stood. He stalked into the corridor as the sound of giggling grew louder with every step.

It led him to the parlor. He paused in the doorway.

Olivia and Miss Theodosia were nestled together on the settee like a pair of schoolgirls, a book laying open between them. Olivia had her hand over her mouth, trying to stifle another burst of laughter, while Miss Theodosia wiped at her eyes, clearly overcome with mirth. Neither of them noticed his approach.

He cleared his throat pointedly.

Olivia's head snapped up, and her eyes widened. "Where did you come from, Brother? You startled me!"

"I live here," he replied, his tone clipped. "Or had you forgotten?"

"I—of course not."

"I was attempting to work in peace, but apparently that is too much to ask." He gestured towards the book in Olivia's lap. "What on earth could be so amusing that it inspires shrieking laughter?"

Olivia flushed and shut the book quickly, as though the cover itself might incriminate her. "It's just a novel," she said with a nervous smile. "A romantic one."

"A waste of time, in other words," he insisted. "You would do better to read something that exercises your mind rather than numbs it."

Miss Theodosia looked up at him, her voice edged with defiance. "I would have to disagree with you, my lord."

He barely spared her a glance. "Of course you would. But I do not recall asking for your opinion."

Her chin lifted. "You did not. That does not make it any less valid."

He turned to her fully now, arms folded across his chest. "You are employed in my household, Miss Theodosia. I suggest you remember that."

"And what does that mean?" she asked. "That I am not allowed to read? Or have thoughts of my own?"

"It means you will do as you are told."

She stood then, slowly and deliberately, as she met his gaze head-on. "Or what? You'll dismiss me?"

"If necessary."

Her eyes narrowed. "Did we not agree that I was free to speak my mind?"

"On matters that concern you, yes."

"And you don't believe this concerns me?" she asked, her voice rising ever so slightly.

"No," he responded. "Because contrary to what you may believe, the world does not revolve around you."

Color flared in her cheeks. Her entire posture stiffened. "You are a pompous jackanapes."

He scoffed. "Resorting to name-calling? I expected better of you."

She stepped closer, undaunted by his height or the sharpness of his glare. "It is not name-calling if it's the truth."

His voice dropped dangerously low. "You want the truth, Miss Theodosia? You are merely a country bumpkin who ought to be grateful for the opportunity to reside in a respectable household."

She stared at him, stricken—but only for a breath. Then her expression hardened. "I quit," she said softly.

He blinked. "What?"

"I said, I quit!" she snapped, her voice ringing with emotion. "You may keep your money. I will find my own way home."

She turned without another word and swept from the room.

Richard remained rooted where he stood, stunned by her sudden departure, and more so by the realization that she might actually go. That would ruin everything.

Olivia, still seated on the settee, broke the silence. "That was poorly done."

"She's merely overreacting," Richard said dismissively. "She'll come around."

"No," Olivia responded calmly. "You were in the wrong. You were acting like a jackanapes."

"Olivia—"

She held up a hand. "You brought her here as part of some elaborate scheme, didn't you? And you still need her."

His jaw tensed. "Yes, but—"

She interrupted him again. "Then make it right. I believe in Dosia. She's not the liar you've painted her to be."

"You can't be serious."

"I am. You may not trust her, but I do. And I won't stand by and let you ruin this because of your pride."

He exhaled sharply and looked towards the ceiling in frustration. "What do you suggest I do?"

Olivia shrugged. "Fix it, and quickly. I don't think she's bluffing."

Without another word, Richard turned and strode from the parlor. His conscience prickled, but so did something else—something uncomfortable and vaguely unfamiliar. Regret.

He reached the entry hall just in time to see Miss Theodosia speaking to the butler, likely arranging for transport.

"Miss Theodosia," he called out. "A word."

She turned and sighed. "No, thank you. I have no interest in hearing anything further from you."

She pivoted towards the stairs.

"You're being unreasonable," he said, following her.

She stopped midway, back still to him. "And you are being your usual arrogant self."

"I take offense to that."

"And I take offense to your whole person," she said, whirling around to face him. "You don't get to dictate every aspect of my life simply because you pay my wages."

"You are under my employ—"

"Not anymore!" she snapped. "Or have you forgotten already that I quit?"

"You don't mean that. This is a perfectly respectable position for someone of your—"

"Of what?" she challenged, stepping towards him. "My station?"

He hesitated. "Yes."

She laughed, but there was no humor in it. "You forget that

I didn't need this position. I have a profitable estate of my own. You're the one who practically begged me to come."

"I did not beg," he said stiffly.

"No, of course not. That would require humility," she responded. "You think yourself above me."

"I never said that."

"You don't have to. Why did you truly want me to come here if you think I'm so much beneath you?"

"My reasons are my own."

"You are an infuriating man."

He leaned closer until their faces were inches apart. "And you are the most obstinate young woman I have ever had the misfortune of knowing."

She didn't shy away from him as she said, "Fortunately for you, I will be on my way shortly. And we will never have to cross paths again."

Something inside him twisted at that. He couldn't let her go. Not yet.

His voice lowered, more hesitant this time. "Don't go."

"Why not?"

He didn't answer immediately. He couldn't say the real reason—that he needed her to lure Mr. Smith out of hiding. That he needed her to stay.

He swallowed hard, his throat suddenly dry. "Because... I want you to stay."

Miss Theodosia's expression did not waver. "No, you don't," she challenged.

"I do," he insisted, though even to his own ears the words sounded too raw, too vulnerable.

She arched a single brow. "You can hardly tolerate being in the same room with me. I suspect you despise me just as thoroughly as I despise you. It is better if I go."

But it wasn't. Not now. Not when the mere scent of lavender clinging to her skin had muddled his thoughts, or when the afternoon light revealed unexpected flecks of amber in her green eyes. It was maddening how much he noticed her and how quickly his carefully constructed walls began to splinter when she was near.

"You were right to be angry," he said at last. "I spoke out of turn. I was wrong."

She tilted her head slightly. "Was that meant to be an apology?"

"It was," he replied, somewhat stiffly.

Her lips twitched, though the expression held little mirth. "You are truly terrible at apologizing, my lord. Typically, one begins with the words 'I'm sorry.' You might try it sometime."

Insufferable woman.

He exhaled slowly, tempering the urge to snap back. "Do you accept it or not?"

For a moment, she simply looked at him—really looked at him. Her eyes searched his face, lingering on his features as though trying to determine if there was truth buried beneath his pride. Whatever she saw, it softened her expression just slightly.

"I do," she said. "But that does not change the fact that I should probably leave."

"Give me one more chance," he said, the words rushing out before he could rein them in. "Please."

A flicker of surprise crossed her face at his plea. "I shall think on it."

He gave a short nod. "That is enough for me... for now."

She made no move to step away, and neither did he. The silence stretched between them, thick with unspoken things. And as he stood there, far too aware of the closeness of her presence, he found himself once again lost in the green depths of her eyes—and all the uncertainty they held.

"Does that mean Dosia is staying?" came Olivia's voice from behind him, bright with hope and just a hint of mischief.

Startled, Richard stepped back, instinctively putting a safer distance between himself and Miss Theodosia. "She is... considering it."

Olivia wasted no time, turning her full attention on her friend. "You must stay. I should be dreadfully bored without your companionship."

Miss Theodosia glanced sidelong at Richard, her expression guarded. "I suppose I can remain for now."

A delighted squeal escaped Olivia as she clasped her hands together. "What wonderful news! Come—we should dress for dinner. I've just had a new gown delivered, and I want your opinion on the sleeves."

"I think that is a fine idea," Miss Theodosia replied, allowing Olivia to loop their arms together.

The two women began their ascent up the staircase, their heads bent together in quiet conversation, as though the tension from moments before had never occurred.

Richard, however, remained where he stood, unmoving.

What had just happened?

He was almost relieved she had chosen to stay. With him. And it was not just because of Mr. Smith and his elaborate ruse. A part of him was softening towards her. It was maddening. Impossible.

Yet, if he truly wished to keep her in London, he would have to try. He would have to make a genuine effort... to be less guarded. To speak with her, not just interrogate. To see her as more than a complication.

Being open with her would not come easily.

But for the first time in years, Richard found himself willing to try.

Theodosia stepped out of her bedchamber, smoothing a hand down the pale pink gown Olivia had lent her. The fabric shimmered faintly in the candlelight as she moved down the corridor. The dinner bell had not yet rung, but she had no desire to linger alone in her room with her thoughts. The drawing room, she decided, would be a suitable place to pass the time—provided she didn't encounter a certain marquess.

When she entered the drawing room, she came to an abrupt halt.

Lord Wilton stood near the tall window, his hands clasped behind his back, gazing into the darkness beyond the pane. The flickering wall sconces cast golden light over his form, highlighting the tension in his shoulders and the solemn set of his jaw. He hadn't noticed her yet.

Botheration.

Theodosia considered retreating quietly before he turned around but that would be cowardly. She was not a child to be cowed by a man simply because he was insufferable. They were adults. They could exist in the same room without snarling at one another... in theory.

But something about his expression gave her pause. There was a heaviness in his gaze, a shadow that had not been there before. The Lord Wilton she knew wore arrogance like a second skin, but now... now he looked almost human. Vulnerable, even.

He turned abruptly, and their eyes met. Whatever softness she had glimpsed vanished beneath a familiar mask of cool detachment.

"Miss Theodosia," he said with a terse nod and an even stiffer bow.

She dropped into a graceful curtsy. "Lord Wilton."

An awkward silence stretched between them, thick and uneasy. She remained rooted to the floor, unsure whether to stay or go, and he seemed equally unsure of what to do with her presence.

At last, he cleared his throat. "I trust you rested before supper?"

"I did, thank you." She could have left it at that and let the silence reclaim the space between them. But her curiosity got the better of her. "Something troubles you."

His jaw tightened. "No."

She studied him, undeterred. "You seem rather... sad."

His entire frame went rigid. "Do you always speak your mind so freely?"

"I do."

"It is vexing."

She smiled sweetly. "We shall have to agree to disagree, my lord."

He took a step towards her, the movement slow and deliberate. "The women of my acquaintance do not speak to me in such a familiar manner."

"Then I daresay you're acquainted with the wrong women."

His lips thinned. "You are a maddening young woman."

"Thank you."

"That was not meant as a compliment."

"I chose to take it as one."

He exhaled through his nose, exasperated. She took a step forward, narrowing the space between them to mere inches.

"You never answered my question," she said.

"Because it is none of your concern."

She arched a brow and placed a hand on her hip. "I thought you intended to make an effort to be civil."

"I did. Then you opened your mouth."

"I could say the same of you."

His eyes narrowed. He stepped close enough that she could see the faint crease between his brows and the turmoil flickering in his gaze. "The difference is that I am a marquess."

Her brow arched higher. "Is your title supposed to impress me? Because I assure you, it does not."

For a moment, he simply stared at her, as if trying to decipher a language he didn't speak. "No one has ever spoken to me so plainly," he murmured. "It is... oddly refreshing. Most women hide behind coy smiles and flutter their lashes."

"I've never fluttered my lashes a day in my life."

That drew the faintest twitch at the corner of his mouth. "I believe you."

Her hand dropped from her hip. "We are not friends, I know. But you did look... well, sad."

He let out a frustrated growl. "Miss Theodosia..."

"Why is it," she asked, unbothered, "that whenever you say my name, it sounds like a curse?"

A chuckle escaped his lips. "Perhaps because I intend it as one."

She tilted her head, her voice softening. "What troubles you, my lord?"

He turned away, shoulders drawn taut. She saw the flicker of indecision on his face before he looked back at her. "I miss my father," he admitted.

The quiet admission stole her breath. "I understand that sentiment more than you know," she responded.

His expression twisted. "I wasn't ready to take on his title. He died too young and left behind a legacy I can't possibly match."

"Why do you say that?"

His hands clenched into fists at his sides. "He was revered. In the House of Lords. Among our tenants. Even the servants adored him. And I—" His voice cracked with frustration. "I can't even pass a single bill. I feel like I'm failing him... and myself."

Moved by the raw honesty in his voice, Theodosia felt an

urge to comfort him, though she dared not reach for him. Instead, she offered what little she could.

"You must give it time," she encouraged.

"I don't think that will make a difference," Lord Wilton responded. "And I feel like I am drowning in the accounts."

"I could look over the accounts for you."

His head snapped towards her, incredulous. "You?"

"I'm rather good with numbers," she said. "I run a profitable estate. Modest, yes, but thriving."

He scoffed. "No, thank you. I don't need your help."

"I didn't say you did. But why won't you accept it?"

"Because accepting help would be admitting I can't manage. That I'm failing."

She met his eyes without flinching. "It would mean you are wise enough to recognize when support is needed. That takes more strength than struggling alone."

He shook his head, raking a hand through his hair, leaving it terribly disheveled. "You can't imagine the pressure I'm under. Everyone watching. Expecting me to be him."

"I do imagine it," she retorted. "I'm a young woman managing an estate. And everyone in my village is waiting for me to fail."

He looked at her then, as if he noticed her for the first time. "Perhaps," he said, "you understand more than I gave you credit for."

Theodosia smiled. "Was that a rare compliment from you, my lord?"

The corners of Lord Wilton's mouth lifted ever so slightly. "I suppose it was."

His smile, genuine and unguarded, caught her off guard. As their eyes held, something shifted between them. A thread of understanding, perhaps, woven from shared burdens neither had intended to reveal. She saw in him not just the irritable, arrogant marquess but a man shaped by grief, duty, and silent expectations. And he, in turn, saw her not merely as an impertinent nuisance, but as someone who might actually understand the weight of standing alone.

The moment fractured at the sound of a familiar voice.

"Good heavens," Olivia said from the doorway, her tone light and teasing. "I do hope you two are plotting each other's downfall. It would be the only logical explanation for this level of intensity."

Lord Wilton broke their gaze first, stepping back with a faint clearing of his throat. "We've come to something of an understanding."

"Did you?" Olivia narrowed her eyes, her voice laced with mock suspicion.

Theodosia turned towards her. "It's true. Your brother even offered me a compliment."

Olivia gasped theatrically. "Is he bottle-weary? Should I summon the physician?"

"I haven't touched a drop this evening," he said with a long-suffering sigh.

Before the banter could continue, Lady Wilton entered the room and asked, "Shall we adjourn to the dining room?"

"Yes," her son muttered under his breath, already turning towards the door.

As they filed out of the drawing room, Theodosia found herself walking beside Lord Wilton once more. The air between them felt curiously lighter, less fraught than it had just moments ago. She glanced sideways at him and, before she could think better of it, said, "I had lemon ice today."

The words left her mouth and immediately struck her as absurd. Of all things to say...

He turned his head just slightly towards her. "Did you enjoy it?"

"I did," she said. "I can now understand why Gunter's Tea Shop is all the rage."

"Next time, you should try the lavender ice. It's rather underrated."

"Lavender?"

He nodded. "It is oddly satisfying."

"If I had my way, I'd go to Gunter's every day," she mused aloud, not entirely joking.

His lips quirked. "There is nothing stopping you."

"I imagine Lady Olivia might have something to say about that."

Ahead of them, Olivia turned her head slightly and called over her shoulder, "Au contraire. I have no objections to daily lemon ice indulgence."

"Then it is settled," Lord Wilton said, his voice touched with mock formality.

Emboldened by the ease between them, Theodosia glanced at him again. "Would you care to join us tomorrow?"

She held her breath, expecting him to politely refuse. But to her astonishment, he replied without hesitation, "I would enjoy that."

"You would?" Olivia asked.

Lord Wilton glanced between the two women, his tone dry but not unkind. "Even a marquess is allowed to enjoy lemon ice, is he not?"

"I suppose I shall allow you to join us," Olivia said. "But no brooding allowed."

"I do not brood," he stated with a note of injured dignity.

Theodosia was unable to resist the opportunity to tease him. "You most definitely brood, my lord."

He came to a halt just outside the dining room door and turned to regard her with a mixture of mild offense and amusement. "I assure you, I am a man of profound thought, not brooding."

"That is precisely what a brooding man would say," Theodosia quipped.

With a muttered sound that may have been a laugh—or perhaps a grumble—he stepped aside and gestured towards the open doorway. "After you, Miss Theodosia."

Inclining her head in thanks, she stepped into the dining room and she moved to take her seat beside Olivia. Lord Wilton took his place at the head of the table, his posture stiff.

Moments later, a footman entered and set bowls of soup before each of them. The clink of silverware began as they ate, the room falling into a companionable, if slightly awkward, silence.

Lady Wilton was the first to speak, setting down her spoon with a soft tap against porcelain. "How was the circulating library today?"

"It was wonderful," Olivia said with a bright smile. "I found two novels I've been wanting for weeks."

Theodosia nodded in agreement. "I must concur. I have never seen so many books in one place before. It felt like discovering a hidden treasure trove."

"It is a magical place," Lady Wilton agreed. "Which is why I am pleased to be among its patrons. As is Richard."

Theodosia turned her gaze to Lord Wilton. "You are?"

He straightened slightly, as if preparing for a challenge. "Indeed. I do not know why that seems so unexpected. I have no objections to women reading. Quite the opposite, I encourage it."

"But this afternoon..." she began, remembering his comment about frivolous reading material.

He cut in smoothly, setting down his spoon. "Had nothing to do with you reading, and everything to do with what you were reading. Surely, there are more enlightening choices than scandalous French romances."

Theodosia opened her mouth to protest, but before she could respond, Lady Wilton added with a pointed nod, "I quite agree with Richard. Those books are written for shock and little else."

"I daresay that they are written to entertain," Theodosia argued. "And sometimes, that is enough."

"Is it?" Richard countered. "Surely one's time could be better spent with works that sharpen the mind."

"My mind is plenty sharp, my lord. And I enjoy indulging it in both politics and passion," she declared.

His lips twitched as if he were restraining a grin. "That sounds rather dangerous."

"Perhaps," she replied, raising her spoon to her lips. "But you might consider trying it sometime."

Lady Wilton let out a soft, almost resigned sigh, and Olivia smothered a laugh behind her napkin. The conversation moved on, but Theodosia couldn't help noticing the way Lord Wilton's eyes lingered on her just a moment longer than necessary—thoughtful, and perhaps just a touch intrigued.

11

R ichard sat hunched over his desk, frowning down at the rows of figures that stubbornly refused to make sense. Numbers had always eluded him. As a boy, he'd muddled through his lessons with the help of patient tutors and his father's gentle encouragement, but even now, with years of experience behind him, columns still blurred and balances never quite added up as they should. He had long since learned to rely on his man of business to handle the more intricate aspects of estate management, but pride insisted he at least make the attempt before surrendering the ledger.

The door creaked open and his mother's voice broke the silence. "Do you intend to remain in here all morning, or will you join us for breakfast?"

Glancing up at the long clock in the corner, Richard blinked in surprise. "Is it that time already?"

"It is," she said with the faintest smile, her eyes sweeping the cluttered desk.

With a rolling of his shoulders, he rose. "I suppose I could use a reprieve."

"Good." She turned as if to leave, then paused at the threshold. "Before you sit down, go fetch Miss Theodosia from the gardens. She's been out there drawing for hours, and I daresay she will miss breakfast."

He sighed inwardly. "Is that truly necessary?"

"I believe you promised to be more civil."

That was true enough. "Very well," he said with little enthusiasm.

Her expression softened. "I've noticed a change in your manner towards Miss Theodosia. You've been less... brusque."

With a dismissive shrug, he replied, "It's self-preservation. If I drive her away, Olivia will never forgive me, and I, quite frankly, would never forgive myself."

"Regardless of the motive, I am pleased," she said. "I find her to be rather delightful."

His jaw tightened. "Do not let her deceive you, Mother. She may charm you as she tried to do to me, but she is not what she pretends to be."

"We've discussed it—Olivia and I—and neither of us believes it's a pretense."

"That is rarely a good sign," he muttered.

She ignored him and continued. "She seems sincere."

"You are both too tender-hearted," he replied, though without much conviction.

His mother fixed him with a thoughtful gaze. "I do not know why you are so jagged about her, Richard, but be careful. You may be wrong."

"I know what I'm doing," he said firmly. "You must trust me."

"I do," she said, "but part of me hopes you are wrong. If Miss Theodosia is innocent, then she'll be exonerated. And you won't have to challenge Mr. Smith to a duel."

He stiffened. "I am doing this for Olivia. For her future."

Her eyes searched his face, as if weighing how much of that was truth and how much was something else. Finally, she spoke. "And how, precisely, is this helping Olivia's future?" she asked. "We are already contending with the disgrace of her elopement and Mr. Smith's heartless abandonment. The whispers in Society have not yet faded. What do you suppose will happen if you hunt the man down and challenge him to a duel? If you kill him, we will not merely be dealing with whispers. We will be drowning beneath a fresh tide of scandal."

He drew a breath. "We cannot let Mr. Smith win." The words came out harsher than he had intended.

His mother's expression was a mixture of exasperation and desperation. "And what, pray tell, will happen if you are killed?" Her voice broke slightly on the last word, though she quickly mastered herself. "Have you considered that, Richard? If you fall, the marquessate will pass to some distant cousin who knows nothing of our affairs, nor cares for Olivia or me. We would be left to fend for ourselves, ruined both socially and financially. Is that the future you envision for your sister? For me?"

His chest rose and fell in a deep, uneven breath. "No," he admitted, voice roughened by emotion. "Of course not. But what choice do I have? It is the only way I see to resolve this—" He broke off, his fists curling at his sides. "Mr. Smith married Olivia under false pretenses and cast her aside like rubbish. I cannot—*will not*—stand by and do nothing. I must set this right. For her sake... and for mine. It is my duty."

For a long moment, his mother said nothing. Then she merely nodded and left him with a parting, "I'll see you in the dining room."

Closing the ledger, Richard made his way through the townhouse and out the rear door, which a footman opened with a bow. The crisp morning air was laced with the scent of roses.

Ahead, beneath the shade of a sycamore, he saw Miss Theodosia, seated on a blanket with her sketchbook resting on her lap. Her brow was furrowed in concentration, her hand moving swiftly across the page.

He didn't wish to startle her, so he called out softly, "Good morning."

She turned, and to his pleasant surprise, she did not scowl at him. "Good morning, my lord."

"I've been sent to retrieve you for breakfast." He gestured towards her book. "May I see what has so captured your attention?"

A faint flush crept into her cheeks as she closed the book protectively. "I would rather not."

"Now I am intrigued. What secrets are you hiding in those pages?"

"Nothing that would interest you."

He stepped closer, watching her curiously. "So you say."

Rising to her feet, she tucked the sketchbook firmly against her chest. "It's not ready to be seen."

He inclined his head, not wanting to press her. "Very well. My mother insisted I fetch you, so here I am, performing my duty."

"That was thoughtful of her."

He gave her a crooked smile. "What about me? Am I to receive no credit for braving the outdoors on your behalf?"

"Your contribution is marginal, my lord," she replied.

He offered his arm. "May I escort you in?"

Taking a step back, she said, "I can walk just fine, thank you."

"I've no doubt. Still, I am endeavoring to be a gentleman."

Her gaze dropped to his arm. "I suppose it wouldn't kill me to accept your offer."

"Spoken like a true optimist," he said with a quiet chuckle.

She rested her fingers lightly on his sleeve, and together they strolled towards the house. After a pause, he asked, "How did you sleep?"

"Well, thank you. And you?"

He kept his gaze ahead. "Surprisingly well."

"Good. Now, since that topic is out of the way, shall we discuss the state of the gardens?" she asked lightly.

He gave a mock shudder. "I would rather not."

"Then what subject would you prefer?"

He glanced sideways at her. "Are you enjoying London?"

She perked up, and her eyes brightened. "Oh, yes. Everything is so vibrant and full of life."

"I'm glad to hear it."

"What do you enjoy most in Town?"

He considered before replying. "Vauxhall Gardens. The grounds are magnificent, especially during the fireworks displays."

A wistful look crossed her face. "My mother would have loved to see that. I do not believe she ever saw fireworks."

"Were you close with her?"

"I was. But she died when I was still quite young."

"I'm sorry."

She gave a small, appreciative nod. "My parents married for love, despite their families' objections. It caused quite the scandal in their day."

He held the door open for her. "Love matches are rare."

"They are, but I wish they weren't."

"In our circles, marriages are more about security than sentiment."

Miss Theodosia furrowed her brows. "Do you not aspire for love, my lord?"

"Heavens, no. My parents had a marriage of convenience and eventually found affection. I hope for the same."

"And if affection never grows?"

He shrugged. "Then mutual respect must suffice."

She stopped in the entry hall and turned towards him. "That's a rather bleak outlook."

"No, it's a pragmatic one," he replied. "My duty is to marry well and produce heirs to carry on my legacy."

She tilted her head. "Out of curiosity, what do you consider a suitable match?"

"A well-bred lady with a generous dowry," he answered honestly.

"How romantic," she muttered.

Richard heard the sarcasm in her voice, but he chose to ignore it. Instead, he asked, "And what of you? Do you dream of marrying for love? Perhaps even marrying a wealthy lord?"

"No, I don't care for titles or wealth. I merely want a husband who is kind and present—someone who would raise a family with me in the countryside."

He studied her. "Why are you not married, then? I am sure there are men lining up to marry you."

She laughed. "That is kind of you to say, but I'm considered an oddity in my village. I manage an estate, and most men find that... unsettling. Intimidating."

"Why not let your husband take it over?"

The humor on her face faded. "Because I'm perfectly capable of doing it myself."

He lifted his hands. "I meant no offense."

"Forgive me," she said with a wry smile. "I can be defensive where my father's estate is concerned."

He stepped closer. "It's your estate now, is it not?"

"Technically, yes, considering my sister has all but abandoned it... and me," she admitted.

"Then I commend you. Not many women could manage such responsibility."

Her eyes narrowed. "Are you complimenting me?"

"Yes. At least I'm trying to."

A slow smile curved her lips. "I'm not used to this truce between us. I keep expecting an insult."

"There won't be one. Not today."

She eyed him curiously. "Did your mother put you up to this?"

He let out a slight chuckle. "She may have hinted at it, but I'm speaking of my own accord."

Before she could respond, Olivia's voice rang out from the staircase. "Why do you two insist on waking before the fashionable hour?"

"You could have requested a breakfast tray in your room," Richard said, turning to his sister.

"And miss your lively sparring matches? Never." Olivia descended with a grin. "It's better than any French romance I've read lately."

"Well, I hate to disappoint, but Miss Theodosia and I haven't argued once this morning."

"There's still time," Olivia said as she swept past them.

Miss Theodosia laughed. "We do tend to be at odds with one another."

"Perhaps it's time we tried something else," Richard said.

Her gaze turned curious. "What are you proposing?"

He leaned in ever so slightly, his voice quiet, as though sharing a confidence. "That we try to be friends."

Miss Theodosia's brow lifted in skepticism. "Are you quite certain you wish to attempt such a feat? It sounds terribly ambitious."

A faint smile played at the corner of his mouth. "I am."

She studied him, no doubt in an attempt to discern his sincerity. "Friendship requires effort. A degree of trust. And a willingness to withhold judgment from time to time."

"I am aware," he replied. "And I am willing."

She hesitated for only a moment. "Very well. I am willing to give it a try... assuming you are in earnest and do not plan to revoke the offer the moment I say something impertinent."

"I suppose I shall need to grow more tolerant of impertinence," he said, softening his words with a smile.

"Then let us attempt to be friends. However, I must warn you that Olivia will be dreadfully disappointed. She thrives on our disagreements."

"I tend to disappoint Olivia rather frequently," he said with a shrug. "She'll survive." He extended an arm towards the corridor that led to the dining room. "After you, Miss Theodosia."

She dipped her head in graceful acknowledgment and began walking. "Thank you, my lord," she said over her shoulder, her voice warm with amusement.

And for the first time, he saw something extraordinary. Her smile lit up her features and it stirred something deep within him.

As he followed her down the corridor, Richard found himself troubled by his own impulsive offer. He hadn't planned to suggest friendship—hadn't even considered it until the words had left his mouth. It might have been an attempt to keep her near, to keep her cooperative... but even as he told himself so, he knew it wasn't the truth. Not entirely.

He was starting to enjoy her company far more than he should.

And that was not part of his plan.

Theodosia sat curled into the corner of the drawing room settee, the afternoon light streaming in through the windows as she turned the page of her book. A slight rustle drew her gaze upward. Olivia, lounging in a nearby armchair, was staring at her with an almost mischievous smile playing at the corners of her mouth.

Lowering the book to her lap, Theodosia tilted her head. "Is something amiss?"

Olivia shook her head, her smile deepening. "Not at all. I was merely watching you read."

"You do realize how peculiar that sounds?"

"Oh, undoubtedly," Olivia remarked. "But I find myself quite curious about what exactly is happening between you and my brother."

Theodosia lifted a brow but remained composed. "We have agreed to attempt a friendship, nothing more."

Olivia let out a thoughtful hum. "That is... interesting."

Knowing her reading would not continue until the conversation had run its course, Theodosia sighed softly and set the book aside on the table. "And why, pray tell, is that interesting?"

"My brother is not exactly the friendly type," Olivia explained. "He maintains a small group of friends—tolerates them, really—and he doesn't take to people easily. Or at all, in most cases."

Theodosia couldn't help but grin. "I had rather suspected as much."

Before Olivia could reply, the butler appeared at the doorway with a slight bow. "Madame Duchon has arrived and is setting up in the parlor."

At once, Olivia leapt to her feet, her eyes bright with excitement. "Oh, splendid! I cannot wait to see what gowns she's brought this time."

Rising more slowly, Theodosia smoothed down the borrowed pale pink muslin she wore and gave a small smile. "It will be a relief to have a wardrobe of my own. Not that I haven't appreciated your generosity, of course."

"It's truly no trouble," Olivia said with a wave of her hand.

"You are kind to say so, but your brother did promise me a new wardrobe," Theodosia reminded her.

"Then let us go spend my brother's hard-earned money," Olivia declared, looping her arm through Theodosia's as they exited the drawing room.

As they strolled towards the parlor, they passed Lord Wilton's study. Theodosia cast a fleeting glance through the open doorway. There he sat, hunched over a ledger, quill in hand, the furrow between his brows speaking to the weight of his thoughts.

"My brother works entirely too hard," Olivia murmured.

"That is a commendable trait."

"Perhaps," Olivia said with a shrug, "but not if he ever hopes to find a wife."

They entered the parlor, and Theodosia halted for a moment, taken aback by the flurry of activity. Fabrics in every color imaginable lay draped across settees and chairs, and two young assistants flitted between the bolts. At the center stood a woman with striking black hair, keen dark eyes, and a commanding presence.

"Lady Olivia," the woman greeted, extending her arms. "I brought your gowns, as promised. I do hope you'll find them satisfactory."

Olivia made a delighted noise and reached for a maroon gown with a black overlay. "This is exquisite," she declared, holding it up to her figure.

"I am pleased to hear it," the woman said before turning to Theodosia with a knowing smile. "And you must be Miss Theodosia Smith."

"I am," she confirmed, stepping forward.

"I am Madame Duchon. I understand Lord Wilton has commissioned an entire wardrobe on your behalf."

Theodosia gave a tentative nod. "Yes—if it isn't too much of an inconvenience."

Madame Duchon let out an amused laugh. "Inconvenience? My dear girl, Lord Wilton is paying me handsomely for my time. It is no trouble at all."

She stepped closer, appraising Theodosia from head to toe

with a discerning eye. "You are a pretty little thing. Unmarried, I presume?"

"I am," Theodosia replied.

"Then we shall favor soft hues—pale blues, blushes, creams. They will suit you beautifully. Have you been presented at Court?"

"Heavens, no," Theodosia responded. "I am merely Lady Olivia's companion. I've no ambition to be presented to the queen."

"Well, I daresay you shall be the most fashionable companion the *ton* has ever seen," Madame Duchon declared with a flourish.

"That really isn't necessary—"

"Oh, but it is," Olivia interjected. "I've no wish to be seen about Town with a dowdy companion."

Madame Duchon beamed. "Then it's settled. I shall begin with your measurements."

An assistant stepped forward and handed her a long measuring tape. As Madame Duchon began her work, she kept up a pleasant stream of questions.

"Where do you hail from?"

"A small village in Sussex," Theodosia answered.

"And how are you enjoying London?"

Theodosia attempted to quell her enthusiasm. "It's all quite marvelous. I had no idea so many people could live in one place."

Madame Duchon laughed. "The novelty does fade rather quickly, especially when the Thames begins to smell."

"We're going to Gunter's this afternoon," Olivia piped up from where she was comparing two silk sashes.

"A fine establishment," the modiste remarked.

"It is," Theodosia said. "Though this time, Lord Wilton will be joining us."

Why had she said that? It was hardly worth mentioning. Yet she felt Olivia's eyes land on her with amusement.

"I've been trying to coax my brother to accompany me for weeks," Olivia said, lifting a brow. "But one polite invitation from you and he agrees."

Theodosia's cheeks flushed. "I merely asked. There was no persuasion involved."

Mercifully, the subject dropped, and a more comfortable silence fell over the room as Madame Duchon continued taking measurements.

Once finished, she stepped back and gestured towards the bolts of fabric. "Would you like to examine the material I brought with me?"

Theodosia approached the settees, letting her fingertips glide over the fine muslin. "They're so soft. So beautiful."

"I only use the best," Madame Duchon said, joining her. "Nothing less will do for a young lady's first impression."

Theodosia hesitated. "Are you sure that's... wise?"

"I am," the modiste replied with a confident nod. "I have an excellent team of seamstresses working night and day. With any luck, you'll have the first gowns delivered tomorrow."

"That sounds rather expensive," Theodosia said, but then a voice spoke from the doorway.

"You needn't concern yourself with the expense, Miss Theodosia," Lord Wilton said, stepping into the room. "I gave my word."

Madame Duchon dipped into a graceful curtsy. "My lord, a pleasure, as always."

He inclined his head in polite acknowledgment. Olivia rushed to his side, a rich green gown draped over one arm.

"Look at this one," she said. "Is it not the loveliest?"

He studied it for a moment, then replied dryly, "It is... certainly a gown."

Olivia merely smiled. "Why do I even bother? You haven't the faintest appreciation for fashion."

"I never claimed to," he said. "Are we to depart for Gunter's now?"

"Just one more moment while I speak to Madame Duchon," Olivia said over her shoulder, already turning back to the modiste with a sparkle of excitement in her eyes. The two women fell into easy conversation, animatedly discussing sleeve lengths and hem embellishments.

As Olivia became engrossed, Lord Wilton stepped beside Theodosia. "Are these muslin fabrics to your liking?" he asked, his gaze sweeping over the assortment with polite interest before settling on her.

"They are," she replied, allowing her fingers to glide over the soft weave of an ivory muslin. "I've never seen anything so fine. The fabrics available in my village were more practical than pretty."

"Then I'm pleased you'll have the opportunity to wear something worthy of you."

She turned her head, regarding him with playful suspicion. "Another compliment, Lord Wilton?" she asked lightly. "If you're not careful, all this flattery might go to my head."

His answering chuckle was low and genuine—the sort of sound that invited a smile in return. "I merely speak the truth. Would you prefer I lie?"

"No," she responded. "I prefer the truth."

He reached out then, his fingers brushing along a bolt of pale blue muslin that lay unfurled across the settee. "This one," he murmured. "I believe this would suit you exceedingly well. It would bring out the color in your eyes."

It was the way he said it—quiet, unforced, utterly sincere—that made the words land with unexpected weight. Her breath caught just slightly, and to her mortification, warmth rushed to her cheeks. She ducked her head in an attempt to hide the flush.

Why was she reacting this way? They were only words. Kindly meant, perhaps. But still, only words.

Before she could muster a reply, Olivia's voice rang out from behind them. "I am ready to depart!"

Relieved by the timely interruption, Theodosia turned towards her a touch too quickly. "Let us depart, then," she said, her voice perhaps a little louder than it needed to be.

Yes, far too loud.

But if Lord Wilton noticed her discomposure, he made no mention of it. Instead, he merely offered his arm with the easy politeness of a gentleman.

And, after a brief pause, she took it.

She allowed Lord Wilton to lead her from the parlor. They walked in silence through the corridor, and for that she was grateful. Her thoughts were still far too muddled by the strange flutter she'd felt in his presence just moments ago. It had been the most ordinary of compliments, yet it had left her oddly unsettled.

Why?

She stole a glance at him as they reached the entry hall, but his expression was unreadable—composed, as always. Did he know how easily he'd flustered her?

The butler straightened as they approached and gave a dignified nod. "The open drawn carriage is out front, my lord."

"Thank you," Lord Wilton replied.

They stepped outside and the open carriage stood ready at the base of the steps, the horses tossing their heads impatiently. Without hesitation, Lord Wilton turned to assist the ladies. Olivia climbed in first and then Theodosia placed her gloved hand in his. His grip was warm and firm as he helped her up, steadying her with more care than was necessary. Once she was seated beside Olivia, he circled around and took his place opposite them.

With a lurch, the carriage set off, wheels creaking as they rolled onto the bustling street. The familiar clatter of hooves and distant murmur of London life surrounded them, yet within the carriage lingered a moment of quiet.

It was Olivia who broke it, her voice light with interest. "I was thinking we should attend Lady Warwicke's ball in a few days."

"A ball?" Lord Wilton repeated, lifting a brow. "Do you truly think that is wise, given the current murmurings about our family?"

Olivia waved a hand dismissively. "The gossip will fade. It always does. And what better way to remind Society that we are not hiding in shame than to be seen at one of the Season's most anticipated events?"

His gaze sharpened slightly, but he made no immediate rebuttal. Instead, he turned his attention to Theodosia. "And what say you? Does the idea of a grand ball appeal to you?"

She felt herself sit a little straighter beneath the weight of his scrutiny. "I have never attended a ball in London," she admitted, a tinge of excitement creeping into her voice despite her best efforts to remain composed. "I imagine it would be quite the experience."

His lips quirked in a way that might have been amusement —or approval. "Then I suppose we shall accept the invitation."

Olivia clasped her hands together. "What fun we shall have! I simply adore a good ball."

Theodosia smiled faintly, but her thoughts had already begun to drift. Despite her initial hesitations about London Society, she found herself genuinely eager for the upcoming ball. Would a gentleman ask her to dance? Would *Lord Wilton*?

She tried to imagine it: his gloved palm reaching for hers, the press of his hand at her back, the strength of his arm as he guided her through the elegant steps of a waltz. The closeness of such a thing—of him—was enough to make her breath catch. It was foolish, of course. And yet... the thought carried with it a strange, undeniable allure.

"Wouldn't you agree, Miss Theodosia?" Lord Wilton asked.

His voice cut through her reverie like a blade, and she blinked. "Pardon?" she said. "I'm afraid I was... woolgathering."

He looked amused. "Anything you'd care to share?"

"No," she replied swiftly, a touch too quickly. "Nothing of importance."

Olivia's brows lifted, clearly intrigued, but to her credit, she said nothing.

Theodosia folded her hands in her lap and fixed her gaze out at the bustling street, willing the warmth in her cheeks to fade. Whatever had possessed her to woolgather about dancing with Lord Wilton—of all people—needed to be banished.

He was her employer's brother. Nothing more.

As the carriage rattled forward, she knew no good would come from dwelling a moment longer on the infuriatingly handsome Lord Wilton.

12

Richard adjusted his top hat with a brisk tug, settling it more firmly on his head as the open carriage rolled through the streets of London. The sun was bright and cheerful, but his jaw was clenched as he recalled his last conversation with Miss Theodosia.

What in the blazes had he been thinking telling Miss Theodosia that she would look lovely in a blue gown?

He didn't care what she wore. He couldn't afford to care. And yet, the very thought of how that particular shade complemented her eyes had formed on his tongue before he could stop it. Madness. Absolute madness. She was not even a proper guest in his household—merely installed there under the guise of being Olivia's companion. And here he was, thinking about the way her eyes sparkled when she smiled.

Dangerous territory indeed.

The last thing he needed to do was develop feelings for her.

The carriage slowed and came to a halt before Gunter's. Patrons were already gathered beneath the establishment's distinctive green awning, many of them pausing to note their arrival. Richard's gaze swept over the assembly, daring anyone to voice their opinions aloud. Let them stare. He would not have Olivia subjected to ridicule—at least, not in his presence.

Across from him, Olivia looked about nervously. "Why did I agree to this outing?" she asked under her breath.

"Because the lemon ice is divine," Miss Theodosia replied with a teasing smile. "And because you deserve to indulge in a little sweetness now and again. Besides, why should we care what these people think?"

"I do care," Olivia admitted. "I care very much. They are judging me... as harshly as I judge myself."

Without hesitation, Miss Theodosia nudged Olivia's shoulder affectionately. "Then it sounds to me like you need a distraction. I could read to you. Or—if you're lucky—I might even juggle."

Richard huffed. "You do not juggle."

Miss Theodosia arched a brow at him. "And how can you be so certain, my lord?"

"Because women do not juggle," he said in a tone that suggested the matter was beyond debate.

She gave him a slow, smug smile. "I am many things, Lord Wilton, but a liar is not one of them."

He leveled a skeptical gaze at her. "Are you honestly expecting me to believe that a genteel-born daughter of a baronet has mastered such a skill?"

"I am," she said simply.

Before he could press further, a male server from Gunter's approached the carriage with a polite bow. "Are you ready to order, my lord?"

"We'll have three lemon ices," Richard replied, "and three oranges."

The man looked surprised by the request. "Three whole oranges?"

"Yes," Richard confirmed, his tone brooking no questions.

As the server turned away, Miss Theodosia leaned towards him with narrowed eyes. "Do you truly intend for me to juggle in front of Gunter's, on a crowded afternoon?"

"Is that a problem?" he asked with feigned innocence.

She met his gaze. "Not at all. Though I ought to warn you, it will attract attention."

"I believe that's the entire point," he said dryly. "Unless, of course, you care to admit that you fabricated the whole thing."

"And why would I do that?" she countered. "It sounds to me as though someone is afraid of being proven wrong."

"Juggling is not a drawing room accomplishment," Richard said stiffly. "It belongs to the circus."

Olivia turned in her seat to regard her companion with sudden eagerness. "Wait—can you truly juggle?"

"I can," Miss Theodosia replied. "Though it's been some time since I last attempted it. I might be a touch rusty."

Just then, the server returned with a small wooden tray bearing three glossy oranges. He extended them towards Richard. "Will these do, my lord?"

"They are perfect," Richard said, handing them over to Miss Theodosia. "Might I trouble you for a demonstration?"

She accepted the oranges and adjusted them in her gloved hands. "If you insist."

"I do."

Without another word, she tossed one orange into the air and caught it smoothly. Then the second followed. And finally, the third. Within moments, all three oranges danced between her hands in a swift, fluid rhythm that defied expectation. Her posture was effortless, and her movements were precise.

The surrounding patrons—many of whom had pretended not to notice their arrival—began to murmur and gawk openly.

After a few passes, she caught the oranges neatly and

returned them to her lap with a triumphant smirk. "Are you satisfied now, my lord?"

He stared at her, quite dumbfounded. "How did you come by such a skill?"

"My uncle taught me," she said with a casual shrug. "Much to the mortification of my mother and father. It amused him to see how quickly I could master it, but my mother made me swear never to do it in public again. She was terrified of what the villagers would think."

Miss Theodosia turned her head, taking in the widened eyes and scandalized expressions of Gunter's patrons, and continued. "It would appear I've gone and attracted quite the audience."

Olivia laughed, clearly delighted. "At least they're staring at you now instead of me."

"I don't mind," Miss Theodosia said. "You deserve kindness, Olivia. Not the judgment of people who are too proud to examine their own faults."

The server returned with three glass bowls filled with lemon ice. "Will there be anything else?"

"No," Richard said, handing the desserts to the ladies. "This will do nicely."

As they began to eat, the atmosphere grew lighter, the ice a welcome reprieve from the warmth of the day.

Miss Theodosia dabbed her lips with a napkin. "Does anyone else have a hidden talent they've kept secret?"

"I can play the pianoforte," Olivia offered, reaching for her spoon.

"That is hardly a shocking revelation," Miss Theodosia remarked.

"No, but what most people don't know is that I'm quite good at it," Olivia replied. "I always play the simpler pieces in public. I don't care to perform for an audience."

Richard nodded. "She's telling the truth. Olivia plays with remarkable skill when no one's watching."

"I never learned," Miss Theodosia confessed. "The pianoforte never held my interest."

Olivia's eyes widened in disbelief. "Not at all?"

"I'm afraid not. My interests... wandered elsewhere," she said with a mischievous twinkle in her eyes.

He shook his head, a reluctant smile tugging at his mouth. What a curious, infuriating, impossible woman. However, the image of her juggling oranges—utterly unrepentant and proud —refused to leave his mind.

Richard had just polished off the final spoonful of his lemon ice, savoring the lingering chill on his tongue, when he caught sight of a familiar figure weaving through the crowd. Mr. Addington, impeccably dressed as always, approached the carriage with a purposeful stride.

Lifting a hand in greeting, Richard called out, "Addington."

His friend halted beside the carriage and offered a polite bow. "Good afternoon, Wilton." His gaze shifted to the others. "Lady Olivia." He bowed again, this time with greater courtesy.

"Mr. Addington," Olivia returned with a cordial smile.

But Richard noted the brief, inquisitive pause in Addington's gaze when it settled on Miss Theodosia.

Without hesitation, Richard gestured towards her. "Mr. Addington, allow me to introduce Miss Theodosia Smith— Olivia's companion during her stay in Town."

Addington tipped his head. "Miss Theodosia. A pleasure to make your acquaintance."

"The pleasure is mine, sir," she answered, responding in kind.

Olivia leaned slightly forward. "I believe I heard you are now a Fellow at Oxford. Is that true?"

Addington puffed out his chest in pride. "Indeed. I received the appointment last month."

"How very impressive," Olivia said. "Your parents must be pleased."

At once, his expression faltered, and he offered a rueful smile. "Ah, I'm afraid not. My father considers it a waste of time. He believes a proper Englishman should be acquiring estates, not lecturing about ancient Rome to distracted students."

"I'm sorry to hear that," Olivia said.

He waved a hand as if brushing away her sympathy. "No need. I reconciled myself to disappointing him long ago. Besides, it's far too pleasant a day for complaints, is it not?"

Richard gave a faint nod of agreement, though his attention was more fixed on the subtle change in his sister's demeanor. She was toying with the lace of her sleeve, her gaze distant.

"How is Lord Harwood enjoying married life?" Olivia asked.

"He and his new bride are still enjoying their wedding tour. I'm told they are somewhere along the coast now—Devonshire, perhaps," Addington replied.

Olivia dropped her gaze, and in that instant, Richard saw the brightness leave her eyes. A shadow passed over her features—pain, or perhaps longing. The transformation was swift but unmistakable.

He furrowed his brow. *What was it about that comment?* Was it the mention of a honeymoon? Of Lord Harwood content in marriage? Whatever it was, Olivia was clearly unsettled.

Taking a step back, Addington said, "Well, I should be on my way. I hadn't meant to intrude."

"You're not," Richard responded. "You're welcome to stay and join us."

"That is kind of you, but I shall have to decline."

Richard noticed Addington's gaze drift once more towards Miss Theodosia. This time it lingered—just a moment too long, with a spark of appreciation that Richard found oddly unwelcome.

The reaction was irrational, of course. Miss Theodosia was

young, strikingly beautiful, and carried herself with a confident grace. It was of little wonder that Addington would notice. Any man would.

So why was Richard's jaw tense?

Something about the idea of Addington—charming, well-positioned, and altogether eligible—showing interest in Miss Theodosia unsettled him far more than it ought to have.

He forced a polite smile. "Perhaps we'll see you at Warwicke's ball?"

Addington tipped his hat. "If I can finish my work before then, I'll be there."

With one last look at Miss Theodosia—this time paired with a parting smile—he turned on his heel and disappeared into the crowd.

Silence descended over the carriage, and Richard saw Miss Theodosia eyeing him curiously.

"Is something wrong, my lord?" she asked.

"Not at all," Richard replied briskly, though his tone lacked conviction. "I simply find it curious how many gentlemen discover their manners when introduced to you."

Her lips curved faintly. "And do you object to good manners?"

"I object to someone ogling you."

"And you think Mr. Addington was ogling me?" Miss Theodosia asked with amusement in her voice.

He adjusted the cuff of his coat. "It was merely an observation."

She said nothing, but the look in her eyes told him she saw more than he wished to admit.

Much more.

Olivia spoke up. "Mr. Addington is not capable of ogling anyone. I daresay you are mistaken, Brother."

"I know what I saw," he replied, a touch too forcefully.

"Perhaps you need spectacles, then," Olivia remarked lightly.

Richard did not want to prolong this line of conversation, especially under his sister's perceptive gaze. She would see through him—just as Miss Theodosia had.

Theodosia sat near the window in the parlor, her needle moving in and out of her embroidery. A shaft of golden afternoon sunlight illuminated her stitches, though her concentration faltered now and then—not from difficulty with the pattern, but from the music filling the room. Olivia was seated at the pianoforte, her fingers gliding across the keys with graceful mastery. The melodies were light and elegant, yet tinged with something more wistful beneath the surface.

Still, since their visit to Gunter's, a question had been gnawing at the edge of her thoughts, refusing to be silenced.

The final note drifted into silence, and Olivia let her hands fall into her lap. She rose from the bench with a soft sigh and crossed to the settee, flopping onto it with none of the polish expected of a lady.

"What shall we do now?" she asked, brushing a stray curl from her face.

Lowering her needlework to her lap, Theodosia said, "We could speak about what happened at Gunter's earlier."

Olivia made a face and sank deeper into the cushions. "I would prefer not to." She pointed towards the chessboard on a side table. "We could play a game instead."

Theodosia gave her a knowing look. "I take it the gentleman you once loved is Lord Harwood."

Olivia stiffened slightly. "Was it so obvious?"

"Not to most," Theodosia replied. "But I've never known you to appear uneasy around anyone. Today was... different."

With a resigned sigh, Olivia clasped her hands tightly in her lap. "Yes. I once believed I was in love with Lord Harwood. Foolishly, of course."

"And you no longer believe it?"

"Not when the man is married to another," Olivia said bitterly. "That has a way of stripping away illusions."

Theodosia offered a faint, understanding smile. "Feelings don't vanish the moment someone becomes unavailable. It simply means you mustn't act upon them."

"Oh, I would never," Olivia said, her voice laced with scorn. "The man is a blackguard. He promised me everything—devotion, a future, even marriage. And then he married another without a word of explanation."

Theodosia's smile faded. "I'm sorry, Olivia. That must have been painful."

Olivia waved a hand dismissively, though the motion lacked its usual liveliness. "It's over now. He made his choice, and I must live with it."

"You didn't deserve to be treated so callously."

"No, I didn't. But that's the world we live in, is it not? Where trust is a fool's currency."

Theodosia met her gaze. "You can trust me."

"Can I?"

"Why are you surprised?" Theodosia asked. "I want only what is best for you."

There was a pause, and then Olivia spoke carefully. "Are you acquainted with my husband?"

Theodosia blinked, taken aback. "No. Why would I be?"

"It's just..." Olivia hesitated. "My brother seems convinced that you know more than you're letting on about Luke Smith."

Setting her embroidery aside on the nearby table, Theodosia straightened. "I have told your brother—repeatedly, in fact—that I do not know this Mr. Smith. He is not my brother, nor any relation to me. The name is a mere coincidence."

Olivia tilted her head, studying her, as if gauging her sincerity. After a long moment, she nodded. "I believe you."

"Good," Theodosia said. "Now perhaps you can knock that truth into your brother's thick skull."

Adopting a more rigid posture, Olivia deepened her voice in imitation. "'You cannot insult me. I am a marquess!'"

Olivia's impersonation was so uncanny that Theodosia burst out laughing. "He does announce it rather often, doesn't he? Do you think he ever forgets?"

"I highly doubt it," Olivia replied, giggling.

Just then, the parlor door opened and Lady Wilton swept in and lightly chided, "Do leave your brother alone, Olivia."

"I cannot help myself, Mother. He is just so terribly stuffy."

Lady Wilton made a sound between a laugh and a sigh as she took a seat beside her daughter. "He is very much like his father in that respect. Stiff and stubborn, but both with hearts of gold."

Turning her attention to Theodosia, she asked, "How are you settling in here, dear?"

"I'm enjoying myself greatly," Theodosia replied with genuine warmth. "Everyone has been most welcoming."

Lady Wilton's face lit with pleasure. "Wonderful. I'm so pleased to hear it."

At that moment, the butler entered, bearing a silver tray with a single letter atop it. "A letter for Miss Theodosia."

She rose, accepted the letter with a murmur of thanks, and glanced down at the handwriting. Her heart lifted. "It's from my dearest friend, Penelope."

"Will you read it now?" Lady Wilton asked.

"I shall, in a little while," Theodosia replied, slipping the missive into a concealed pocket in her gown as she returned to her seat.

Lady Wilton held her gaze and asked, "Have you heard from your man of business recently?"

"Not yet," Theodosia said. "But before leaving, I gave him a very thorough list of what I expect to be managed in my absence. I'm quite detailed when it comes to estate affairs."

Lady Wilton nodded with a look of impressed approval. "You must have a remarkable head for business."

Olivia straightened suddenly, her eyes bright. "Do you think I could manage an estate?"

Without looking at her, Lady Wilton answered, "No."

Olivia's mouth fell open. "Well, that was rather rude."

"I meant no offense, darling," her mother said, clearly amused. "But you and Richard both inherited my lack of skill with numbers. We tend to mix them about, even when we try very hard not to."

Olivia gave a theatrical sigh and flopped back against the settee. "So much for my future as a shrewd landowner."

"I daresay that you shall manage," Lady Wilton said.

Just then, a maid entered the room, balancing a gleaming silver tea service upon a tray. She moved with silent efficiency and placed it carefully upon the low table before Lady Wilton.

"Shall I pour, my lady?" the maid asked politely.

Lady Wilton gave a shake of her head. "That won't be necessary. Lady Olivia shall see to the tea."

Olivia straightened at once and reached for the teapot with exaggerated seriousness. "So I cannot be trusted with numbers," she muttered, "but I am deemed fit to serve refreshments."

"Precisely," Lady Wilton said with a smile. "An invaluable skill."

Olivia poured three cups of tea and distributed them. Theodosia took a sip of her tea and then lowered her cup to her lap, turning her gaze to Lady Wilton.

"I understand," she began slowly, "that your marriage to the late Lord Wilton was... a practical arrangement?"

Lady Wilton did not appear startled by the question. Her gaze turned contemplative. "Yes, it was. A marriage of convenience, arranged by our families. There was no courtship to speak of. We barely knew each other."

"But it changed over time?"

Lady Wilton's expression softened. "Yes. Respect came first. Then affection. And eventually, something far deeper. When he passed, I found myself quite lost. I could not imagine my life without him by the end."

"I think that's rather beautiful," Theodosia murmured.

"You will have your own love story one day," Lady Wilton encouraged. "I've no doubt of it."

Theodosia's fingers tightened slightly around the teacup. "I often wonder... what I would have to give up to be married."

Lady Wilton considered her thoughtfully. "Perhaps you are looking at it the wrong way. What if, instead, you asked yourself what you might gain?"

"I wish it were that simple."

"Sometimes," Lady Wilton said, setting her cup down, "it can be. Two good people, committed to one another, can create something wonderful together. But both must bring sincerity to the table."

Theodosia's voice lowered. "If I were to marry, my husband would almost certainly insist on managing my estate. And I... I could not abide that."

Lady Wilton nodded with understanding. "Then the right man would not ask it of you. He would recognize that managing your estate brings you joy, and he would wish for you to keep doing so."

Theodosia gave a soft laugh, more wistful than amused. "And where might I find such a man?"

A knowing smile touched Lady Wilton's lips. "He may be closer than you think."

The butler appeared in the doorway and cleared his throat discreetly. "Pardon the interruption, my lady. Mr. Pritchett has come to call on Miss Theodosia Smith. He requests a few moments of her time."

Lady Wilton lifted a single brow. "And who, precisely, is Mr. Pritchett?"

Olivia set her cup down and leaned forward with interest. "He proposed to Dosia before she came to London. She refused him."

Lady Wilton turned to Theodosia and asked, "And what would you like to do, my dear?"

Theodosia glanced towards the open doorway, her features composed, though her stomach tightened. "I suppose there's no harm in allowing him a few minutes."

"As you wish," Lady Wilton said, giving a slight nod to the butler. "Show Mr. Pritchett in."

The butler bowed and disappeared. A few moments later, the parlor door opened again to admit Mr. Pritchett, who had perspiration gleaming at his temples. He clutched a handkerchief in one gloved hand and offered a shallow bow upon entering.

"Forgive me," he said with a sheepish smile, dabbing at his brow. "It is rather warm out this afternoon."

"I hadn't noticed," Theodosia replied, rising from her chair. Her tone was cordial but she didn't wish to encourage the man. She had refused his offer of marriage for a myriad of reasons. She gestured to an armchair across from hers. "Please, do sit down, Mr. Pritchett."

"You're looking well, Miss Theodosia," he said, his gaze lingering on her face with unmistakable admiration. "Quite well, indeed."

"Thank you," she replied.

An awkward silence hovered for a breath too long before Lady Wilton leaned subtly towards her daughter and murmured, "Dear, we have a guest. I am certain he would appreciate a refreshment."

Olivia gracefully reached for the teapot. "Would you care for a cup of tea, Mr. Pritchett?" she asked sweetly, though her smile did not quite reach her eyes.

He waved a hand. "Most kind of you, Lady Olivia, but I fear I must decline. The very thought of tepid tea on such a warm day turns my stomach."

Knowing what was expected of her, Theodosia gestured between their guest and Lady Wilton. "Mr. Pritchett, allow me to introduce you to Lady Wilton."

Mr. Pritchett scrambled to his feet and gave a stiff, awkward bow in the older lady's direction. "My lady. A true honor."

Lady Wilton responded with a courteous nod, though her expression remained neutral. Her eyes quickly returned to her tea.

Once Mr. Pritchett had reseated himself, Theodosia asked, "To what do I owe the pleasure of your visit today, sir?"

He gave a rueful smile and leaned forward slightly, elbows resting on his knees. "Only the pleasure of your company, Miss Theodosia. I happened to be in the area and thought I might pay my respects."

Theodosia forced a smile to her lips as she attempted to come up with a believable lie to end this visit. "That is... thoughtful of you. But I'm afraid we cannot linger long since Lady Olivia insists upon a daily turn about the gardens with her dog before we begin preparations for supper."

Olivia, ever quick to catch a cue, nodded with feigned earnestness. "It is quite true. I find that if my dog does not take the air at least twice a day, he becomes rather insufferable to those around him. It's how I manage his excess energy."

Mr. Pritchett gave a short nod, dabbing his brow again. "I

understand. I would not dream of imposing upon your routine." But his eyes flicked towards Theodosia once more, his disappointment only thinly veiled.

Theodosia shifted slightly in her seat, the angle of her posture growing a fraction more formal. She had no wish to wound Mr. Pritchett's feelings outright. He had never been unkind, only persistent—and woefully mismatched. Still, that did not obligate her to offer warmth where there was none to give.

Politeness, yes.

Encouragement, no.

And she would not make the mistake of blurring the line between the two.

13

Richard sat at his desk, his gaze fixed on the columns of numbers that danced mockingly across the page. The ledgers sent over by his man of business should have been straightforward, yet the figures blurred and shifted no matter how often he blinked. With a frustrated exhale, he leaned back in his chair and pinched the bridge of his nose. His temples throbbed with a dull ache. Why did it have to be so infernally difficult?

A soft voice broke the silence.

"You missed dinner," Miss Theodosia said from the doorway, holding up a small plate. "Your mother asked me to bring you pudding."

He didn't glance up. "We have servants for that sort of thing," he muttered, his tone sharper than he intended.

Unbothered, she stepped into the room with a weak smile. "I know. But I didn't mind. I was on my way to retire for the evening, and I thought you might appreciate something sweet."

He gestured to the corner of the desk, his voice still curt. "You can put it there."

She approached and carefully set the plate down. "You look tired," she observed. "And frustrated."

Something in him snapped. "It is none of your concern," he said, the words flung with more force than he'd meant.

There was a brief pause. Then, calmly, she replied, "No, it is not. But I am asking as a friend. That is what we agreed to be, is it not?"

He raked a hand through his hair, fingers catching in the unruly strands. "We did," he admitted gruffly, "but I'm not in the mood to talk. Not with you, not with anyone."

"I understand." Her gaze dropped to the cluttered papers. "Still, if you're struggling with the accounts, perhaps I might offer some assistance."

His eyes narrowed. "And why would you think I need your help?"

"I never said you did."

"I am perfectly capable of handling my own accounts, Miss Theodosia," he said, his voice tight with defensiveness.

A flicker of emotion crossed her face—perhaps disappointment or restraint. She bowed her head slightly. "Of course. Good night, my lord."

She turned and made her way towards the door, her steps light, unhurried. But before she reached it, the weight of guilt tugged at him.

"Wait," he called out.

She stopped and turned, her expression guarded.

He rose, tugging down his waistcoat as though to steady himself. "I'm sorry. I had no right to speak to you in that manner."

"It's all right," she said quietly and moved to leave again.

"No, it isn't," he said, stopping her once more. "You did nothing wrong. I—" He faltered, ashamed. "I was taking out my frustrations on you."

She studied him for a long moment. "Dare I ask what has you so vexed?"

His pride warred with his honesty, but in the end, honesty won. "I struggle with numbers," he admitted, his voice low. "Always have. My mind switches them around somehow. It's like chasing smoke trying to get them to line up properly. I've had this issue since I was a boy."

He braced himself for ridicule or condescension. Instead, her eyes softened with something dangerously close to understanding.

"My dearest friend, Penelope, is the same way," she said. "Arithmetic was always a struggle for her. Her mother used to say she had a mind built for stories, not sums."

He gave a humorless chuckle. "Yes, well, I'm expected to manage an estate. What use is a lord who cannot even read the blasted ledger?"

"There is no shame in that," she said simply.

He frowned. Was that pity he heard in her tone? He couldn't abide that. "Don't look at me like that."

"Like what?" she asked, appearing genuinely puzzled.

"Like I'm broken."

Her expression turned solemn. "I don't pity you, if that's what you're implying."

His brow furrowed. "You don't?"

She stepped closer to the desk. "Everyone has strengths and weaknesses, my lord. Some are merely more visible than others. Struggling with something doesn't make you broken. It makes you human."

He looked away, jaw tight. "I shouldn't have weaknesses. Not ones that matter."

"'To err is human,'" she quoted. "There's no disgrace in it."

He stared at her, scarcely able to believe what he was hearing. "Surely, you are mocking me," he said. "Just as the boys did at Eton when they learned of my so-called limitations. They mimicked my struggles, laughed behind my back and some-times to my face."

Her eyes did not waver from his. "I am truly sorry they treated you so cruelly. But I assure you, I am in earnest. They had no right."

Richard exhaled and sank back down into his chair, the strength seeming to drain from him. He dragged a hand down his face, as though wearied by years rather than minutes. "My father tried everything," he murmured. "Tutor after tutor. Each promising miracles, each failing. None of it made any differ-ence. You cannot mend something that is fundamentally broken."

Miss Theodosia stepped closer, her expression firm. "You must stop saying that you are broken. You are not. Struggling with one task does not render you less capable, less worthy, or less whole. So what if you cannot read a ledger? That does not prevent you from managing your estate or leading your house-hold with competence and wisdom."

He let out a frustrated breath. "You don't understand."

"You are right—I don't," she said with unflinching honesty. "Because I see a man who has every advantage, every resource, and yet insists on wallowing in his sense of inadequacy instead of doing something about it. You're not a failure. You're simply too determined to feel sorry for yourself to see the truth."

He shoved back his chair again and rose. He crossed the room with quick, agitated strides and stared out into the dark-ened night beyond the window.

"I am a marquess," he said quietly, almost to himself. "Men look to me—to guide, to inspire. To lead by example. And I—I cannot even read a blasted column of numbers."

A silence stretched between them before she asked, "Why do you believe that disqualifies you from leading them?"

"Miss Theodosia—" he started.

She cut him off. "Enough of the excuses. There is nothing

wrong with you, save for the fact that you insist on seeing yourself through the lens of childhood shame. If your brain scrambles numbers, then hire someone who can read them clearly. Delegate that task and focus on the many duties only you can fulfill. That, my lord, is what a wise leader does."

He stood there for a long moment in the flickering lamplight. Then, slowly, he swallowed, his throat working. "You truly don't think less of me? Not even a little?"

"Of course not," she said without hesitation. "Why would I? You've entrusted me with a truth most men would never dare voice aloud. That takes courage, not weakness."

Richard's chest felt tight, not with embarrassment, but something dangerously close to relief. For so long, he had lived with the fear of exposure, of being seen and judged. Yet now, standing before this woman who met his flaws with strength instead of scorn, he felt... lighter.

Miss Theodosia regarded him with a quiet intensity. She said nothing further, but something shifted in the space between them—something fragile and profound.

He didn't feel quite so alone anymore.

For the first time in what felt like years, he felt truly *seen*— not as a title, or an obligation, or a disappointment—but as a man. Someone understood him. Someone *heard* him. It was a startling sensation, one he had not experienced since his father had been alive.

Miss Theodosia glanced at his cluttered desk. "If you'd like," she began, "I would be happy to help you review your accounts tomorrow."

"You would?"

A soft smile curved her lips. "As I've said before, I am quite good with numbers. I find it rather satisfying to bring order to a chaotic ledger."

He chuckled. "You are rather peculiar, but in the most agreeable way."

"Thank you," she murmured, a faint flush coloring her cheeks.

Without meaning to, he stepped towards her. One step, then another, until only a breath separated them. She looked up at him, her chin lifting to meet his gaze, and her expression a mix of uncertainty and curiosity.

A stray tendril had escaped her otherwise neat chignon, curling against her cheek. His fingers itched with the urge to reach out, to tuck it gently behind her ear. It was a ridiculous impulse—intimate and absurd—but he couldn't shake it.

Her eyes searched his face. She wasn't retreating, but she wasn't drawing closer either. He could see the question in them: *why are you standing so near?*

"I should go," she said softly, though she made no move to step away.

"Yes," he agreed. His voice was hoarse, and his feet remained stubbornly in place. "You should."

Nevertheless, neither of them moved. He should have stepped back. He should have remembered his manners, remembered who they were.

But he didn't want to. Not just yet.

Not when standing this close to Miss Theodosia felt like the first right thing he'd done in a very long time.

She took a breath. And that breath stole his. He had never been so tempted by a young woman before. Not in all of his life.

His sister's voice rang out from the doorway. "Good heavens, what am I interrupting?"

Startled, Richard stepped back at once, his movements swift and stiff. "Nothing," he said—far too quickly to sound convincing.

Olivia's brow arched in clear disbelief as she sauntered into the room. "It didn't look like nothing," she said, her tone lilting with barely concealed amusement. "In fact, it looked quite like something."

He clenched his jaw, resisting the urge to roll his eyes. Trust Olivia to appear at the most inopportune moment.

He risked a glance at Miss Theodosia, who now had both hands raised to her cheeks. Her gaze had dropped to the floor, and she seemed to be willing it to swallow her whole. The usually composed woman looked thoroughly flustered—an expression he hadn't seen on her before and found oddly endearing.

Olivia, of course, noticed everything. Her eyes sparkled with delight as she looked between them. "Well," she drawled, "it's a bit late in the evening for private consultations about account ledgers."

Richard cleared his throat, his expression now stern. "That's quite enough, Olivia."

But his sister only grinned wider, unrepentant as ever. "Of course. I shall let you two resume nothing, then." She turned with a swish of her skirts and disappeared down the corridor, humming as she went.

Silence fell again, heavy with all that had nearly been said —and all that had nearly happened.

Richard looked back at Miss Theodosia. Her hands slowly dropped from her face, though the pink still lingered on her cheeks. Their eyes met, and for a moment, neither of them could summon a single word.

"It is late," Miss Theodosia said, her voice a touch unsteady. "I should retire for the night."

Richard gave a small nod, though he couldn't seem to look away from her. "Yes," he agreed. "I believe that would be wise."

She lingered a moment longer, as if considering whether to say more, then offered him a weak smile. But it didn't quite reach her eyes—not this time. With a graceful dip of her head, she turned and made her way to the door, her footsteps hushed against the carpet.

She didn't glance back. Not once.

As soon as the door clicked softly shut behind her, Richard exhaled the breath he hadn't realized he'd been holding and sank heavily into the nearest chair.

He stared at the now-closed door, his mind racing, his chest still tight with the echo of what might have been.

What in the blazes had just happened?

One moment they were speaking of ledgers, and the next, he had been drawn to her. Compelled. And she had not pulled away. Not until Olivia's untimely arrival shattered the spell like glass.

And that was the question that haunted him now, the one that refused to be silenced: *what would have happened if his sister hadn't walked in when she did?*

Would he have touched her cheek? Leaned in to kiss her? Would Theodosia have let him?

He scowled at the very thought. It was madness. She was here to lure Mr. Smith out of hiding. Nothing more.

His gaze drifted back to the fire, now burning low. One thing was certain: whatever that moment between them had been, *it could not happen again.* He would make certain of it. He must.

Even if a part of him—an insistent, unruly part—very much wanted it to.

Theodosia sat near the window as she gazed out over the gardens below. The early morning sun hovered just above the horizon, casting a soft golden light across the dew-laced hedges and waking blossoms. The air was still, hushed, and it suited her unsettled thoughts.

She had slept more soundly than she had in weeks, her rest untroubled but for the one persistent thread of memory that tugged at her consciousness the moment she opened her eyes: *Lord Wilton.*

What had nearly happened between them last night?

Whatever it was must not happen again. She was Olivia's companion, a position of trust and propriety, and she had no business entertaining any sort of entanglement with her employer's brother. Certainly not with a man as infuriating, arrogant, and utterly exasperating as the Marquess of Wilton.

And yet...

She had seen something in him the night before. A glimpse of the man beneath the title. His usual shields—his pride, his aloofness—had slipped for just a moment, revealing someone unexpectedly vulnerable. A man who, despite his wealth and status, seemed to hunger for acceptance—not for what he represented, but for who he was.

It had stirred something in her. Something foolish and inconvenient.

Drat.

She'd done it. She'd gone and developed the tiniest, most inconvenient affection for a man she had no intention of ever loving.

Theodosia huffed softly and turned her face from the sun. She was being utterly ridiculous.

A firm knock at the door broke through her thoughts.

"Enter," she called, her voice composed.

Mary stepped inside with her usual brisk cheer. "Good, you're awake. Shall we ready you for the day, Miss?"

With a nod, Theodosia rose and moved to the dressing table. As Mary began brushing and pinning up her hair, she allowed her mind to drift again—though now she kept her thoughts carefully guarded, even from herself.

Once she was dressed in a soft morning gown of lavender muslin, she made her way down the staircase and towards the dining room. With every step, her heart seemed to knock a little harder against her ribs. She had no desire to see Lord Wilton this morning. Or... perhaps she had too much desire, which was the greater danger.

She stepped into the dining room and found him precisely as she had expected—seated at the head of the table, newssheets in hand, his expression as unreadable as always.

Theodosia hesitated for only a moment before squaring her shoulders and crossing the room with practiced composure.

Lord Wilton immediately started to rise at her entrance.

"There's no need to stand, my lord," she said quickly, lifting a hand to forestall him.

He inclined his head and resumed his seat, offering her a folded section of the newssheets. "It seems your juggling display yesterday has garnered you a mention. Mr. Fairchild has written a short article about it."

She blinked in surprise as she accepted the page, her eyes scanning the neat columns of print. "I've never appeared in the Society pages before."

"It's rather less exciting than one imagines," he said dryly.

Theodosia laughed under her breath and set the newssheets down. "I can only imagine Penelope's reaction when she reads this in a few days. The newssheets always arrive late in the village, but we devour them the moment they come —every article, every ridiculous rumor."

Lord Wilton leaned back slightly, amusement glinting in his eyes. "And what will Penelope say when she learns you've been publicly juggling in front of Gunter's?"

"She won't be surprised in the least," Theodosia replied with a shrug. "She's seen me juggle many times."

"Well, I found it rather impressive," he admitted. "I don't believe I've ever encountered another young woman who could juggle with such confidence."

"I also possess the rare talent of skipping stones across a lake with near-perfect accuracy," she added with mock pride.

He chuckled, a warm, genuine sound that made her stomach flip in the most inconvenient way. "A woman of many talents, indeed."

Theodosia smiled and looked down at her plate, hiding the blush that was threatening to warm her cheeks. This version of Lord Wilton—this easier, smiling man—was far too dangerous. He made her feel at ease. He made her laugh. He made her wonder if perhaps... just perhaps... there was something real beneath all the propriety and posture.

And that, above all, was what worried her most.

Lady Wilton swept in and seated herself at the far end of the table. "Good morning," she said pleasantly.

"Good morning, my lady," Theodosia returned with a polite smile.

A footman appeared and set a cup of chocolate before her. Theodosia reached for the cup and took a sip.

Lady Wilton turned her attention towards her son. "I was thinking—"

"A dangerous pastime," Lord Wilton interjected, his eyes still fixed upon the newssheets.

Lady Wilton ignored the jibe and continued. "As I was saying, I believe it would be rather pleasant for Miss Theodosia to enjoy a carriage ride through Hyde Park during the fashionable hour."

Lord Wilton didn't even glance up. "That is a grand idea," he agreed.

"Wonderful," Lady Wilton replied at once, her tone brightening. "Then you will take her."

That made him look up. He lowered the newssheets with deliberate slowness. "I beg your pardon?"

She gestured towards Theodosia with a mild wave of her hand. "You cannot expect Miss Theodosia to go to Hyde Park alone."

"Of course not," he responded. "Olivia can accompany her."

Lady Wilton's expression didn't waver, but her lips pressed into a firmer line. "I would feel much more at ease if you were to accompany them. For appearances, naturally."

Lord Wilton gave a quiet sigh and folded the newssheets before setting them aside. "Very well," he said with a reluctant nod. "Though I maintain it is entirely unnecessary."

"Oh, you three will have such a delightful time," Lady Wilton declared, clearly pleased.

"Now hold on for a moment," Lord Wilton said, turning to Theodosia. "I've yet to hear whether Miss Theodosia actually wishes to go."

Theodosia lowered her cup to its saucer and glanced between mother and son. "I believe it sounds lovely," she responded. "I have always wanted to see Hyde Park."

Lord Wilton gave her a pointed look. "You do understand, of course, that Rotten Row is less a scenic stroll and more a theatrical parade? A place for the *ton* to observe and be observed."

"I suppose that sounds... delightful," she said, though a note of hesitation slipped into her voice.

"Then I must have misrepresented it," he said with a dry smile. "Because there is nothing delightful about it."

"Oh, hush," Lady Wilton chided gently. "It's a ritual for any young woman with even the slightest association to Society."

"But I'm not in Society," Theodosia protested, her brow furrowing.

"No," Lady Wilton conceded, "but you are the companion to the daughter of a marquess. That alone places you within its peripheral circles. Appearances must be made."

Theodosia bit back the first response that came to mind. Wasn't a companion meant to be discreet, unobtrusive? Present but not prominent?

She opened her mouth to voice her thoughts, but Lord

Wilton spoke before she could. "There's little use in protesting. My mother tends to get her way."

Lady Wilton offered an unapologetic smile. "It is true."

With a faint sigh, Theodosia picked up her fork and murmured, "Are companions always expected to be quite so... visible?"

"Do you object?" Lord Wilton asked. "Because if so, we might be forced to lock you up in the townhouse and deny you access to fresh air and polite company."

A laugh escaped her lips. "Well, when put in those terms, I suppose appearing in Society is the lesser punishment. At least there, one is allowed a bonnet and the occasional lemon ice."

Lord Wilton cast a glance towards the long clock in the corner. "If you've no pressing engagements this morning, I had hoped you might assist me in reviewing the estate accounts."

Setting her fork down on her plate, Theodosia pushed back her chair and stood with barely contained eagerness. "I would love nothing more. We can go now—"

He held up a hand to still her, his lips twitching. "There is no urgency, Miss Theodosia. You should finish your breakfast first."

"My apologies," she said, returning to her seat. "I do tend to become rather overenthusiastic when ledgers are involved."

Lord Wilton regarded her with evident amusement. "Of course. A perfectly ordinary reaction."

She grinned. "My instructors at my boarding school certainly didn't think so, but at least they never discouraged me."

Lady Wilton, who had been quietly buttering her toast, glanced up with interest. "And your father? Did he approve of your intellectual prowess?"

"He did more than approve. He believed, quite firmly, that one day women would be educated alongside men in every subject. He always told me never to dull my mind simply to fit into the expectations of others," Theodosia said.

"A fine sentiment," Lady Wilton responded, "though I fear it may be some time before such a notion is widely accepted."

Lord Wilton reached for his glass of water. "And does your sister share your fascination with numbers?"

"Heavens, no. My sister detested school and left as soon as she could. She pursued other... interests."

"Dare I ask what those interests entailed?"

Theodosia grew quiet. "I couldn't say with certainty. We're not particularly close. Our meetings are infrequent and often too brief to speak of anything meaningful."

"That is unfortunate," Lady Wilton murmured, her expression thoughtful.

A new thought sparked in Theodosia's mind. "I do wonder if she will read the article about me in the newssheets. At the very least, she'll know I am enjoying myself."

Lord Wilton studied her intently. "And are you enjoying your time here?"

"I am," she said.

He held her gaze a moment longer, something unreadable passing through his expression before he cleared his throat. "Well then. Shall we eat before we adjourn to the study?"

She reached for her fork again. "I suppose that would be the sensible thing to do."

Leaning in slightly, he lowered his voice to a conspiratorial whisper. "Unless, of course, you'd prefer to abandon breakfast entirely and go work on the accounts now?"

She sprang from her seat in mock delight. "The accounts, without question!"

Lord Wilton chuckled, standing as well. "Very well, Miss Theodosia. Come along. We have lots of work ahead of us."

They had just crossed the threshold when Lady Wilton's

voice called after them. "I shall send a maid into the study, of course. For propriety's sake."

Lord Wilton paused, turning just enough to address his mother over his shoulder. "Whatever you think best, Mother."

Theodosia glanced back as well and couldn't help but notice the twinkle in Lady Wilton's eyes. It was the sort of look that suggested amusement mingled with mischief, as though she were two steps ahead of them both in a game they hadn't realized they were playing.

14

Richard paced the length of his study, his steps agitated, the soft tread of his boots muffled by the thick carpet. Behind him, seated at his desk, Miss Theodosia bent over his account books, her head tilted in concentration, and her brows drawn into a tight line. The quill in her hand scratched across the page as she made another notation, pausing now and then to compare figures between the receipts and the leather-bound ledger.

It had been this way for over an hour—perhaps longer—and the silence, punctuated only by the occasional rustle of paper, was beginning to fray his nerves.

Finally, unable to bear the suspense any longer, Richard halted and turned to face her, his voice more clipped than he intended. "Well?"

She sighed, setting the quill aside and leaning back in her chair. "You are not going to like what I'm about to tell you."

A sinking feeling settled in his stomach. "What is it?"

Her expression sobered, her eyes meeting his. "I fear that your man of business has been embezzling funds from your estate."

The words struck him like a blow. He blinked, momentarily stunned, before straightening with disbelief. "That is impossible. Mr. Benson would never do such a thing. He's been with the family for years, and he was my father's man."

"I understand," she said gently. "But the figures don't lie."

"My father trusted him implicitly. And so have I," Richard declared, his tone growing defensive. "Your calculations must be wrong."

She didn't flinch. Instead, she calmly reached for a receipt from the pile beside her and held it up. "This document shows a charge of ten pounds from the haberdashery. But here"—she flipped open the ledger and pointed—"it's recorded as one hundred and ten pounds."

His brow furrowed. "That has to be an error. A clerical mistake."

"I thought the same," she admitted. "But it isn't isolated. There's a pattern—consistent discrepancies, always rounded in a way that benefits the ledger. The errors are too numerous and too specific to be accidental."

"How long?" he asked, his voice low.

"From what I can determine," she said, "since shortly after your father's death."

Richard dragged a hand down his face, his mind whirling. "You must be wrong. This can't be true."

"I wish I were," she replied, sincerity etched into every line of her face. "But based on my review, I believe Mr. Benson has stolen well over ten thousand pounds."

"No," he said again, his voice a whisper of disbelief. "I don't believe you."

She nodded slowly, as though she had anticipated the reaction. "I thought you might say that. Which is why I've documented every discrepancy. If you'll allow me, I can show you precisely what I found."

He hesitated, then gestured for her to continue, though his eyes remained wary.

She stood, holding out both the receipt and the open ledger. "This line here," she said, pointing. "Ten pounds owed. And here in the ledger, it's recorded as one hundred and ten pounds."

He peered at the figures, squinting slightly. Numbers had always eluded him, swimming on the page, but even he could make out the damning difference.

Still, he resisted. "Perhaps... perhaps someone else recorded it incorrectly. A clerk. A simple transcription error."

She met his gaze, firm but not unkind. "It happens too often to be a simple error. Always in Mr. Benson's hand. And always in his favor."

Richard's jaw tightened. "You expect me to believe that I've been so blind? That I've allowed this to happen under my nose?"

"That is not what I'm saying," she replied. "You had no reason to suspect deceit. You trusted him. That is not a flaw, my lord—it is the mark of someone who believes the best of people."

"You think me incompetent," he snapped.

She took a measured breath. "I think you are angry. Hurt. And I understand both. But I would never call you incompetent."

"You didn't have to," he muttered.

"Please," she said. "Don't take my word alone. Look at the records yourself. Ask your steward. Cross-check these amounts with estate expenditures. The truth will be evident."

"And why should I believe you? For all I know, you could be inventing this entire tale."

It was evident that her patience had cracked slightly by the inflection in her voice. "To what end? What would I gain by fabricating theft? I care for this household. For the people who depend on you. And whether you believe it or not, I care what happens to you."

The room fell silent.

After a long moment, Richard reached for the documents, and he studied the numbers again. He didn't want to believe her, but deep down, he could see it. The evidence was damning. And it pointed to betrayal from someone he had once considered above reproach.

He dropped the papers to the desk and let out a slow breath. "You better be right. If you are wrong..." His words trailed off.

"I'm not," she replied. "I'm sorry. I truly am."

And for the first time, Richard found he believed her.

He hung his head. The truth had struck like a blow to the chest, knocking the breath from his lungs. He knew now what he must do—there was no avoiding it—but the knowledge hollowed him. He had placed his faith in the wrong man, and the betrayal stung more bitterly than he cared to admit.

As he grappled with the enormity of it, he felt the gentle pressure of a hand resting lightly on his sleeve. Miss Theodosia stood beside him, her touch steady and unflinching.

"It will be all right," she said, her voice a balm against the storm gathering within him.

"How could I have been so blind? So utterly stupid?" he asked, his voice rough with emotion.

He expected censure, or worse—pity. But when he looked into her face, there was only warmth, only understanding. Her eyes held none of the judgment he feared.

"You must not blame yourself," she responded.

His lips curled into a bitter line. "Then who should I blame?"

A flicker of wry amusement touched her mouth. "I would start with Mr. Benson."

Her attempt at humor was met with silence. He didn't have

the heart to return the smile, though he recognized the effort behind it. Not now. Not when everything he had believed about his business, his instincts, had been turned on its head.

Her fingers tightened slightly on his arm. "You are a good man. Honorable. Trusting someone does not make you a fool. What happened is not your doing."

He looked down at her hand that was still resting against his sleeve. Every nerve seemed to come alive beneath her touch. He should chide her for being too familiar. But he couldn't. He didn't want to. Her touch was the only thing anchoring him to the moment, keeping him from unraveling completely.

"I should have seen it," he murmured, more to himself than to her. "I should have known."

"It is not wrong to place your faith in someone," Miss Theodosia said. "You trusted me enough to allow me into your home as Olivia's companion—and again when you asked for my help with your accounts."

Richard winced. Her words were meant to console, to reassure. But instead, they pierced him with guilt. It wasn't as simple as she believed. He hadn't truly trusted her—not fully. Not with the gnawing suspicion that she still concealed the truth about Mr. Smith. And she, in turn, had no idea that she had been summoned to London under false pretenses. Her position in his household had been orchestrated, not offered in good faith.

He should tell her.

No.

He couldn't. Not yet.

If she knew, if she left now, they would lose their only advantage. The trail to Mr. Smith was already faint; without her, it would vanish altogether. His silence, however distasteful, was necessary.

A faint breeze stirred through the window, carrying the soft scent of lavender to his senses. It clung to her—subtle, clean, and distinct. He inhaled deeply. It was her. Unmistakably her. He wanted to draw it deeper into his lungs, to remember it, to remember this—whatever this was.

Her voice pulled him back. "What are you going to do now?"

He looked at her. The question was practical, but her tone was not. He felt a powerful urge to take a step closer, to close the space between them. To cup her face in his hand and—

Good gads! What was he thinking?

He could not afford distractions, least of all this one. Kissing her would be madness. Dangerous, entangling madness.

Steeling himself, he cleared his throat and replied with far more resolve than he felt. "I need to speak to Mr. Benson. At once."

"I think that is wise," she responded. "Would you like me to stay with you when confronting him?"

He paused, surprised by how much he wanted her there. "Would you mind?"

"Not at all."

Out of the corners of his eyes, he caught sight of the maid standing discreetly by the door. He was suddenly, keenly aware of just how close they stood. How improper it was. But he could not bring himself to move.

Fortunately, Miss Theodosia appeared to sense the growing tension between them—or perhaps she possessed better judgment than he did—for she took a step back, releasing his sleeve at last.

"I should probably go see if your sister requires anything," she said, her words sounding rushed.

Richard gave a curt nod. "I think that is wise."

She attempted a smile, but it faltered at the edges. "If you need anything from me, my lord, you have only to ask."

"I appreciate that," he replied, more stiffly than he intended. "You've already been of great help."

"Yes, well... good day," she said.

As she started walking towards the door, Richard called out after her. "Thank you."

Glancing over her shoulder, she gave him a small, genuine smile this time. "I should be the one thanking you. I find I rather enjoy combing through ledgers and solving puzzles. There's something comforting in numbers since they always tell the truth, eventually."

He chuckled, despite himself. "You are an odd one, Miss Theodosia."

She turned fully at that, eyes dancing with amusement. "So I've been told... by you, repeatedly, I might add."

With a parting smile, she dipped into a graceful curtsy and slipped through the doorway. He dropped into the nearest chair. What was wrong with him?

He had developed feelings for Miss Theodosia. Real ones. Inconvenient, entirely inappropriate feelings. And the most maddening part was that he had known about them for some time, known about them and ignored them, or perhaps pretended they would pass.

But they hadn't. Those feelings had only deepened.

He leaned back in the chair, staring at the ceiling as if it might offer some sort of wisdom. What sort of fool falls for the very woman he suspects of harboring secrets? The woman he had deceived into coming to London under false pretenses.

The worst part wasn't that he cared for her. It was that he knew, with unwavering certainty, that he would do absolutely nothing about it.

Miss Theodosia was the last woman he could ever consider for a wife. She was unsuitable for a myriad of reasons, and, worst of all, dangerous to his peace of mind.

No. He could not act on these feelings.

He wouldn't.

But heaven help him, he wanted to.

Theodosia paused just outside the door to Lord Wilton's study, her back pressing lightly against the paneled wall as though she needed its support to remain upright. Her pulse still fluttered with agitation, her thoughts befuddled. What had just transpired between them? One moment they had been speaking of figures and ledgers, and the next... it had shifted. Subtly. Powerfully. Irrevocably.

She closed her eyes for a brief moment, willing her heartbeat to slow. It was utterly maddening—this effect he had on her. Lord Wilton, with his abrupt manner and guarded expression, was the last man she ought to feel drawn to. And yet, when his façade slipped, when a flicker of vulnerability crept into his voice... it stirred something deep within her. Something dangerous. Something undeniably compelling.

Her reverie was broken by the familiar voice of Olivia. "Oh, there you are," she called as she approached. "Some of your dresses have arrived."

Theodosia pushed away from the wall and straightened her shoulders. "Already?"

"Yes, and we must see them at once," Olivia said eagerly. "The maids have laid them out in the parlor for your inspection. Come along—Madame Duchon has surely outdone herself."

Theodosia managed a smile, grateful for the distraction. "Wonderful," she murmured, though her thoughts still tangled stubbornly around Lord Wilton.

They made their way down the corridor, and Olivia chattered happily as she opened the parlor door. Inside, sunlight streamed through tall windows, catching on the delicate fabrics draped over the settees. Four gowns—muslin and lace, adorned with careful embroidery and fine netting—were displayed.

Theodosia moved closer, running her fingertips along the edge of a sleeve. "These are exquisite," she murmured in genuine awe.

Olivia nodded, folding her arms with satisfaction. "She truly surpassed herself. And this is just the beginning. There is more to come, including your ball gown. Though I do believe she mentioned a delay in delivery."

Theodosia's gaze lingered on a pale blue gown with puffed sleeves and a scooped neckline. "This one might suit for a ball," she suggested hopefully.

Olivia let out a laugh. "Hardly. That is an afternoon gown. Lovely, yes, but not nearly dramatic enough for the ballroom."

"I have never worn anything so fine before," Theodosia admitted, brushing a bit of lace between her fingers.

"You deserve every stitch," Olivia said, then added with a grin, "especially since you've had to endure my brother's charming moods."

Theodosia's cheeks warmed at the mention of him, and her thoughts flew back to the moment in the study—the way his eyes had searched hers, unguarded. "It isn't all bad," she said before she could think better of it.

Olivia narrowed her eyes, clearly intrigued. But before she could press the matter, the butler appeared in the doorway and announced, "Mr. Addington has requested a moment of your time, my lady. He is in the drawing room."

"We shall be there shortly," Olivia replied.

With a nod, the butler withdrew. As soon as he was gone, Olivia turned back with her brow arched. "Did something happen between you and Richard?"

Theodosia offered a swift, practiced smile. "No," she lied.

She wasn't entirely certain what had happened—but something had.

Olivia gave her a long, knowing look. "Very well. I'll let it go... for now. But you know I always manage to uncover the truth."

Rather than reply, Theodosia inclined her head. "Should we not go to Mr. Addington? It would be impolite to keep him waiting."

Olivia acquiesced with a sigh. "I am terribly curious to learn what brings him here."

They walked to the drawing room together, and as they entered, Mr. Addington stood. His expression brightened instantly upon seeing Olivia.

"Olivia," he said warmly, bowing.

She dropped into a graceful curtsy. "Evander."

But when his gaze shifted to Theodosia, the warmth faded noticeably. "Miss Theodosia," he offered, with far less enthusiasm.

"Mr. Addington," she replied with a polite nod.

He barely waited for her words to fade before turning back to Olivia. "Might I speak with you privately?"

Olivia waved her hand in front of her. "You may speak freely. Dosia is my companion and utterly trustworthy."

He hesitated but pressed on. "You seemed upset earlier at Gunter's. I came to ensure you were well."

"I am perfectly fine," Olivia said, too swiftly.

"Perhaps—but is it the truth?"

Her posture stiffened. "Yes. And I'm glad your friend has found happiness with his new wife."

Mr. Addington stepped closer, his voice gentling. "He is no longer my friend. Not after what he did to you. We both know he had affection for you."

"*Had*," Olivia repeated firmly. "The past tense is key."

"Olivia—"

"I appreciate your concern, Evander, but Lord Harwood is in my past. That is where he shall remain."

"I know he made promises—"

"And broke them," she cut in. "What does it matter now?"

There was sorrow in his eyes. "I don't wish to cause you more pain. I only want you to know I'm here if you need to talk."

Olivia shook her head, blinking rapidly. "Thank you, but I have no desire to dwell on him. I am a married woman now."

He pressed his lips together. "Yes, I have heard."

Olivia gave him a brittle smile. "Shall we enjoy a cup of tea and speak of more pleasant things?"

But Mr. Addington did not sit. His eyes, filled with quiet intensity, remained fixed on her. "Feelings are not so easily dismissed, Olivia. I've known you since childhood. I can tell when you're pretending."

Olivia met his gaze with open defiance. "And what would you have me do? Languish over a man who discarded me like yesterday's newssheets?"

The pain in her voice struck Theodosia like a blow. She could feel her friend's heartbreak pulsing in the very air.

Mr. Addington's voice was heavy with regret. "I know how much he meant to you..."

Olivia's hand came up, stilling his words. "He lied. He promised me a future, and then he married another. That is the whole of it."

He took another step towards her. "Tell me how I can make it right."

"You can't," she whispered, her voice tight with unshed tears. "And that is the greatest cruelty of all. Excuse me."

She turned abruptly and fled the room, her skirts brushing the doorframe as she disappeared.

Theodosia made to follow, but Mr. Addington's quiet words halted her.

"Poor Olivia," he murmured, gazing after her. "She's always been so brave."

Theodosia remained silent, unsure of what to say.

Mr. Addington continued. "She once fell from a tree and broke her arm clean through. She didn't shed a single tear—not even when the doctor set the bone. But heartbreak... heartbreak is harder to hide."

Curiosity tugged at her. "Why did Lord Harwood marry another?"

Mr. Addington's expression darkened. "Because he's selfish. Always has been. I suspect it had to do with his new wife's dowry."

"But Olivia had a dowry of twenty thousand pounds. That is no small sum."

With a frown, Mr. Addington revealed, "His bride brought forty."

Theodosia drew in a quiet breath. So that was the price of a broken heart.

"I believe I should take my leave," Mr. Addington said, his voice tinged with regret. "It seems I may have only added to the distress rather than soothed it."

"You meant well," Theodosia responded. "You are a loyal friend."

At that, a shadow flickered across his face, and his jaw tightened. "Yes... a friend," he echoed. "Olivia and I have been through a lot over the years, and I need to know she is all right."

There was something in the way he said it that gave Theodosia pause. He might not have declared it aloud, but his feelings for Olivia surely went deeper than friendship. She opened her mouth to respond, but before she could speak, a familiar voice cut through the room.

"Addington," Lord Wilton said from the threshold, his tone unmistakably curt. "What brings you by?"

Mr. Addington turned towards Lord Wilton. "I came to speak with Olivia."

"And yet you are here alone... with Miss Theodosia," Lord Wilton replied, each word slow and clipped.

"Olivia was present," Addington explained. "Until I upset her. That was not my intent, but the conversation proved... difficult."

"Then perhaps you are right to take your leave."

Addington inclined his head, making no attempt to argue. "Miss Theodosia," he said, "it was a pleasure to see you again."

"The pleasure was mine, sir," she replied, her voice composed, though she could feel Lord Wilton's gaze like a weight upon her.

As Mr. Addington passed, he paused beside Lord Wilton. "We should have that drink soon."

"Tomorrow?" Lord Wilton suggested, his tone still tight.

"That would do. I'll send word to the others."

And with that, Mr. Addington departed, leaving behind a silence that prickled with unsaid things. Theodosia turned to find Lord Wilton's eyes fixed upon her, his expression far from warm.

He crossed his arms over his chest. "The rules of propriety may be more forgiving in the country, but in London, a young lady does not remain unchaperoned with a gentleman. Surely even you must be aware of that."

"I was not meeting with Mr. Addington," Theodosia returned, her spine stiffening. "He came to speak with Olivia. She excused herself, and I remained. That is all."

"Regardless," he said, tilting his head slightly, "the result remains the same—you and he, alone together."

Her temper flared. "Yes, and quite unintentionally. Are you accusing me of some impropriety, my lord?"

He didn't answer at once. Instead, he approached her, his

eyes narrowing slightly. "I would have to be blind not to notice that Mr. Addington holds a certain fondness for you."

That startled a laugh from her. "Then I fear your eyesight is in question, for you are entirely mistaken."

"Am I?" he asked. "He is the second son of an earl, with excellent connections, and he is a Fellow at Oxford. You could do far worse."

"I have no intention of marrying Mr. Addington."

"You say that now—"

"I will say that always," she interrupted, her voice firm.

A discreet throat clearing from the doorway broke the taut silence between them.

Both turned. Mr. Addington stood there, his expression strained and his posture awkward, as though he regretted returning at all. "Forgive me," he said. "I appear to have left my hat."

Theodosia followed his gaze to the table near the window, where a well-brushed black top hat rested beside a porcelain vase. "Indeed." She crossed the room, retrieved the hat, and handed it to him with a polite smile. "Here you are."

For a moment, Mr. Addington lingered, glancing between them with his brow slightly creased. "Good day, Wilton. Miss Theodosia," he murmured, bowing briefly before taking his leave.

Theodosia turned back towards Lord Wilton. "If you will excuse me, I should check on Olivia." She took a step, then paused. "That is... assuming I have your permission to go unchaperoned," she added, her tone laced with mockery.

"By all means, do as you please. But keep in mind what I said about propriety."

"I shall never forget it," she said dryly, sweeping towards the door.

She left without a backward glance and hurried up the

stairs. But even as her steps carried her towards Olivia's room, her thoughts lingered stubbornly in the drawing room.

She didn't understand him.

Lord Wilton had looked almost... possessive. Irritated by Mr. Addington's presence. Perhaps even jealous? But that was absurd. Entirely absurd.

What possible reason could Lord Wilton have to be jealous of another gentleman's attention?

She paused in front of Olivia's bedchamber and gently rapped her knuckles against the door.

"Olivia," she called softly. "It's me."

There was a brief silence, followed by the soft scrape of a bolt being drawn back. The door opened, and Olivia appeared, her face pale and her eyes rimmed with red. It was clear she had been crying, though she made no attempt to conceal it.

"I'm about to lie down," she said quietly, her voice thick with exhaustion. "I don't feel much like talking."

Theodosia's heart ached at the sight of her friend's pain. "Of course," she replied. "We can speak later, if you feel up to it."

Olivia gave her a faint, grateful smile before slowly closing the door again.

The latch clicked softly into place, and Theodosia continued down the corridor, feeling unusually helpless. If there were something she could do—something to ease Olivia's heartache—she would do it without hesitation. But heartbreak was not a wound easily tended, and words were a poor balm for betrayal.

And worse still, her mind was anything but steady. For no matter how hard she tried to focus on Olivia, Lord Wilton's voice continued to echo in her memory. His sharp words. His narrowed gaze. That flash of something she hadn't quite dared to name.

It was exasperating. Infuriating.

And far too telling.

She pressed a hand to her temple, determined to master her thoughts—particularly those that revolved around one infuriating marquess who, despite all logic, had found a way to occupy far too much space in her heart.

15

Richard sat rigidly at his desk, his eyes fixed on the papers strewn before him—figures and inked notes that now represented far more than financial discrepancies. They were a betrayal. One he had failed to see. One he had allowed.

How could he have been so blind?

The door creaked open, and his mother stepped inside, her expression touched with concern. "Is something amiss?"

Richard didn't look up. Instead, he asked, "How well do you know Mr. Benson?"

"Mr. Benson," his mother repeated, sounding caught off guard. "Quite well. He's been with our family for decades. Your father trusted him implicitly."

Richard finally met her gaze. "Then Father was deceived. Benson has been embezzling from me."

A sharp breath escaped her. "No. That cannot be right."

"It is," he said, lifting the papers slightly. "Miss Theodosia reviewed my ledgers and found the discrepancies. I plan to confront him soon enough."

There was a pause before she asked, "You had Miss Theodosia review your accounts?"

He nodded. "Yes. She offered to help."

"But I thought you didn't trust her."

His jaw tensed. "It's complicated."

His mother moved to the chair across from him and settled into it gracefully. "Then by all means, enlighten me. Because it hasn't escaped my notice how often you've sought out her company of late."

"I have done no such thing," he said, more defensively than he intended.

A knowing smile touched her lips. "Of course not. But it's obvious to everyone but you—though even that, I suspect, is changing. You care for Miss Theodosia."

Richard scoffed. "I don't wish her to be run over by a carriage, if that's what you mean."

"That is not what I mean and you know it," she said with a teasing gleam in her eyes. "You have feelings for her."

He shifted uncomfortably in his chair. "You know not what you speak of."

"You can pretend all you like, Richard, but a mother knows."

"Well, a mother can be wrong," he said stiffly. "Even if I did feel something—which I assure you, I do not—she's the daughter of a baronet and serves as Olivia's companion. Hardly a suitable match for a marquess."

His mother tilted her head, her smile widening. "So now we're discussing marriage?"

He sighed and looked heavenward. "That was not what I meant."

"You said the *ton* would not accept her," she said. "But I've seen the way she holds herself, and how others respond to her. She would win them over... just as she's already won over you."

"She hasn't won me over," he muttered.

"Hasn't she?" came her retort as she rose to her feet.

Before he could respond, Sterling appeared at the door. "Mr. Benson has arrived, my lord," he announced.

Richard straightened. "Send him in. And please ask Miss Theodosia to join us as well."

"Are you sure about Mr. Benson?" his mother asked.

"I am."

His mother gave him an approving look as she started walking to the door. "Then I wish you good luck," she said.

Moments later, Mr. Benson entered the study. Tall and long-faced, his silver-streaked hair was neatly slicked back, and he wore the calm smile of a confident man.

"Good afternoon, my lord," he said with a bow.

Richard gestured towards the empty chair in front of the desk. "Have a seat, Mr. Benson."

The older man hesitated only briefly before taking the proffered chair. "Is something the matter?"

"There is," Richard replied. "But I would prefer to wait until Miss Theodosia arrives before addressing it."

"Miss Theodosia?" Mr. Benson asked, his brow furrowing.

"She is my sister's companion."

"I see... and why would she need to be present for our conversation?"

"You'll understand in a moment."

Mr. Benson settled back, seemingly unbothered. "How is Lady Olivia faring?"

"As well as can be expected," Richard replied tersely. "Given everything."

Mr. Benson's expression turned solemn. "It was a terrible misfortune, what befell her. I was truly grieved to hear it."

Richard studied him closely. He was smooth, practiced, and his voice steeped in sympathy that now felt hollow. No wonder his deceit had gone unnoticed for so long.

The door opened again, and Miss Theodosia stepped

inside. Richard stood as she entered and said, "Miss Theodosia Smith, allow me to introduce Mr. Benson. He is my man of business." He tripped over those last words.

Mr. Benson rose and gave a courteous bow. "Miss Theodosia."

She curtsied. "Mr. Benson." Her gaze slid to Richard with subtle apprehension.

"Come stand by me," Richard invited, gesturing to the space beside him.

She complied, moving to stand at his right.

"I asked Miss Theodosia to review the estate accounts," Richard began, "and she made a rather troubling discovery."

Mr. Benson's smile barely faltered. "And what would that be?"

"That you've been siphoning funds from my accounts for years," Richard replied. "And based on Miss Theodosia's calculations, you have stolen nearly ten thousand pounds."

There was a brief silence before Mr. Benson asked, "You had a woman examine your accounts?"

"I did," Richard said. "Miss Theodosia is precise and extremely capable."

Mr. Benson chuckled softly. "I don't doubt her intentions, my lord, but estate accounts are not simple. I fear she may have misunderstood them."

"I assure you, I did not," Theodosia said, her voice even but firm.

He raised a placating hand. "I meant no offense, Miss Smith. But these matters are complex. You haven't been trained—"

"I can still read a receipt," she interrupted, "and I know what one should look like. Especially when a ten pound bill is entered in the ledger as one hundred and ten."

Mr. Benson stiffened. "An oversight, nothing more."

"Once or twice, perhaps," she countered. "But the same

'mistake' appears monthly for three years. And always on lesser sums, to most likely avoid drawing attention."

"I believe you're mistaken," he said tightly.

She met his gaze without flinching. "I believe I am not."

Turning back to Richard, Mr. Benson asked, "And you believe her over me? A man who served your father loyally and has stood by you since you came of age?"

Richard met his eyes squarely. "Yes. I do."

Mr. Benson's composure slipped. "This is absurd. She is not qualified—"

"I've heard enough," Richard cut in. "I will be contacting the constable shortly. You would do well to use the time to put your affairs in order. I daresay I am being exceedingly generous, considering the circumstances."

Mr. Benson paled. "My lord, surely you are not in earnest," he said, taking a hesitant step backward. "This is all a misunderstanding—nothing more than a series of innocent errors. You must see that."

"I see clearly for the first time," Richard replied. "Miss Theodosia uncovered the inconsistencies. I reviewed them myself and I came to the same conclusion as her."

The older man's composure began to unravel. "But... surely you must realize the consequences of making this public," he said, his voice turning desperate. "What will people say when they learn a *woman*—a mere companion, no less—was entrusted with managing your estate accounts? Think of the scandal. Not only for yourself, but for her."

"That is not your concern," Richard said. "Nor will I allow you to use societal opinion as a shield for your deceit."

Mr. Benson's expression contorted into a frown. "Your father never would have allowed a woman to interfere in such matters."

"Did you steal from him as well?"

Mr. Benson bristled. "Never," he said with a sharp swipe of his hand, as though the very notion were offensive.

"Only from me, then?" Richard asked, the accusation laced with bitter irony.

There was a pause, then a sigh—wary, evasive. "You've never been comfortable with numbers," Mr. Benson said carefully, his tone sliding into condescension. "I fear Miss Theodosia has preyed upon that weakness. She's misled you, whether intentionally or not."

Richard's hands curled into fists at his sides. "Do not speak of her as though she were a scheming opportunist. She has done nothing but assist me with patience and clarity—something you, for all your years of service, never did."

"I meant no insult," Benson said quickly. "It's just that managing an estate of this size is no small feat, my lord. The ledgers alone—balances, projections, investments—those are complex matters. A woman cannot possibly be expected to—"

"You would be wise to stop right there," Richard interjected. "If you insist on underestimating Miss Theodosia, then that shall be your downfall. She is every bit as capable of running an estate as a man."

Mr. Benson's mouth opened, then closed, as though searching for a retort he no longer believed himself capable of defending.

Richard took a breath and said more quietly, "You took advantage of me. You believed I would never notice. You relied on my limitations. But *she* noticed. And now I see you for what you are."

The silence that followed was thick and damning.

Mr. Benson stared at the floor, his shoulders beginning to sag. "You would see a man ruined by the word of a woman?"

"I would see a man ruined by his own actions, and I expect you to return the funds you stole from me," Richard replied. "Now get out of my sight."

Mr. Benson did not wait to be dismissed a second time. With his face pale and his dignity in tatters, he bowed stiffly and exited the study in hurried strides.

Richard exhaled slowly, then turned towards the woman who had made the confrontation possible. "Thank you."

Miss Theodosia's eyes searched his. "Did you mean what you said... about me?"

He didn't hesitate. "Every word."

Her eyes glistened with the barest sheen of emotion, and the corners of her lips curved upward. "Then I believe it is I who should be thanking you. Very few men—particularly men of your rank—would have spoken so openly in a woman's defense. Let alone a companion with no wealth or consequence."

"You are a woman worth defending," he said, taking a step closer.

Her smile grew. "Careful, my lord. I could grow quite accustomed to such compliments."

Richard chuckled, though the sound caught slightly in his throat. His eyes dropped to her perfectly formed lips.

For a moment, he was no longer the Marquess of Wilton burdened by responsibility and pride—but simply a man standing before a woman who saw him, understood him, challenged him in ways no one ever had.

And he very much wanted to kiss her.

But he didn't. Not yet.

Not while questions still lingered about Mr. Smith and her past involvement with him.

With great reluctance, Richard took a single step back, putting space between them. "I should return to my work," he said, though even to his own ears, his words sounded gruff.

Her brow creased, clearly puzzled by the sudden shift in his demeanor. "Yes, and I should return to my reading."

"Very good," he murmured, already turning towards the

desk, feigning focus on the scattered documents as though the confrontation with Mr. Benson demanded his immediate attention. It was easier than facing the regret in her expression.

She quickly exited the study. The door clicked shut behind her, and the silence that followed was stifling.

Richard exhaled and dragged a hand through his hair in frustration. What in the blazes was he doing?

She had stood by him, defended him in her quiet, composed way. She had seen what others could not, and still, he had sent her away. Because of fear. Because of propriety. Because of Mr. Smith.

He stared at the closed door, torn between responsibility and something far more dangerous—hope.

And for the first time, he realized just how much he wanted her to walk back through that door.

———

The late afternoon sun filtered through the lace curtains of the parlor as Theodosia sat on the settee, a book from the circulating library open upon her lap. Yet, despite her best efforts, her eyes lingered on the same sentence again and again, the words blurring as her thoughts drifted elsewhere—namely, to Olivia.

She had scarcely turned another page when the door opened with a quiet creak. Olivia entered, her expression weary and her eyes red-rimmed, as though she'd fought back tears too long.

Theodosia set the book aside and asked, "How are you faring?"

"I am... doing well enough," Olivia replied, her voice flat.

"And what, precisely, does that mean?"

A slight shrug lifted Olivia's shoulders. "I don't rightly know. Everything feels... too much and not enough all at once."

Theodosia patted the cushion beside her. "Come sit with me."

Slowly, Olivia crossed the room and lowered herself onto the settee. Her hands twisted together in her lap, betraying her restlessness.

"I was such a fool," she whispered. "Falling in love with Lord Harwood was the most stupid thing I've ever done."

"You were not a fool," Theodosia responded.

But Olivia shook her head. "Oh, but I was. We were engaged —secretly, of course. He insisted we keep it between us for a time, and I believed him. I trusted him." Her voice broke. "The only one who knew was our friend, Evander."

Theodosia's eyes widened. "You were engaged?"

Olivia nodded, her lips trembling. "And I believed every promise he whispered to me. I thought we would marry and spend our lives together, and I allowed him liberties I never should have."

Theodosia's stomach clenched. "What sort of liberties?"

"Nothing more than kisses," Olivia rushed to assure her as a shadow crossed over her expression. "Lord Harwood didn't even have the decency to tell me himself that he was marrying another. I read about it in the Society pages."

Theodosia's heart ached. "Oh, Olivia..."

"I married Mr. Smith to preserve what little dignity I had left," Olivia continued, her tone tinged with bitterness. "I met him at the circulating library that same day and, for some inexplicable reason, I told him everything. He offered a solution— Gretna Green—and I was so despondent I followed him without question."

"Mr. Smith preyed upon your vulnerability," Theodosia said.

"He did," Olivia admitted. "But at the time, it seemed like

the only option. I am five and twenty years old, and I thought no one else would want me. I felt unlovable."

Theodosia reached out and gently clasped Olivia's hand in her own. "I understand now why you did what you did."

Olivia glanced down at their joined hands, her voice quiet. "It hasn't been easy, pretending everything was well. I am glad you're here, Dosia. Truly."

"You haven't told anyone? Not even your mother?"

A humorless smile flitted across Olivia's lips. "She would no doubt tell Richard, and I couldn't bear another of his lectures about propriety and decorum."

Theodosia squeezed her hand. "Your brother may surprise you. He has surprised me of late."

Olivia scoffed. "My brother? He is nothing but predictable. He has been telling me what to do since my hair was in braids."

"He is... different now," Theodosia mused. "Beneath that gruff exterior, I see a tenderness he tries so very hard to hide."

"That's only because you're beautiful. If you were toothless and bald, I daresay he wouldn't be quite so kind."

Theodosia laughed. "I don't think that's the reason."

As if summoned by their conversation, the door opened and Lord Wilton stepped inside. "I have made a decision," he announced. "We are going to Vauxhall Gardens this evening."

Theodosia's lips parted in surprise. "Truly? That sounds positively delightful."

He smiled, clearly pleased by her response. "I thought you might approve."

Theodosia sprang to her feet. "Then I must change into one of my new gowns immediately."

Olivia, however, remained seated. "I don't know that I am in the mood for such an outing."

"You must come," Theodosia urged. "A diversion will do you good."

"I fear I shan't be very good company."

"Then come exactly as you are. I expect nothing more," Theodosia asserted.

Lord Wilton clapped his hands together. "It is settled, then. I shall see that the coach is brought round."

As he strode from the room, Olivia watched him go with narrowed eyes. "My brother detests crowds. Why is he dragging us to Vauxhall Gardens?"

"Does it matter?" Theodosia asked.

"I suppose not."

Looping her arm through Olivia's, she gave her a gentle tug. "Come, let us change. We mustn't keep your brother waiting for too long."

Olivia allowed herself to be led, a soft chuckle escaping. "You're far too eager for a trip to Vauxhall Gardens."

"I've only ever read about it," Theodosia replied. "The gardens are lit with hundreds of lamps, which are disposed in different figures of suns, stars, and constellations. The very idea sounds like something out of a fairy tale."

"I always loved the statues," Olivia replied, a wistful smile touching her lips.

As they descended into the entry hall, they found Lord Wilton and Lady Wilton in quiet discussion with the butler.

Lady Wilton turned towards them with a fond smile. "You shall have such fun tonight, my dears."

"Would you care to accompany us?" Theodosia asked.

"Heavens, no," Lady Wilton replied. "You do not want an old woman coming along. Go and enjoy yourselves, and I expect a full report tomorrow."

"You are not old," Theodosia protested.

With a grin, Lady Wilton said, "I knew I liked you."

Lord Wilton stepped to his mother's side. "Do not waste your breath, Miss Theodosia. My mother is most insistent that she remain home."

"It is true," Lady Wilton agreed. "I prefer going to bed at a reasonable hour and not staying up until the sun rises."

Just then, the butler stepped forward. "The coach is waiting, my lord."

Theodosia glanced at her gown. "I still need to change. I hope that won't delay you."

"Take all the time you need," Lord Wilton encouraged.

"Thank you, my lord," Theodosia said, holding his gaze longer than what would be considered proper.

Olivia broke the moment by tugging lightly on Theodosia's arm. "Come," she urged. "Let us change. We shall be down shortly."

They ascended the staircase together, their footsteps muffled against the carpet runner. Once they reached the upper landing, Olivia leaned in, her tone hushed but pointed. "Do you wish to explain what that was about?"

"I beg your pardon?"

Olivia gave her a look of long-suffering incredulity. "Do not pretend ignorance. That exchange between you and Richard. You looked at each other as if no one else existed in the world."

"We are merely friends," Theodosia replied, though her voice lacked conviction.

Olivia snorted. "Oh, is that why he allowed you to review his accounts? Because I have been trying to peek at his ledgers for years and he guards them more fiercely than a dragon protects its hoard."

"I offered my assistance," Theodosia said. "And he accepted. It was nothing more than that."

"Mmm," Olivia murmured, clearly unconvinced. "And the matter with Mr. Benson? I heard whispers from below stairs that you uncovered his embezzlement."

"It's true."

Olivia stopped just shy of Theodosia's chamber door and asked, "So my brother is indebted to you?"

"Not in the slightest," Theodosia replied. "I was simply helping him. He finds figures troublesome."

"As do I," Olivia muttered as she pushed open the door and stepped inside ahead of her. "You should wear the new blue gown tonight—the one Richard said you'd look lovely in." Her grin turned mischievous. "You know the one."

"You heard that?"

Olivia's smile widened. "The servants hear everything, and they are far from tight-lipped. You would be wise to remember that."

Inside, Mary was busily straightening the dressing table, arranging hairbrushes and ribbon spools with practiced efficiency. She turned as they entered and gave a knowing smile.

"I understand we've only a short time to prepare for Vauxhall Gardens," she said, already eyeing Theodosia's hair with a critical gleam. "We must make haste."

Olivia took a step back. "I shall leave you in Mary's capable hands while I see to my own gown. Do try not to keep Richard waiting too long since he gets awfully cross when women dawdle."

With a teasing wink, she exited, leaving Theodosia alone with her maid.

Mary patted the back of the dressing chair. "Let's begin by arranging your hair into something more elegant. Perhaps a coiled chignon with a few artful curls?"

Theodosia lowered herself into the chair. "Whatever you think best."

After Mary gently removed the final pin from Theodosia's hair, setting it aside in a tidy row upon the dressing table, she began brushing through the dark strands. "I've never been to Vauxhall Gardens before. I've heard it's like stepping into a dream."

"Nor have I," Theodosia replied, her voice light with anticipation. "And I find myself quite eager to see it with my own eyes."

Mary twisted her hair into an elegant chignon. "You must tell me all about the pavilions when you return. And the orchestra. I heard once that the Prince Regent himself was spotted there."

"I shall try to recall every detail," Theodosia promised. "Though I suspect my thoughts will be too scattered to retain much."

Once her hair had been intricately arranged, Theodosia stood and slipped out of her gown. Meanwhile, the maid fetched her new blue gown and held it out to her. She accepted it and stepped into it.

The process of fastening the back began—button by button, each one tugged and secured with care. As Mary worked, Theodosia ran a slow hand down the front of the gown, smoothing the muslin against her figure.

Her eyes lingered on her reflection in the looking glass. A strange flutter stirred within her chest. Would Lord Wilton approve? Would there be a flicker of admiration in his gaze when he saw her? And why, in all reason, did that matter?

She bit the inside of her cheek. *It doesn't matter,* she told herself firmly. *I wear this because I like it. Because I feel confident in it. Not because of him.*

Mary gave the final button a firm press and stepped back, inspecting her handiwork with a nod of satisfaction. "There. That was the last one."

Theodosia turned slowly to face her. "Thank you, Mary," she said, offering a grateful smile. "I don't know what I would have done without you."

Mary's expression softened. "That is the job of any good maid, Miss."

With one last glance in the looking glass, Theodosia

straightened her posture and reached for her gloves. She was ready, at least outwardly. But within, her heart still beat a little faster than usual.

Vauxhall Gardens awaited. And so did he.

16

———

Richard strolled at a measured pace along the graveled paths of Vauxhall Gardens, his hands clasped behind his back, the soft crunch beneath his boots a quiet counterpoint to the distant strains of music and laughter. Colorful glass lanterns flickered above their heads, suspended like stars caught in a whimsical net of wire and silk. He watched Miss Theodosia with veiled intensity, noting the way her eyes shimmered with unabashed wonder as she took in the fantastical scene around her.

When his mother had first suggested that he accompany Olivia and Miss Theodosia on this excursion, he had scoffed. The very idea had seemed absurd. He had more pressing matters to attend to—accounts to review, correspondence to manage, and Mr. Smith to unmask. But then he had recalled the gleam in Miss Theodosia's eyes when she spoke of Vauxhall Gardens, and against his better judgment, he had agreed to go.

And here he was, entirely at odds with himself.

Botheration.

His heart was becoming far too entangled with Miss Theodosia. It was dangerous—foolish. Perhaps the wisest course would be to send her away altogether, to sever this growing attachment before it bound him too tightly. But that would also mean forfeiting the only remaining link to Mr. Smith. No, he needed her still. At least until Smith returned to claim her. And Richard would be waiting.

Miss Theodosia might present the image of innocence, all bright smiles and eager curiosity, but Richard remained unconvinced. She knew more than she had admitted. He was certain of it. It was only a matter of time before he would uncover the truth.

His thoughts were interrupted by Olivia's voice. "You are being awfully quiet, Brother."

"I am merely enjoying the gardens," he replied, keeping his tone light in hopes of deflecting her scrutiny.

Miss Theodosia turned towards him, her face alight with excitement. "Aren't they magical? I have never seen anything quite like them."

"They are rather extravagant," he admitted, though his eyes lingered more on her than their surroundings. "But you've yet to see the stone and thatched pavilions. They are quite a sight."

She pointed towards a nearby sham castle, where ladies swung from ropes and umbrellas were tucked neatly beneath ivy-laced trellises. "Look at that! And those umbrellas—how quaint."

"They're for shelter," Olivia explained with a smile. "In case of sudden rain."

But Miss Theodosia barely acknowledged her. She had already turned her attention to the colorful lanterns strung from the branches above, their hues dancing like fireflies across her face. "I feel as though I've stepped into a fairy tale," she declared.

"Wait until you see the Grand Walk," Richard said, unable to resist responding to her delight. "A wide avenue flanked by elms, with even more lanterns overhead."

Her eyes widened. "Oh! I must get a closer look," she said, darting off.

Richard chuckled under his breath. "Her enthusiasm is remarkably contagious."

"Good heavens," Olivia muttered with a shake of her head. "We shall never leave if Dosia insists on inspecting every lantern and flowerbed."

"I think it's rather endearing."

She turned a narrowed gaze on him. "I daresay you're blinded by affection."

He stiffened. "I do not hold affection for Miss Theodosia."

"Of course not," Olivia replied, feigning innocence. "You always volunteer for outings to crowded pleasure gardens. And you certainly do not hate people."

"I do not *hate* people," he said defensively. "Merely... most of them."

"Mm." Olivia raised a single brow. "It's still telling that you're here."

"Mother suggested that I accompany you, for propriety's sake," he replied. "It was a far better option than Mother's proposed Hyde Park excursion."

"Regardless, do you not recall that I am a married woman? I require no chaperone."

Richard cast a glance towards Miss Theodosia, who now stood beneath a cluster of lanterns, her hand lightly touching one as if to test its reality. "I know I don't ask it enough, but how are you, truly?"

All humor faded from Olivia's expression. "I am well."

"The truth, Olivia."

She looked away, her voice soft. "It's been difficult... but I'll survive."

He turned towards her fully, his tone more earnest. "I've no doubt. You're one of the strongest women I know."

She blinked at him. "Was that a compliment?"

"It was."

Olivia smirked. "Dosia said you've been rather free with compliments lately, but I hadn't expected to receive one myself."

He looked heavenward. "You're making a fuss over nothing."

"Perhaps. But thank you, Brother. It means a great deal to know I have your support."

"You have it. Always."

Just then, Miss Theodosia returned, her cheeks flushed from the cool night air. "There's a hedge maze just ahead. Shall we try it?"

"We could," Olivia said. "Or we might go see the tightrope performers. I believe they're starting soon."

"Can we do both?" Miss Theodosia asked eagerly.

"We most certainly can," Richard said, smiling. "We have the whole night ahead of us."

"Thank you, my lord," she said brightly, and with that, she was off again.

He watched her go, amused. "I've never seen anyone so excited over a hedge maze."

Olivia nudged him playfully. "You'd best keep up."

As they followed the winding path, Olivia glanced sideways at him. "And how are you faring?"

"I'm well."

She arched a brow. "Truthfully?"

He hesitated. "I've no right to complain."

"Nor do I," she said wryly, "but I manage it just fine. Do you still believe Dosia is hiding something?"

"I do."

Olivia tsked. "I think you're wrong. I don't believe she's capable of deception."

"She knows more than she admits."

"And if she doesn't?" Olivia pressed.

Richard exhaled in exasperation. "Why does everyone keep asking me that?"

She came to a halt and turned to face him. "Because I see the way you look at her. It's not suspicion, but rather, love."

He scoffed. "Don't be absurd. I do not love Miss Theodosia. She is—she is a liar. A deceiver."

Olivia didn't flinch. "I've been in love before. I know what it looks like."

"And what do you know of love?"

She gave him a wistful smile. "I was in love once and it didn't end well."

Furrowing his brows, he asked, "Did you love Mr. Smith?"

"Heavens, no," she said with a laugh devoid of mirth. "I barely knew the man."

"But you eloped with him?"

She looked down at the gravel. "It was a mistake. One I regret."

He stepped closer. "I will fix this. When Mr. Smith comes for Miss Theodosia, I'll be waiting. I'll challenge him to a duel for what he did to you."

"You don't need to fight my battles."

He met her gaze with firm resolve. "It's a brother's duty to defend his sister's honor."

Olivia gave a dramatic roll of her eyes. "And what if Luke proves to be an excellent shot and manages to kill you?" she asked, her voice tinged with a mixture of jest and genuine concern. "I might complain about you often, but I'd rather like to keep my brother alive."

Richard gave a half-smile, hoping to reassure her. "You're not going to lose me so easily. I'm not that obliging."

"Good. Because I suppose you aren't a terrible brother."

He tilted his head, scrutinizing her with mock suspicion. "That may be the highest praise I've ever received from you.

But, pray tell, who was this mysterious man you once loved? And how did I not hear a word of it at the time?"

Her smile faltered, and she gave a dismissive wave of her hand. "It is of little consequence now."

"It is not," he said more gently. "You can trust me with the truth, Olivia. You know that."

She paused, her eyes flickering with old pain. "Very well. I was foolish enough to fall in love with Lord Harwood."

Richard's jaw clenched. "Harwood? That scoundrel? He's a rake of the first order."

"I know," she whispered, blinking rapidly. "But he made me feel seen. As though I were the only woman in the world. I know it sounds foolish, but I believed him. I believed we had a future together."

"You deserved far better than that preening popinjay," Richard said firmly, his brows drawing together in a frown.

"I don't know what I deserve anymore," she admitted, her voice barely above a whisper. "I've made one disastrous decision after another. And now I fear I've ruined everything. My reputation. My prospects. My life."

He placed a hand on her sleeve. "The past is set in stone, Olivia. We cannot alter it, no matter how desperately we might wish to. But the future... the future is still yours to shape."

Her eyes filled with tears as she asked, "Do I even have a future? Truly?"

"You do," he asserted. "But only if you refuse to surrender to despair. Do not let one mistake—or even several—define your worth. You are stronger than that."

"I wish I could believe you," she murmured.

"Then believe in me," he countered. "Let me believe on your behalf until you can do so yourself. I will fight for your future. I swear it."

She gave a small, shaky nod, blinking away tears. "All right. I can do that."

He released her arm and reached into his jacket pocket, producing a crisp white handkerchief.

"There," he said, extending her the handkerchief. "You've been spared the rest of the speech I had so carefully prepared. It was quite moving, I assure you."

A laugh burst from her lips. "Spare me, I beg you. I've endured enough theatrics for one evening."

Just as Richard's lips quirked with amusement, he glanced around—and froze. His amusement vanished in an instant. "Wait... where is Miss Theodosia?"

Olivia turned to look and then shrugged. "I wouldn't worry. She's likely wandered into the hedge maze."

Still, an uneasy sensation tugged at him, one he could not dismiss. "I do not like not knowing where she is."

Olivia arched a brow. "You've grown quite protective."

He didn't reply to that. Instead, he took a purposeful step forward. "Come. We should go find her."

***

Theodosia stepped lightly along the gravel path, her slippers crunching softly as she navigated through the towering hedgerows of the gardens' maze. The moon hung low above Vauxhall Gardens, casting a silvery sheen upon the sculpted greenery and lending the night an otherworldly glow. Laughter and the distant strains of a violin floated in the air, but here, at the heart of the maze, the world had gone still.

She emerged into the center clearing, where a marble statue of Venus rose from the middle of a stone pedestal, her pale form bathed in moonlight. Theodosia paused, momentarily awestruck. Her mother had once described Vauxhall Gardens as a place of enchantment, and now she understood why. Everything—the lanterns, the music, the scent of roses blooming even at night—felt like something out of a dream.

She inhaled deeply, trying to still the flutter in her chest. It was almost too much to believe that she was finally here. For so many years, she had read of Vauxhall Gardens in the newssheets, imagining the elegance, the spectacle. Tonight, it had exceeded her every expectation.

Footsteps crunched behind her. She turned slightly, smiling to herself, expecting Lord Wilton and Olivia to appear from the hedges, no doubt ready to scold her for rushing ahead.

But the voice that spoke near her ear was neither warm nor welcome.

"Were you waiting for me, my dear?" The words rasped against her skin, sending a chill straight through her.

No.

That was not Lord Wilton.

She stiffened and turned sharply, only to find herself face to face with Mr. Pritchett.

Her heart sank, dread tightening in her chest. Taking an instinctive step back, she squared her shoulders. "What do you want?"

He dipped into a mockery of a bow. "Merely the pleasure of your company."

"Mr. Pritchett—"

"Adam," he interjected smoothly.

She lifted her chin. "I would never presume to address you so informally. We are not acquainted in such a manner."

He chuckled, a sound that sent unease crawling along her spine. "We know enough. I've admired you from afar for years, Miss Theodosia. Surely you must see that we would suit admirably."

"I do not share that opinion."

He stepped forward. "We are both practical people. You

must admit that a marriage between us would serve us both. Our estates—"

"I am not seeking a practical arrangement," she asserted. "I want a marriage founded on respect. On affection."

He scoffed. "Love? Is that truly what you believe you'll find among the *ton*?"

An image of Lord Wilton flickered in her mind—his dry wit, his thoughtful gaze—but she pushed it away. He had given no indication that he cared for her. "I believe I might. And even if I do not, I would rather remain alone than marry someone I do not care for."

His expression hardened. "You would choose spinsterhood over marrying me?"

"Yes."

"Why?"

She glanced around the quiet maze, hoping that someone would appear. "I mean no offense—"

"Then how did you mean it?" His voice dropped lower.

"I should return to the main gardens," she said quickly, stepping past him.

But he moved into her path, blocking her escape. "Not until you agree to marry me."

Her stomach twisted. "I am not going to marry you."

"Then we are at an impasse," he replied coolly. "But I am convinced I could make you happy."

"And how, precisely, would you accomplish that?"

He leaned in, his breath unpleasant. "Between our lands, we would be the most prominent landholders in the county."

"So that is what this is truly about," she retorted. "You want my estate."

"I never said that."

"You didn't have to."

He ran a hand through his thinning hair. "Perhaps I came on too strong. Let us begin again."

"It will not make a difference," she responded. "I desire a partner, not a transaction."

"You are a fool," he snapped.

Theodosia's eyes darted towards the nearest hedgerow. "It is entirely improper for us to meet in this manner. Come to Lord Wilton's townhouse tomorrow if you wish to speak again. We can discuss the matter properly."

"Only for you to dismiss me again?" His lips curled. "I came to London to make you mine."

Suddenly, he reached for her, seizing her arm and yanking her close.

"You will not succeed," she stated, trying to pull away.

His fingers dug into her flesh. "I don't think so."

"You are hurting me."

He didn't release her. Instead, he crushed his mouth against hers—a kiss without tenderness, without consent.

She reared back and struck him across the face. "How dare you take such liberties!"

"I'll take whatever liberties I please," he snarled. "And when I'm done with you, no one else will want you."

Terror clutched at her throat. She stumbled back, desperate to flee—but then, like a thunderclap in the night, a familiar voice rang out.

"Unhand her!"

Lord Wilton stood at the edge of the clearing, fury carved into every line of his face.

Mr. Pritchett tightened his grip and turned. "Leave us. This doesn't concern you."

"It does," Lord Wilton said, stalking forward. "Miss Theodosia is under my protection."

"Not any longer," Mr. Pritchett shouted. "We are engaged."

Theodosia's voice rang with outrage. "That is a lie!"

"It's a lover's quarrel," Mr. Pritchett insisted. "Leave us be."

Lord Wilton's gaze dropped to Theodosia's arm, still caught in Pritchett's grasp. "I warn you—release her. Now."

"And what if I don't?" Mr. Pritchett sneered. "I doubt you've ever engaged in fisticuffs in your life."

A soft click interrupted them.

Olivia stepped out from the shadows, her face determined, and a small muff pistol raised in her hand. "You heard my brother—unhand her. And trust me, I have no qualms about shooting you."

Mr. Pritchett's face paled. "You wouldn't."

"I suggest you don't test me," Olivia said, cocking the pistol with deliberate precision.

Mr. Pritchett let go of Theodosia at once, and she rushed to Lord Wilton's side, trembling.

"This is all a misunderstanding," Mr. Pritchett stammered, his voice laced with desperation.

"Is it?" Olivia asked, advancing a step. "Because it looks very much like you were taking liberties with a woman who had already told you no."

"We belong together!" he cried. "If she would only think rationally—"

"You have exactly three seconds to leave," Lord Wilton growled. "And I strongly suggest you never return to Town."

"Or what?" Mr. Pritchett demanded.

Lord Wilton took a step forward, his presence towering. "Or I will see to it that every door in London is closed to you."

Mr. Pritchett's eyes narrowed. "Why do you care what happens to Miss Theodosia? She's nothing to you."

"She is my sister's companion," Lord Wilton replied, his voice taut, "and under my household's protection."

"You want her for yourself!" Mr. Pritchett shouted. "And when you tire of her, you'll cast her aside like rubbish."

Lord Wilton's jaw clenched, his hands curling into fists. "Do not speak that way in front of ladies."

"You didn't deny it," Pritchett said, triumphant.

"Because your accusation was so ludicrous, it wasn't worth addressing," Lord Wilton snapped. "I would never treat Miss Theodosia with anything but the respect she deserves."

Pritchett opened his mouth, but Olivia lifted the pistol higher. "Go," she said simply.

This time, he obeyed.

As soon as Mr. Pritchett disappeared around the corner and the sound of his footsteps faded into the distance, Lord Wilton turned towards Theodosia, his thunderous expression still shadowing his features. His voice, though quieter, carried the weight of urgency.

"Are you all right?" he asked.

She managed a small, tremulous smile. "I will be—thanks to you and Olivia."

His gaze dropped to the sleeve of her gown, where the skin beneath the fabric was reddened.

"He hurt you," he said grimly—not a question, but a dark, resolute fact.

She winced slightly as she rubbed at the soreness with her other hand. "Yes. He did."

A muscle jumped in his jaw. Without a word, he turned as if to stride after the man.

Alarmed, she reached out and grasped his arm, her fingers curling around the fine fabric of his coat sleeve. "No—please, don't."

He halted midstep, glancing down at her hand before looking into her eyes. "You're protecting him?"

"Of course not," she insisted, her voice thick with emotion. "I'm trying to protect you."

His brows drew together in confusion. "From what?"

"From doing something rash," she said earnestly. "I couldn't bear it if anything happened to you because of me."

His expression softened, the anger in his eyes fading just

slightly. "I assure you, Miss Theodosia, I am quite capable of defending myself."

"I know that," she murmured, her fingers still clinging to his coat. "But I would prefer it if you stayed here—with me."

The tension in his posture eased. For a long moment, he simply looked at her, as if weighing the meaning behind her words. Then he nodded. "If that is what you would prefer, then here I shall remain."

She exhaled a shaky breath, her grip loosening, but her gaze never wavering from his. His presence steadied her, settled something frantic within her chest. Just having him there, close by, was reassuring and dangerously intoxicating.

Olivia's voice cut through the night air. "Just say the word, and I'll shoot Mr. Pritchett in the foot. Fingers crossed it gets infected and he loses it. Then we can call him 'One-Foot Pritchett.'"

A laugh escaped Theodosia's lips, despite herself. "There is no need to shoot him," she said, though the amusement lingered in her tone.

"A pity," Olivia muttered, tucking the small pistol back into her reticule with a dramatic sigh.

It was only then that Theodosia realized her hand was still resting against Lord Wilton's arm. Embarrassed, she released him and took a small step backward, smoothing the fabric of her gown as if to gather her composure.

"I imagine Mr. Pritchett has finally received the message loud and clear," she said, her voice regaining some of its steadiness.

Lord Wilton's attention shifted to his sister, his tone somewhere between concern and exasperation. "Since when do you carry a muff pistol?"

Olivia shrugged. "London can be a dangerous place. I find it best to be prepared."

He gave her a long look, and a reluctant smile tugged at the corner of his mouth. "I would urge a bit of caution, Olivia. You carry that pistol with such confidence, but one misstep and you might very well be called 'One-Foot Olivia.'"

Olivia huffed with theatrical indignation. "I am far too clever to shoot myself in the foot."

"We shall see," he said dryly.

She rolled her eyes in response, entirely unbothered. "Very well. If your teasing is quite finished, shall we resume our grand tour of Vauxhall Gardens? There is still the Chinese Pavilion and the fireworks display to admire, assuming we haven't missed them entirely."

Theodosia stood silently for a moment, her hands clasped before her as she looked out into the hedged paths beyond. Her heart was still thudding in the aftermath of what had occurred, and though she tried to compose herself, the idea of returning to the public gaiety of the gardens felt overwhelming.

But she would not be the one to spoil the evening again— not after such a dramatic interruption. She straightened her shoulders and forced a pleasant expression, even as her nerves still prickled beneath the surface.

Lord Wilton turned towards her with gentleness in his gaze as if sensing her hesitation. "I believe it would be best if we called it an early night," he said, his tone laced with concern. "There's no need to press on when we can easily return another evening. Vauxhall Gardens will still be here tomorrow."

"That sounds perfect," Theodosia murmured, grateful for his understanding.

With a gracious nod, he extended his arm to her. "May I escort you to the carriage, Miss Theodosia?"

She slipped her hand into the crook of his arm. "I would greatly appreciate it."

"Good," he said, his voice suddenly low and purposeful, "because I don't want you out of my sight."

She looked up at him in surprise, her breath catching at the intensity in his gaze. Then, he blinked and shifted his gaze towards the path leading out of the maze.

Behind them, Olivia's wry voice rang out. "Do feel free to leave me behind. I'm certain I can find my way back to the coach through this charming labyrinth of hedges in the dark."

Lord Wilton glanced back with a chuckle and held out his other arm with a gallant sweep. "My deepest apologies, Sister. Come along—we shall all exit this romantic maze together."

Olivia linked her arm with his and offered a grin. "Much better."

17

The golden light of morning streamed through the tall windows of the study, casting long beams across the surface of Richard's desk. The accounts lay open before him, figures and ledgers carefully arranged, yet entirely unread. His eyes scanned the page, but his thoughts were far removed from the column of numbers. They had returned, again and again, to the events of the previous night—and to her.

Miss Theodosia.

The image of Mr. Pritchett's hand on her arm, of her startled expression, and that faint tremble in her voice, tormented him. What might have happened had they not arrived in time? The thought had robbed him of sleep.

She was under his protection. That had been the arrangement. But it wasn't duty that drove this unrest in his soul—it was something far more dangerous.

He cared for her.

More than he should. More than was wise. More than he dared admit aloud.

He leaned back in his chair, dragging a hand through his

hair in frustration. *Could it be love?* Olivia had suggested as much, and at the time, he had scoffed. But now...

Good gads, no.

He couldn't love Theodosia.

He *wouldn't*.

And yet, he did.

The truth came down on him like a hammer—solid, unyielding, impossible to ignore. He did love her. Somehow, through late-night conversations, shared glances, and her maddening refusal to be anything less than herself, she had become the most important part of his day.

But how had it come to this? He had brought her here under false pretenses—as a companion for Olivia, yes, but truly as bait to lure out the elusive Mr. Smith. He had used her. And still, he had fallen for her.

Madness.

She was entirely unsuitable. A baronet's daughter, formerly in service as a companion. The *ton* would never accept her as a marchioness. *His* marchioness. Furthermore, the scandal would cling to Olivia like a second skin. No, he needed to marry someone whose name was above reproach, whose connections could help restore his family's standing.

A knock interrupted his brooding, and Sterling stepped into the study. "The constable, Mr. Allen, is here to speak with you, my lord."

Richard straightened. "Show him in."

The butler bowed and withdrew. Moments later, a large man with a heavily lined face and a full beard entered the room.

"Good morning, my lord," the constable said with a respectful nod.

"Good morning, Constable. Please, have a seat," Richard offered, gesturing to the chair opposite his desk.

The man shook his head. "No need, I won't stay long. I

came to inform you that Mr. Benson has confessed to embezzling funds. He claims it began shortly after your father's passing. Said he took advantage of your... difficulties with reading numbers."

Richard's jaw tightened. "Splendid."

"He'll remain at Newgate for the foreseeable future. I daresay you won't be troubled by him again."

Richard rose from his seat. "Thank you for your diligence, Constable."

"It was my pleasure, my lord," Mr. Allen replied before taking his leave.

The door shut, and silence reclaimed the room. Richard sank slowly back into his chair, a deep ache blooming behind his eyes. Mr. Benson, whom his family had trusted for years, had preyed upon his weakness. He might never have known had it not been for Miss Theodosia's careful scrutiny. She had saved him more than just money. She had saved his pride.

His mother entered a moment later, her expression mild but observant. "Do you intend to join us for breakfast?"

"In a moment."

She crossed the room to stand before his desk. "Something troubles you."

"Nothing of consequence."

Without the slightest hint of hesitation, she lowered herself into the chair that faced the desk. "Is this about last night? About Dosia?"

Richard's shoulders stiffened. "Partly."

She leaned forward slightly. "Have you finally admitted to yourself how you feel about her?"

He avoided her gaze. "It's irrelevant."

"Is it?"

"She is under my protection. That is all."

"You do realize I was not born yesterday."

He exhaled. "She is merely a baronet's daughter. A companion. Society would see it as a scandal if I were to pursue her. My title demands a marriage that improves our standing."

"And Dosia cannot do that?"

"No," he said, sharper than intended. "Do you think I've forgotten how precarious Olivia's reputation is? I need a bride whose lineage is unimpeachable. Someone who will help restore what was lost."

His mother tilted her head. "And Dosia is not enough for you?"

"She is too much," he admitted. "Too clever. Too honest. Too... everything. But none of it matters."

She stood and approached him, placing a gentle hand on his arm. "You sound very much like your father just now. Strong. Proud. Stubborn."

"I am responsible for this family. I cannot afford to follow the dictates of my heart."

"Even if it costs you your happiness?"

He stared out the window, jaw clenched. "My happiness is not what matters."

"It should be."

"I deceived her," he said. "I brought her here under false pretenses. How could I ask her to forgive that?"

His mother was silent for a long moment before saying, "Tell her the truth."

"And risk the one lead we have on Mr. Smith?"

She met his gaze. "You'll have to choose, Richard—your heart, or your pride."

He flinched. "It was easier when Father was alive."

A shadow crossed her features. "Yes. And I miss him still."

"As do I."

"But I see him in you and Olivia every day. That helps. More than you know."

He saw the sadness in her eyes. "How are you faring, truly?"

"I take each day as it comes."

"Mother—"

She waved him off. "Shall we go to breakfast?"

"If that is your wish."

"It is." She stepped back.

Richard offered his arm, and they departed the study in silence. Once in the corridor, he asked, "How do you plan to pass the day?"

"Well," she said with a smile, "we have Lord Warwicke's ball this evening. And preparations are, as always, plentiful."

He grinned. "Sometimes, I think being a man is far simpler."

"I do hope you will dance with Dosia," she added lightly, as if that thought had just come to her.

"Do you?"

"If you show her attention, the other gentlemen will follow suit. That is how these things work."

The very thought of other men lining up for Miss Theodosia angered him. He offered no reply, but the conversation lingered in his mind long after they reached the dining room.

As they stepped into the room, he saw Miss Theodosia already seated at the long mahogany table with a book in her hand. Her back was straight, her expression intent, and she was utterly absorbed in her reading—until she caught sight of them entering.

She promptly closed the book and set it down. "I do beg your pardon," she said, her tone apologetic, "but we are returning to the circulating library later today, and I was quite determined to finish this before we go."

"No harm done," Lady Wilton replied, waving her hand dismissively as she took her customary place at the head of the table. "A book worth finishing is often worth forgiving."

Richard crossed to stand beside Miss Theodosia's chair. "May I ask what you're reading with such urgency?"

She glanced up at him, her lips curving faintly. "It's one Olivia recommended—*La Princesse de Clèves*. A French novel."

"Ah." He raised an eyebrow, folding his arms. "Fantastical nonsense, then."

Miss Theodosia did not appear amused by his remark. "Not at all. It is, unfortunately, all too grounded in reality. The heroine is torn between the man she loves and the obligations imposed upon her by Society."

He leaned a hand on the table, intrigued despite himself. "And which does she choose?"

"Duty," Miss Theodosia answered, her fingers brushing the closed cover of the book as though reluctant to let it go. "Even after her husband dies, she refuses the duke's proposal. She blames herself for her husband's decline and remains alone, loyal to a sense of honor that, in truth, brought her little happiness."

"Fascinating," he murmured, reaching for the book. He flipped through the pages idly, the soft crackle of paper the only sound for a moment. "Still, it is not uncommon. Those in high Society often find that happiness must be second to obligation. Not everyone is free to follow their heart."

"That is a sad way to live," Miss Theodosia said. "To sacrifice so much, only to please others."

"Indeed," Lady Wilton interjected from her end of the table. "I must agree with Dosia. A life without personal happiness is not one I would recommend. Don't you think so, Richard?"

He knew that tone—it was deliberate. His mother was baiting him. He closed the book and set it gently on the table. "Whether I agree or not is irrelevant. As a marquess, my path is dictated by duty. To my estate. To my family. To my name."

Miss Theodosia's gaze lingered on him for a breath longer than necessary, and in her expression was something perilously close to pity. "And what of your happiness, my lord?"

He forced a smile as he moved to his seat. "I am perfectly

content when my tenants are cared for, my accounts are balanced, and my work in the House of Lords is effective. That is happiness enough for me."

But as he unfolded his napkin and reached for his cup of tea, he felt her eyes on him still. And for reasons he could not name, he could not quite bring himself to meet them.

———————————

Theodosia sat with a small stack of books nestled in her lap as the coach trundled through the cobbled London streets, bound for the circulating library. She adjusted them carefully, her fingers brushing over the tooled leather spines. The promise of new stories stirred a familiar flutter of anticipation within her since there was nothing quite like the prospect of discovering a fresh tale.

Across from her, Olivia sat gracefully, tapping a gloved finger lightly against her chin before speaking. "Well? How did you fare with the books I recommended?"

Theodosia lifted her gaze. "I devoured them. Especially the ones penned by women. Their voices felt... truer somehow. More intimate."

Olivia smiled. "I'm glad to hear it. There's power in those perspectives. You just have to know where to look."

Theodosia shifted the books to her side, then added more softly, "And thank you for coming to my aid last night. I'm not sure what would have happened if you hadn't."

Olivia waved a hand, but there was a terseness in her words. "You owe me no thanks. Pritchett is a coward—accosting a woman in the shadows like some back-alley villain."

"I never imagined he would stoop to such behavior."

"People reveal their darkest sides when they're cornered.

When they think they've lost everything." Olivia's voice took on a pensive quality that gave Theodosia pause.

She studied her friend. "Is that how you feel? Like you've nothing left?"

Olivia exhaled slowly, turning her face towards the window as the city passed them by. "I don't know what I feel anymore. Some days it's despair. Other days... nothing at all."

With gentle care, Theodosia reached across the coach, touching Olivia's gloved hand. "You do have something left. You have yourself, your wit, your courage. Don't let one man's betrayal define your future."

A weak smile flickered on Olivia's lips. "A part of me believes that. But another part, the louder part, insists I've ruined everything beyond repair."

"Then quiet the louder part," Theodosia insisted. "You alone choose which thoughts to believe. That is a power no one can take from you."

There was a long pause before Olivia whispered, "I fell in love with a rake who made me feel seen. I thought I could change him. I was wrong. And the worst part? I feel like a fool."

"No," Theodosia asserted. "You believed in love. That's never foolish. It's brave."

Olivia let out a mirthless chuckle. "Perhaps I should abandon love altogether and take after my brother—practical to a fault."

Theodosia grinned. "There must be a middle path. Somewhere between reckless rapture and rigid reason."

After a moment, Olivia glanced sideways. "I told Richard last night. About Lord Harwood."

Theodosia's brows lifted. "You told him everything?"

"Heavens, no," Olivia said quickly. "Only that I loved him. Had I confessed we were secretly engaged, Richard would've challenged him to a duel before sunrise."

"Well," Theodosia said, "I daresay Lord Harwood deserves a duel."

Olivia laughed—genuinely this time. "Perhaps I should challenge him. It might do Society some good."

"Women are far too practical for duels," Theodosia said wryly. "We use our words as weapons. Far more effective, I'd argue."

"Perhaps," Olivia murmured. "Though a pistol would certainly solve some problems more quickly."

Theodosia's eyes flicked to the small reticule dangling from Olivia's wrist. "Are you carrying your muff pistol now?"

"I am," Olivia said without a trace of shame.

"Well, oddly enough, I feel safer knowing that," Theodosia admitted. "Though your brother insists upon footmen for our protection."

"One can never be too prepared," Olivia replied.

Just then, the coach slowed and came to a gentle halt. Theodosia gathered the books and stepped onto the pavement, nodding for Olivia to follow. Together, they crossed the pavement and entered the familiar hush of the circulating library.

After returning their finished books inside, they wandered among the shelves, the quiet rustle of pages and distant murmurs of other patrons surrounding them like a comforting shroud.

Theodosia had just reached for a novel with a blue cloth cover when a voice, low and unwelcomely familiar, broke through the calm.

"We meet again."

A cold shiver coursed down her spine. Slowly, she turned to face Mr. Pritchett.

"What are you doing here?" she demanded in a hushed voice, her fingers tightening around the book.

"I came to speak with you," he said simply.

"I've no interest in anything you have to say," Theodosia asserted.

Olivia was instantly at her side, her posture stiff with outrage. "You heard her. Leave."

"I will," he said, raising his hands in mock surrender. "But not before I speak my piece."

"Or I could shoot you," Olivia stated.

Mr. Pritchett bristled. "I mean no harm, truly."

A few heads had begun to turn, and Theodosia, aware of the eyes upon them, gave a tight nod. "Say what you will, and quickly."

"May we speak privately?"

His request was almost ludicrous. "You forfeited that right last night," she responded. "You attacked me."

His jaw twitched, but he said, "I wanted you to know that I'm leaving London tomorrow."

Olivia muttered, "Good riddance."

"But I was hoping you'd come with me," he continued.

Theodosia reared back. "You must be mad," she said. "Why would I ever leave with you?"

"You don't belong here," he insisted, stepping forward. "This isn't you. You belong back in our village, managing your estate, not playing dress up and wasting time in the drawing room."

"Who says this isn't me?"

"I know you," he said. "You can pretend all you want, but this life will sour on your tongue. You'll tire of it. You will."

"I don't require your concern," she remarked.

He gave a scoffing laugh. "So you enjoy being a lady's companion? Playing servant to nobility? You think that makes you happy?"

"I don't care what you think."

"But you haven't denied it," he remarked. "Not once. And

I've seen how Lord Wilton looks at you. I daresay he wants you for his mistress."

Theodosia tensed. "He is an honorable man, far above your slander. You don't deserve to speak his name."

Mr. Pritchett took a step back, his expression hardening. "Think on it. You're an interloper here. They'll never truly accept you."

From the side, Olivia leaned in and whispered, "Say the word and I will shoot him in the foot."

"There's no need," Theodosia said tightly. "Mr. Pritchett was just leaving."

He clicked his tongue. "I thought you were clever. But you've let luxury beguile you. And you'll regret that."

"Why the sudden concern?"

His voice softened. "Because... I still believe we could have been happy."

She laughed, but there was no humor in it. "You're delusional."

He didn't deny it. "But a part of you knows I'm right. If you change your mind, I'll be at the Wolf and Badger Inn until morning."

She gave him a pointed look. "Then enjoy your solitude. I won't be coming."

Disappointment flickered in his eyes, but he said nothing more. With a curt nod, he turned and disappeared into the rows of books.

As he vanished from sight, Olivia muttered, "I should have shot him."

Theodosia let out a shaky breath. "Let's just find a novel worth getting lost in."

After a long, contemplative silence, Olivia turned towards her friend, her voice quiet but steady. "Mr. Pritchett was wrong, you know. You do belong here."

"Do I?" she asked, her voice more uncertain than she

intended. "I'm merely the daughter of a baronet. A companion. The *ton* will never truly welcome me, especially not as one of their own."

"Well, then the *ton* is blind," Olivia said. "Because I certainly don't see you that way. You're not just a companion, Dosia—you're my friend. And I, for one, am grateful you're here. London is far more bearable with you in it."

A warmth stirred in Theodosia's chest, softening the sharp edges left behind by Mr. Pritchett's cruel words. "I feel the same," she murmured. "I hadn't realized how much I needed someone like you."

Olivia leaned her shoulder against the nearest shelf. "What say you to a bit of lemon ice after we've chosen our books? I feel we've earned it."

Theodosia's brows arched. "Shouldn't we be preparing for the ball this evening?"

Olivia waved a dismissive hand. "We should, yes. But it won't take long, and I'm firmly of the opinion that lemon ice can mend almost any ailment, especially the emotional sort. Even if only temporarily."

A smile crept across Theodosia's face, her spirits lifting. "In that case, I have no objections."

"Splendid," Olivia said, straightening. "And should Mr. Pritchett appear at Gunter's again, I shall be forced to shoot him."

Theodosia gave a laugh, more genuine now. "I think that sounds more than reasonable."

"Would you like a muff pistol of your own? I have a spare one at the townhouse."

Theodosia considered it for a moment before replying, "Given recent events... yes, I believe I would. It's rather comforting, knowing one could defend oneself if necessary."

Olivia grinned. "Excellent. Just don't tell my brother. He would be most unamused."

"Would he object?"

"Oh, not exactly," Olivia responded. "But I daresay he rather fancies himself your protector."

Theodosia gave her a wary look. "I'm afraid to ask what you mean by that."

Olivia gave a nonchalant shrug, her expression perfectly innocent. "Nothing at all. Only that he seems particularly invested in your safety. Quite touchingly so."

Theodosia's cheeks warmed, but she kept her voice composed. "That is because I'm under his protection as your companion."

"Yes," Olivia said lightly, already turning back to the shelves. "Let's go with that." Her fingers trailed across the spines of the neatly arranged volumes, eyes scanning for titles, though her smirk suggested her thoughts were elsewhere.

18

Richard sat in the coach as it rumbled through the darkened streets of London, its wheels clattering softly against the cobblestones. He was wedged between his mother and the window, but his attention was far from the passing scenery. Opposite him sat Miss Theodosia and Olivia, their skirts pressed close together in the narrow confines of the carriage. Every so often, as the coach jostled over a rut or turned a corner, his knee would bump against Miss Theodosia's. Each accidental touch sent a ripple of awareness through him that he tried—and failed—to ignore.

Olivia shifted in her seat and glanced towards him with a look of trepidation. "I do hope I haven't made a terrible mistake by coming tonight."

"You haven't," Richard rushed to assure her. "I dare anyone to say something unkind in my presence."

Olivia gave a dry laugh. "Oh, they won't say it to your face. They'll whisper it behind their fans, all the while smiling sweetly to me."

Miss Theodosia offered Olivia a reassuring smile. "If at any time you wish to leave, say the word. I'm here for you, not the ballroom."

Olivia's gaze softened. "But this is your first ball in Town. I want you to enjoy it. Perhaps even dance with an eligible gentleman or two."

Miss Theodosia flushed and looked down at her gloved hands. "I should not assume to be so bold."

At that, Lady Wilton nudged her son with her elbow and gave him a look that required no words.

Suppressing a sigh, Richard cleared his throat. "I was rather hoping you might save me a dance this evening."

Miss Theodosia's brows lifted in mild surprise. "I appreciate your kindness, my lord, but you needn't offer me pity."

"Pity?" he repeated, the word tasting foul. "That isn't what this is. I asked because I would like to dance with you."

She regarded him carefully, as if weighing his words. "Very well. I shall consider it, then."

He raised a brow. "You do realize I am a marquess. Most young ladies would be thrilled for the honor."

Olivia snorted. "Good heavens, do you ever hear yourself speak?"

"It's merely the truth," Richard said, puffing his chest out in exaggerated pride. "I am, after all, quite the eligible bachelor."

"Also incredibly humble," Olivia muttered.

Miss Theodosia gave a soft laugh behind her gloved hand. "She isn't wrong."

He clutched his chest dramatically. "*Et tu*, Miss Theodosia?"

The coach slowed, then stopped in front of Lord Warwicke's grand townhouse, ablaze with lights. Richard stepped out first after the footman placed the steps down. He assisted his mother and sister, but when it came time to help Miss Theodosia, he held her hand a moment longer than propriety allowed. Her skin, even through her glove, felt warm against his palm, and it was with great reluctance that he let go.

He stepped back and admired Miss Theodosia. She wore a silver gown that shimmered like moonlight, and her dark hair was swept into an elegant arrangement with soft curls framing her face. She was, quite simply, radiant. He knew she would turn heads tonight—even without a noble pedigree to bolster her status.

And part of him hated that. Hated the vulnerability of it.

He offered his arm to his mother and sister, and they made their way up the steps and into the *crush* of the ballroom. A crystal chandelier hung high above their heads, its many facets scattering light like fire across the chalked dance floor underfoot. The room was packed shoulder-to-shoulder with the best and worst of the *ton*, and Richard felt his jaw tighten at the sheer press of bodies and over-loud laughter.

A voice behind him drew his attention.

"Just pretend we aren't packed in here like cattle," Miss Theodosia said lightly.

He turned his head, grateful for her levity. "It's far too crowded for my tastes."

"But you're here to support your family," she said. "That's what matters."

He nodded, glancing around only to find a half-dozen young women eyeing him like a prized bull, their eyelashes fluttering. Subtlety was clearly out of fashion.

They reached the rear of the ballroom and Lady Wilton slipped her hand off his arm. "Excuse me, I see someone I must speak to."

Richard patted Olivia's hand where it rested on his sleeve. Her eyes were wide, her shoulders tense.

"It's all right," he murmured. "You're not alone."

"Let's hope this night doesn't end in utter disaster," Olivia whispered.

"It won't," he said, hoping he spoke true.

Just then, Lady Granleigh and her daughter, Lady Fanny, swept towards them with bright smiles on their faces.

"Lord Wilton," Lady Granleigh said sweetly. Too sweetly. "Is it not a fine evening?"

"Perfectly pleasant," Richard replied.

"Fanny was just saying how beautiful the gardens are tonight," Lady Granleigh continued. "Perhaps you might escort her for a stroll later?"

"I shall consider it," Richard said with a courteous bow.

The ladies curtsied and moved on.

Olivia leaned in and said, "She didn't even look at me. Her sights are clearly set on your title for her daughter."

"Lady Fanny has a faultless reputation," Richard replied.

"Yes, but Lady Fanny once spent twenty minutes telling me about lavender ribbon," Olivia muttered. "Is that truly what you want? A woman who has nothing of interest to say?"

His gaze drifted towards Miss Theodosia, who was staring up at the chandelier with quiet wonder. No. That wasn't what he wanted.

He wanted *her*.

He wanted the woman who made him laugh and made him think—who made him feel seen.

But she wasn't his to claim.

Olivia nudged him again. "You're staring."

"I was merely woolgathering."

"About Dosia, no doubt," she said. "Why not end your misery and ask her to dance?"

Feigning ignorance, he asked, "With Lady Fanny?"

"Don't be absurd. No—Dosia. You remember her. Dark hair. Opinionated. Beautiful," Olivia said with amusement in her eyes.

Just then, Miss Theodosia turned back to them, eyes alight. "I've never seen a chalked dance floor before. It's almost too beautiful to step on."

"It won't last," Olivia said. "By the night's end, it'll look like someone spilled a paintbox."

"That's a shame," Miss Theodosia murmured.

The musicians struck the opening chord of the waltz to announce that the next set was about to begin.

Richard turned to Miss Theodosia. "Might I have the pleasure of this dance?"

She looked down at his outstretched hand, hesitant. "It's a waltz."

"I noticed. I'm very observant," he said with a teasing smile.

"I've never danced it before."

"It's simple enough," he said, wiggling his fingers. "Just let me lead."

After a pause, she slipped her hand into his. "I only hope I don't make a fool of myself."

"I won't let that happen," he rushed to assure her. "Not tonight. Not ever."

She smiled at him, and something inside his chest clenched. She trusted him. But could he say the same in return?

They took their place on the floor. As the music began, he set his hand at her waist and lifted her other in his. Her frame was stiff, her movements cautious.

"You can relax," he murmured.

"Everyone is watching," she whispered, her eyes roaming over the room.

He met her gaze. "Forget them. It is just you and me."

She drew in a breath, then let it out slowly. "I rather like the sound of that."

"So do I," he said, and he meant it. More than anything, he wanted this moment to stretch forever. However, he was in trouble. Now that she was in his arms, he never wanted to let her go. He knew that he would never be able to escape his heart. Perhaps it was better to listen to what it had to say.

But reality would not be kept at bay. He had a duty to his family and himself. He couldn't marry whoever he desired.

So, just for tonight, he would dance with her.

Then he would have to let her go.

As the final notes of the waltz drifted into silence, Richard released her and stepped back. He bowed. "Thank you, Miss Theodosia, for the honor of the dance."

She dipped into a graceful curtsy, the faintest flush on her cheeks. "You are most welcome, my lord."

Without speaking further, he offered his arm, which she accepted with a gloved hand, and together they made their way across the ballroom floor. The sounds of music, laughter, and murmured conversation swelled around them, but Richard noticed none of it. His only focus was on Miss Theodosia.

As they reached the edge of the room, he immediately noted something amiss. Olivia stood alone, her posture too stiff. Her eyes shimmered, and she blinked rapidly, as if trying to hold back tears.

"What is it?" he asked, his tone low with concern.

Olivia looked up, her voice brittle. "I just saw Lord Harwood... with his wife."

Richard's brows drew together. "He has returned from his wedding tour, then?"

"Apparently so," she muttered.

Miss Theodosia moved instinctively to Olivia's side, her concern plain. "We should go."

"No," Olivia protested. "It's early yet and—"

But Miss Theodosia cut her off. "I am far more concerned about you than I am about Society's expectations. I can attend another ball. But I won't miss the chance to be the friend you need tonight."

For a moment, Olivia's composure crumbled. Her eyes welled, and her lips trembled with gratitude. "Thank you, Dosia," she whispered.

Miss Theodosia turned to Richard. "I'll escort her to the carriage. Would you mind informing your mother about what's happened?"

"Of course," he said, already reaching into his jacket. He produced a neatly folded handkerchief and offered it to his sister.

Olivia accepted it with a soft, embarrassed laugh. "I'm making such a spectacle of myself."

Miss Theodosia placed a comforting hand on Olivia's shoulder. "You are doing no such thing. Now, shall we make a discreet escape through the French doors?"

"I think that's wise," Olivia murmured, already leaning towards her.

As the ladies turned towards the rear of the ballroom, Richard gently touched Miss Theodosia's arm. She paused, and he leaned in just enough to mouth the words, *thank you.*

She gave him a warm smile in return before turning her full attention back to Olivia.

Richard watched them disappear through the French doors before he turned away and threaded his path through the crowded ballroom. His gaze roamed over the room until it settled on a familiar face near the refreshment table.

Lord Alcott stood chatting with his sister, Miss Winslow, who was absently swirling the champagne in her glass.

Alcott spotted Richard first and lifted his glass in greeting. "Good evening, Wilton."

Richard nodded in acknowledgment and gave a curt bow to Miss Winslow. She offered a polite smile but quickly looked away, more interested in her drink than the men's conversation.

"Have you seen my mother?" Richard asked, his tone clipped as his eyes scanned the crowded room once more.

"I believe I saw her last with Lady Warwicke—near the east alcove," Alcott replied.

"Thank you." Richard was about to move on when Alcott's voice stopped him.

"Before you go, I couldn't help noticing you danced with Miss Theodosia Smith," he said with a glint of mirth in his eyes. "You appeared rather taken. I take it your circumstances have changed?"

Richard grew rigid. "You are mistaken. I am not 'taken' with Miss Theodosia."

"Ah, my error," Alcott responded. "Perhaps I should have said you were enchanted. Or captivated. Beguiled, perhaps?"

He lowered his voice. "Miss Theodosia is my sister's companion. And I do not trust her."

"Interesting," Alcott said, folding his arms. "Because men of our standing do not typically dance with companions unless they have a compelling reason."

"My mother requested it."

"A terrible reason," Alcott quipped. "Especially considering that half the ballroom is buzzing about her. Rumors are swirling, and no one seems to know who she really is. Yet there she was, in the arms of Lord Wilton himself."

Richard's lips thinned. "I've no patience for gossips."

"Even when you're the subject?" Alcott asked with a chuckle. "That's admirable. Foolish, but admirable."

"I've no time for this," Richard snapped. "I need to find my mother and leave."

Alcott shrugged. "Very well. I wish you luck with both endeavors."

Without another word, Richard turned on his heel and strode away. But Alcott's words stayed with him, irritatingly persistent. Rumors. Whispered suspicions. And worse—his own betrayal of emotion during that dance.

He could not afford to lose control.

Not over *her*.

The interior of the coach was cloaked in shadows, broken only by the occasional flicker of a gas lamp they passed. Theodosia sat in silence, her hands clasped tightly in her lap. Across from her, Lord Wilton stared unseeingly out the window, and his mother sat beside him, casting furtive, worried glances at her daughter. Olivia sat stiffly at Theodosia's side, dabbing her eyes with a damp handkerchief, her expression one of composed despair.

No one spoke. And the silence was deafening.

At last, the coach pulled up in front of the townhouse. Lord Wilton was the first to step out, turning back to assist each of the ladies with solemn care. When Theodosia reached the gravel drive, she withdrew her hand from his arm but lingered beside him.

He leaned slightly towards her, his voice low. "What can be done?"

She hesitated, watching Olivia from the corners of her eyes. "She's always found comfort in chocolate. I can ask the cook to prepare some."

He gave a faint nod. "A small kindness might help."

"I can hear you," Olivia stated, her voice startling them both. She didn't turn around. "And I wouldn't object to some chocolate, but I want it sent to my room."

"I don't think that's wise," Lord Wilton said. "We should speak and try to make sense of this."

"Not tonight," Olivia replied firmly, already ascending the steps. "Perhaps tomorrow. Right now, I simply want to forget this entire wretched evening."

Lady Wilton took a step forward. "If that is your wish, dearest."

"It is," Olivia said without turning back. "Goodnight."

As they followed Olivia into the townhouse, helplessness washed over Theodosia. She longed to comfort her friend, but sensed such an attempt would only wound Olivia further.

"Should I follow her?" she asked quietly.

"No," came Olivia's answer, firm and echoing faintly from the staircase.

Lady Wilton touched Theodosia's sleeve in silent reassurance. "Let me go with her. You may retire, if you wish."

Left alone in the entry hall, Lord Wilton turned to her with a weary expression. "I'm sorry. This wasn't how I imagined the evening ending."

A small smile tugged at Theodosia's lips. "I rather thought it went splendidly. I danced with a very eligible gentleman. Did you know he was a marquess?"

He chuckled. "I think I did hear that."

"And he was a fine dancer. Not once did I fall."

His gaze softened. "You're safe with me, Miss Theodosia."

She tilted her head. "I do believe you have earned the right to call me Dosia. We are friends, are we not?"

"We are. But only if you'll call me Richard."

Her smile deepened. "That may take some getting used to."

He stepped closer—still careful, still proper—but his presence felt suddenly warmer. "What say you? Shall we see if the cook left us any biscuits?"

"I never say no to a biscuit."

"Nor do I," he said, offering his arm with exaggerated courtliness.

Just as they turned towards the back passage, a sharp knock echoed through the entry hall. Richard paused, brows furrowing. "Who would call at this hour?"

Theodosia glanced towards the door. "Should we answer it?"

"The butler will see to it."

Sterling appeared and went to the door as if summoned by

those words. A moment later, a cloaked figure stepped into the dimly lit entry, his—or rather, her—silhouette familiar in an unsettling way.

The figure removed their hat, revealing a face Theodosia knew better than her own.

Her breath caught. "Lucinda?" she murmured.

But her sister ignored her, speaking instead to Richard in a low, deliberately masculine voice. "I heard you were looking for me, my lord."

Theodosia blinked. Lucinda's dark hair had been pulled back into a crude tie, and her attire was that of a gentleman— waistcoat, breeches, and boots. Her voice was deeper than usual, almost unrecognizable. But her eyes, pleading and defiant, were the same.

Richard's gaze narrowed. "You are Mr. Smith, I presume."

"I am," Lucinda replied.

Theodosia's voice cracked with disbelief. "What?"

Lucinda turned towards her sister. "Before anything else, I must speak with Theodosia. Alone."

Richard looked at Theodosia, suspicion darkening his expression. "You claimed not to know who Mr. Smith was."

"I... I don't. Not really," Theodosia said weakly, knowing how hollow it sounded.

His jaw tightened. "So you have lied to me. All this time."

Pain lanced through her chest. She hadn't meant to deceive him—not truly. But how could she explain something she herself didn't understand?

"I need to speak with Mr. Smith," she said, her voice trembling.

Richard's voice was low and tight. "You have five minutes. Then I speak to 'Mr. Smith.'" He turned on his heel and strode away, his disappointment palpable.

Theodosia faced her sister. "What is going on, Lucinda?"

Lucinda motioned towards the drawing room. "Come. I'll explain."

Once they arrived, the door closed behind them with a soft thud.

"You'd best start from the beginning," Theodosia said, arms crossed.

Lucinda exhaled, adjusting her waistcoat. "It started as a misunderstanding. I wanted to attend a lecture restricted to men. I dressed the part, and no one questioned it. It was... liberating. So I continued."

"And somehow this led to marrying a marquess's daughter?" Theodosia asked incredulously.

Lucinda grimaced. "It was an accident. I met Lady Olivia at the circulating library. She looked so forlorn. I offered her conversation... then comfort... and when I jested about marriage, she didn't laugh. She agreed."

"You knew who she was. And you went through with it? Why?"

"She had a dowry of twenty thousand pounds," Lucinda said, matter-of-factly. "It was a solution. For both of us."

"You tricked her!" Theodosia gasped. "You married her under false pretenses!"

Lucinda shrugged. "But now I take off these clothes and Mr. Smith disappears. No one is the wiser."

"And what of Olivia?" Theodosia demanded. "The scandal... the deception... you've ruined her."

Walking over to the window, Lucinda unfastened the latch. "I have a coach waiting. We can leave tonight," she said.

"You can't be serious," Theodosia stated. "Lord Wilton intends to challenge you to a duel for abandoning his sister."

"Then we must go since I don't intend to die in a duel."

"You could tell Lord Wilton the truth," Theodosia offered desperately. "He might understand."

Lucinda scoffed. "Understand? He'll have me arrested. Is that what you want?"

"No, but you broke the law—"

"I came to rescue you," Lucinda snapped, "and this is the thanks I get."

Her brows lifted. "Rescue me?" she asked. "I do not need rescuing."

Lucinda reached into her jacket pocket and pulled out a piece of paper. "This letter says otherwise. It says that I will never see you again if I don't come to retrieve you personally."

Theodosia retrieved the letter and read the contents, confirming it was true.

Lucinda gave her a pointed look. "Lord Wilton is not so kind anymore, is he?" she mocked.

"There must be a misunderstanding," Theodosia said, her head reeling. "I am Lady Olivia's companion. He asked me to come. He promised me his protection."

"No, he tricked you into coming to lure me out of hiding," Lucinda remarked. "Don't you see? You're a pawn, Dosia. He used you."

"No, Lord Wilton is not that type of man."

Lucinda went to stand on the sill. "Are you going to come with me?"

"I can't... I won't," Theodosia replied.

"Then this is a goodbye, Sister," Lucinda said as she slipped out into the night.

Theodosia stared out after her, not knowing what to believe anymore. Had Richard truly deceived her this entire time?

The door slammed open with a thunderous crack, jolting her from her thoughts.

Richard stormed into the room, and his eyes raked the space until they landed on her. "You let him go?" he bellowed, the fury in his voice reverberating through the drawing room.

"I did—but if you would only give me a moment to—"

He cut her off with a bark of disbelief. "Why should I listen to anything you have to say? You told me you didn't know Mr. Smith, yet he comes knocking at the door asking for you by name!"

"Richard, please—"

"Do not speak to me so familiarly!" he roared. "You lost that right the moment you lied to me!"

The sting of his words hit their mark, but she held her ground. "And you?" she shot back, her voice trembling with righteous fury. "Are you entirely innocent in this? Did you not deceive me as well?"

His brow furrowed. "I don't know what you're talking about."

She took a purposeful step forward. "Did you bring me here under false pretenses? Did you ask me to be Olivia's companion only so you could draw out Mr. Smith?"

He didn't answer immediately, and his silence said more than words ever could.

"I don't owe you an explanation," he said stiffly.

"Then I don't owe you one either, my lord," she responded.

A sharp gasp cut through the air.

"Dear heavens," Lady Wilton exclaimed from the doorway. "What in the world is this shouting about?"

Richard turned towards his mother, his voice still seething. "Miss Theodosia is working with Mr. Smith. She's been deceiving us all along."

"That is not true!" Theodosia cried. "If you'd just stop for one moment and let me explain—"

"To tell more lies?" Richard spat. "I've heard quite enough of those from you."

Her fists clenched at her sides, her whole body rigid with frustration. "You are the most infuriating man I have ever met. I've been trying to help you!"

He looked at her incredulously. "If this is your version of help, I want no part of it."

Lady Wilton raised her hand, her tone firm but even. "Enough. This shouting serves no purpose. Both of you are clearly overwrought. Retire for the night. We can speak calmly and sensibly tomorrow."

Richard didn't back down. "How do we know Miss Theodosia won't vanish in the night as well?"

Theodosia turned to him. "I'm still here, am I not?"

"For now," he said, stepping closer until only a breath of space stood between them. "But understand this, if I don't like your answers come morning, I'll summon the constable myself and have you arrested for your part in this deception."

Her chin lifted defiantly. "And what crimes, pray tell, do you think I've committed?"

"You tell me."

With a breath that shook from the force of her fury, Theodosia brushed past him, refusing to shrink beneath his accusations. "I've had quite enough stupidity for one day. I can only hope you regain some sense by tomorrow."

"Likewise, Miss Theodosia," he called after her.

She didn't look back. Every step up the stairs felt like a strike against her pride. Her hands trembled at her sides, her heart pounded in her chest, not just from anger—but from heartbreak. How could he believe the worst of her? After everything they had shared? After the growing trust, the subtle warmth, the stolen moments?

It hurt more than she could admit, even to herself.

But she would make him understand.

And once she did... she would leave.

Leave him.

Leave all of it behind.

19

Richard sat on the edge of a narrow wooden bench, the air in the boxing club thick with sweat, sawdust. He methodically wrapped strips of linen around his hands, each pull of the cloth a futile attempt to rein in the storm churning inside him. His chest burned with anger. His mind, with betrayal. And his fists itched to make contact with something—anything—that might lessen the ache that words had left behind.

Sleep had eluded him the night before. Every time he shut his eyes, he heard her voice. Saw the look on her face. Theodosia with her careful lies and inscrutable expressions. He had suspected her from the start. Warned himself not to be taken in. And yet... some foolish, idealistic part of him had hoped he was wrong. That she wasn't what he feared.

"Why do you look like you could commit murder and enjoy it?" a familiar voice cut through the haze.

Richard didn't bother lifting his head. "Go away, Alcott."

Lord Alcott crossed his arms and grinned down at him. "Such a warm greeting. You've missed me, haven't you?"

"I didn't sleep."

"That much is obvious. Let me guess—your unrest has something to do with a certain companion with lovely green eyes and a talent for deception?"

Richard's jaw clenched. He finished the last twist of linen around his knuckles and yanked it tight. "I said, *go away*."

Unperturbed, Alcott dropped onto the bench beside him. "You forget that I've known you since we were boys. I can tell when something is bothering you."

"And I said I didn't want to talk about it."

"Well, then, let's not talk. Let's box. You look like you're moments away from putting your fist through a wall."

Richard stood and rolled his shoulders. "Fine. I would love an excuse to hit you."

Alcott chuckled as he followed him towards the chalked ring. "You forget, I survived a French bayonet to the leg. I think I can manage your so-called rage."

They stepped inside the makeshift ring, squaring off in familiar rhythm. Richard raised his fists, waiting.

Alcott gave him a wry smile. "I propose a game."

"I loathe games."

"For every strike that lands, you tell me one thing that's bothering you."

"No."

Alcott's fist shot out and landed a sharp blow on Richard's shoulder. "Consider that the opening round."

Richard swung in retaliation, but Alcott ducked with ease.

"Come now," Alcott said, circling, "what did she do to deserve this delightful mood of yours?"

"She lied," Richard growled, landing a solid punch to Alcott's jaw.

Alcott winced and rubbed the spot, though the amusement never left his eyes. "Didn't you already suspect that from the beginning? Wasn't that why you hired her under false pretenses?"

"Yes," Richard admitted. "But I was hoping I was wrong."

"And Mr. Smith? He came for her?"

Richard's next hit landed squarely on Alcott's chest. "Yes. And she helped him escape."

"But she didn't go with him?" Alcott asked, stepping back.

"No," Richard said, breathing heavier now. "She stayed."

"Why?"

"I don't know. She didn't say."

Alcott raised an eyebrow. "She didn't say, or you didn't give her the chance?"

Richard's hands dropped slightly as he bristled. "Does it matter?"

"To her? Probably."

"I didn't want to hear excuses. She made her choice—she protected him. He got away before I could challenge him to a duel."

"Which means, if what you suspect is true, he'll be back for her," Alcott said. "Sooner or later."

Richard adjusted the linen on his wrist. "Then I'll get my answers. I'll find out exactly how involved she was."

"And when you do?" Alcott asked, raising his guard again.

Richard shrugged. "I'll send her back home. And that will be the end of it."

"Will it?"

"Of course," Richard snapped. "I can't marry a woman I don't trust."

Alcott's lips twitched. "I never mentioned marriage."

Richard glared at him. "You implied it."

"I merely wondered if you finally fell in love."

Richard lunged forward with another punch, but Alcott sidestepped with ease.

"Do we have to discuss this?" Richard muttered.

Alcott's breath was steady despite the bout. "I think we just might," he said with irritating cheer. "Someone has to make sure you don't do something colossally foolish—like sending Miss Theodosia away without hearing her out."

Richard exhaled sharply, his annoyance flaring. "What choice do I have, Alcott? She deceived me."

"This may sound mad," Alcott said, circling slowly with his hands still raised, "but have you considered—just briefly—letting her tell her side of the story?"

Richard scowled. "And what would be the point? So she can perfect her lies? Add to them?"

Alcott didn't answer. Instead, he stepped forward and landed a clean, satisfying blow to Richard's jaw. Not hard enough to damage—just enough to get his attention.

Staggering back a step, Richard growled. "Botheration, Alcott!"

"Perhaps she might be innocent," Alcott said calmly, shaking out his wrist. "Or at least, not the villain you've made her out to be?"

Richard rubbed his jaw but otherwise ignored the pain. "You're daft."

"I've been called worse," Alcott replied. "But I'm not daft—I'm clever. And more to the point, you left yourself open. You never leave yourself open. Which means you're distracted and are not thinking clearly."

Richard rolled his shoulders, trying to shake off the punch and the sting of truth beneath it. "Why don't you just shut up and box like a normal man?"

"Because normal men let their pride ruin perfectly good things," Alcott said, dropping his hands to his sides and stepping in closer. "Someone has to be the voice of reason."

"I'm not wrong," Richard muttered, more to himself than to Alcott.

"Then prove it," Alcott challenged. "Get the facts first. All the facts. Let her speak. Then you can throw her out, if you must, but at least you won't be haunted by what you didn't let her say."

Richard let out a long, frustrated sigh. He hated how easily Alcott could see through him. "Why is this suddenly your crusade?"

"Because I've watched you brood over this woman," Alcott said. "You have changed since she arrived—and not for the worse. Because maybe, just maybe, she matters more than you're willing to admit."

Richard said nothing. He hated how close his friend was to the truth. He'd been so consumed by fury the night before that he hadn't even given Theodosia the dignity of a defense. In spite of everything, her eyes had haunted him, filled not with guilt—but sorrow.

Would she lie to him again? Could he trust her?

Could he risk it?

Alcott placed a hand on his shoulder. "Listen to your heart, Wilton. What is it telling you to do?"

Richard huffed a laugh, though it held no humor. "Since when did you become a hopeless romantic?"

"I haven't," Alcott said, dropping his hand. "When I marry, it'll be for practical reasons. Someone to help with Charlotte. Someone steady."

Richard raised an eyebrow. "Is Charlotte really so terrible?"

"She ignores half of what I say," Alcott responded. "And she's always scribbling in that blasted notebook of hers."

"Is that truly so awful?"

"There are worse vices, I suppose. But sometimes I feel like I'm guardian to a whirlwind."

A small line was forming beside the ring. Richard glanced over and noticed several men waiting for their turn. "I think I've had enough boxing for today."

Alcott inclined his head, following him out of the ring. "How is Lady Olivia handling all of this?"

Richard paused beside the bench and sat heavily. "She doesn't know. She'd already retired to bed when Mr. Smith arrived."

"You need to tell her," Alcott said. "Soon."

"I know," Richard murmured as he began to unravel the linen from his knuckles. "But once she learns what Theodosia's done—or what I think she's done—she'll be devastated. She trusted her."

Alcott sat down beside him. "Are you sure she did something?"

Richard shot him a look.

Alcott held up his hands. "All I'm saying is... I'm not convinced she's the villain in this story."

"She *acts* innocent," he said quietly. "Too innocent."

"Or," Alcott countered, "she *is* innocent. You just don't want to believe it because then you'd have to face what you feel for her."

Richard gave a hollow laugh. "You're infuriating, you know that?"

"Constantly," Alcott agreed cheerfully. "But I also happen to be an excellent judge of character. And something tells me Miss Theodosia deserves better than your current opinion of her."

"I would prefer," Richard said, raking a hand through his damp hair, "if we talked about something else. Anything, really."

Alcott, to his credit, didn't press. He simply nodded as he settled back on the bench. "Very well. How is your bill coming along?"

"Warwicke and I are drafting it now, but I'm not optimistic about its reception."

"That doesn't sound like you," Alcott remarked. "You're usually more stubborn than that."

"This isn't about stubbornness," Richard replied, reaching

down to untie the last strip of linen from his wrist. "It's reality. If this were my father's bill, it would pass without debate."

Alcott leaned forward, elbows on his knees. "Yes, well, your name is attached to it, not his."

"Exactly," Richard remarked. "My father had sway on both sides of the aisle. Tories and Whigs alike deferred to him. He spoke, and votes followed. I'm not afforded that same courtesy."

Alcott studied him a moment before replying, "You will have that influence. It doesn't come overnight."

Richard shook his head. "I'm not so sure. The House of Lords still sees me as my father's son, not my own man. And they're watching—waiting for me to misstep."

"They're also watching to see if you rise to the occasion," Alcott pointed out. "Which you will."

"That's wishful thinking."

Alcott's mouth tugged into a grin. "Then it's a good thing you've caught me on an unusually optimistic day."

Richard glanced at him sideways. "Remind me to ask again when you're in a foul mood. Perhaps then I'll get the truth."

Alcott chuckled. "You'll get the same truth, just with a lot more sarcasm."

With a weary sigh, Richard pushed to his feet, stretching his shoulders as though preparing for battle rather than a quiet return home. "I suppose I ought to head back," he said, his tone dry. "It's time I faced what I've been putting off... even if I dread every moment of it."

Alcott stood as well, brushing imaginary dust from his sleeves. "I don't envy you," he replied, his tone turning sincere. "But I do wish you luck. You're going to need it."

"Thank you," Richard said before turning towards the door, the weight of what awaited him pressing heavily on his shoulders.

Theodosia sat on the floor beside one of her trunks as she folded a gown with trembling fingers. Her wardrobe lay in scattered disarray, the contents of her life hastily thrown about the chamber in her attempt to leave before she lost her nerve. She couldn't stay here. Not after what had happened.

She had to leave—needed to, if she hoped to preserve even a shred of her heart. Last night, while waltzing beneath the glittering chandelier, she had realized with painful clarity that she had fallen in love with Richard. It had stolen into her awareness like a thief in the night—subtle, inevitable. However, no sooner had her heart acknowledged it than it had been shattered. Richard had dismissed her so coldly, so swiftly, never once allowing her to explain the truth about her sister. His anger had been cutting, his words sharper than any blade.

She blinked back the sting of fresh tears. She deserved better than to be so easily discarded.

A firm knock at the door jolted her from her thoughts.

"Enter," she called, not even bothering to glance up.

The door creaked open and Olivia stepped inside, halting at the threshold as her eyes fell upon the chaos in the room. "What are you doing?" she asked, her voice filled with confusion and rising alarm.

"I'm leaving," Theodosia said simply, continuing to fold a chemise and tuck it beside her boots.

"Leaving?" Olivia echoed, walking farther into the room. "Why? What's happened?"

Theodosia finally looked up. "I cannot stay under the same roof as your brother."

Olivia lowered herself slowly onto the edge of the bed, frowning. "Did something happen last night?"

Theodosia let out a long, unsteady sigh. "Yes. It did."

"Then tell me," Olivia urged. "Please. Let me help fix it."

"There's no fixing this," Theodosia said, rising to her feet. "Richard brought me to London under false pretenses. He made me believe I was needed as your companion when in reality—"

Olivia's face fell. "He told you that?"

"No," Theodosia replied. "Mr. Smith did."

Color drained from Olivia's cheeks. "You spoke with Luke?"

Theodosia nodded. "Last night. He came to... rescue me, I suppose. But there's something you must know."

Suspicion sparked in Olivia's gaze. "You do know Luke. Even though you denied it."

"I do," Theodosia admitted. "But Luke isn't who you think he is. The man you know as Mr. Smith is my sister, Lucinda."

Olivia shot to her feet, her mouth falling open. "That's... impossible. I would have known if Luke were a woman."

"I'm sorry, but it is true," she replied. "I will admit that she looked the part of a gentleman, but I would recognize my sister anywhere."

Olivia pressed a hand to her forehead as though warding off a headache. "Did you know she was pretending to be a man?"

"Heavens, no," Theodosia said. "I hardly see Lucinda, and we are not close. But I knew instantly when I saw her last night... despite the disguise."

Olivia sank back onto the bed, shaking her head. "This is madness. Am I truly that gullible? How could I not have seen it?"

Theodosia stepped closer, her voice filled with remorse. "Lucinda admitted she married you for your dowry."

"I thought you said your family had a profitable estate," Olivia said.

"We do," Theodosia replied. "But Lucinda receives only a small allowance, and I never quite understood how she managed. Now I know."

Olivia stared at her, her expression a storm of disbelief and hurt. "Are you absolutely certain?"

"I am," Theodosia responded. "I tried to tell Richard last night, but he wouldn't let me speak. He was furious that I let her escape."

"Did you?" Olivia asked, her voice strained.

"I tried to stop her," Theodosia said, emotion cracking through her words. "I begged her to stay and confess, but she panicked and climbed out the window. I never imagined my sister could be so heartless."

Olivia buried her face in her hands. "I'm ruined. Once the *ton* hears I married a woman, I'll be a laughingstock."

Theodosia placed a hand on her shoulder. "Perhaps, but at least you can have the marriage annulled. You could reclaim your dowry."

"And what if Lucinda's already spent it?" Olivia asked bitterly.

Theodosia didn't answer. She couldn't.

Olivia rose and began to pace the room. "Blast it, it all makes sense now. It was why Luke was so distant. Why he—she —never touched me. How easily she vanished without a trace."

"I swear to you," Theodosia said, "if I had known, I would have told you everything."

"I believe you," Olivia murmured, pausing in her steps. "But you still can't leave."

Theodosia offered a wan smile. "I must. Richard despises me now. He made that perfectly clear."

"Then we'll convince him otherwise. Together."

"I don't think he wants to be convinced. He's already made his judgment."

Olivia's expression hardened. "My brother is a fool."

"I'm not going to disagree," Theodosia said with a small, sad laugh. "I hope to be on the mail coach by this afternoon. It is best if I leave, and quickly."

"Best for whom?"

"Your brother thinks the worst of me. You should have heard the way he turned on me last night."

Glancing towards the open wardrobe, Olivia asked, "You're not taking your new gowns?"

Theodosia shook her head. "No. I don't want reminders of this place. Or of him."

Olivia's voice dropped. "But what if there's still hope?"

Theodosia turned away, her throat tightening so painfully it felt as though she could scarcely breathe. "There is no hope," she responded, "at least not where Richard and I are concerned."

"You care for him," Olivia said, a statement rather than a question.

Theodosia felt the sting of tears pressing against her eyes and blinked them back furiously. She would not cry now—not in front of Olivia, not when she still had so much packing left to do. Those tears, the ones that threatened to undo her, would have to wait until she was alone. Until she was far, far away.

Olivia continued. "You're giving up too soon. I know my brother. He may be stubborn and prideful, but he's not unfeeling. He cares for you."

"He threatened to send me to prison." Her voice cracked slightly, but she steadied herself. "He was ready to call the constable."

"Well... I never claimed my brother was a smart man."

That drew a faint, fleeting smile from Theodosia. "Thank you," she said. "For being my friend. I will always treasure the time I spent with you."

"You were the best companion I ever had," Olivia replied, her voice breaking.

Just then, a knock sounded at the door, and before either of them could speak, it opened to reveal Lady Wilton. Her expression was solemn, but her eyes held only compassion.

"The coach is waiting out front to take you home," she said.

Theodosia turned towards her. "That won't be necessary. I intend to take the mail coach back to my village."

"Nonsense," Lady Wilton replied, waving a dismissive hand. "We have a perfectly suitable coach already prepared. You shall take it."

Theodosia hesitated. "Will Lord Wilton object?"

A knowing smile tugged at the corners of Lady Wilton's lips. "Let me worry about my son."

Olivia threw up her hands in exasperation. "Why are we even discussing this? Dosia can't leave. She's done nothing wrong!"

"I agree," Lady Wilton said. "She told me everything this morning."

"Then why aren't you stopping her?" Olivia demanded. "Why aren't you encouraging her to stay and make things right with Richard?"

"Because," Lady Wilton said, turning to Theodosia, "it is her choice. And hers alone. We do not get to decide what she must endure."

"Thank you, my lady," Theodosia replied.

A kind smile came to Lady Wilton's lips. "If you intend to leave, you should go soon—before Richard returns from the boxing club."

Olivia groaned. "This is ridiculous! Why are you sneaking off like a thief in the night? You did nothing wrong."

Theodosia returned to her trunk, folding one of her gowns. "Perhaps not. But Mr. Pritchett was right about one thing—I don't belong in this world."

Olivia's eyes filled with pain. "You do. You belong with us. With me."

"No. I was pretending. Pretending I fit in, pretending I mattered. But last night, Richard made it abundantly clear what he truly thinks of me."

Olivia came beside her and began folding gowns with brisk efficiency. "This is a mistake, but I shall help you."

"Duly noted," Theodosia said, her voice tight.

A short while later, Theodosia descended the stairs, her blue traveling gown rustling softly as she walked behind the footmen carrying her trunks to the waiting coach. Her hair had been hastily pinned into a loose chignon and a bonnet was in her hand.

The main door opened suddenly, and Richard stepped into the entry hall, his cravat askew. His eyes fell immediately on the trunks—and then on her.

"Where do you think you are going?" he asked, his voice sharp with disbelief.

"I am going home, my lord."

"Like hell you are," he snapped, striding towards her. "You will remain here until you tell me the truth about Mr. Smith."

Olivia's voice echoed down from the top of the stairs. "Let her go, Richard. She told me everything and she is innocent."

He scoffed. "And you believe that?"

"I do," Olivia said firmly. "Once Theodosia leaves, I will explain everything to you. But you will not stop her."

Theodosia made to move past him, but Richard reached out, his hand closing gently around her arm. "I'm sorry it came to this."

She stilled, surprised by the sincerity in his tone, and turned to meet his gaze. "As am I."

He let his hand fall away but remained close, his jaw clenched. "If only you had told me the truth from the start, we could have avoided this."

"You don't understand," Theodosia began. "From the moment we met, you have been waiting for me to disappoint you. I tried to prove myself useful, to show you I wasn't some scheming woman. And still, when it mattered most, you believed the worst."

He grew silent. "Thank you for helping me with the accounts."

Despite the ache in her chest, she offered him a small, resolute smile. "I do believe you're a good man. Misguided. But not without decency."

He bowed, stiffly, formally. "Safe travels, Miss Theodosia."

She inclined her head and turned away, stepping out into the crisp morning air. The coach loomed ahead. She paused for a moment and looked back at the grand townhouse. It had once been so full of promise, but now, it was a reminder of what might have been.

With a quiet sigh, she climbed inside, ready to leave this chapter behind. Ready to return to a life that, while not extraordinary, was hers.

And if her heart felt a little heavier with each turn of the wheel, no one need ever know.

20

Richard stood at the window, arms folded tightly across his chest, as he watched the coach rattle down the drive and disappear around the bend. Theodosia was gone. He should have felt relieved—after all, she had upended his household and undermined his trust. And yet, all he felt was a hollow ache in his chest. A leaden sense of dread settled over him, and with it came the irrational, maddening urge to run after her... to stop the carriage and fall to his knees like a desperate fool.

But he remained frozen, his pride a shackle he could not seem to break.

"She lied to me," he muttered aloud, though the words sounded less like conviction and more like an excuse.

A voice snapped from behind him. "You are an idiot."

He didn't have to turn to know it was his sister. With a sigh, he pivoted slowly to face her. "So that's how this conversation is going to begin."

Olivia stood in the middle of the entry hall, her stance rigid, one hand firmly planted on her hip, her expression ablaze with fury and disappointment. "Dosia never lied to you," she said sharply. "And you treated her with contempt."

"I don't know what she told you, but—"

"She wasn't protecting Mr. Smith," Olivia cut in. "Because Mr. Smith never existed."

Richard stared at her, frowning. "What are you saying?"

"When he came for her, Dosia realized who he truly was. Her sister, Lucinda, was masquerading as a man," Olivia revealed. "Dosia was trying to explain everything to you, but you wouldn't give her a chance."

Richard barked a humorless laugh. "That's absurd. I saw Mr. Smith myself. He was clearly a man."

"Lucinda deceived us all," Olivia countered. "She was determined to keep up the charade. And it worked."

He shook his head. "Even if that were true, you don't honestly expect me to believe that Theodosia did not know of it."

"I do believe it," Olivia replied fiercely. "She begged Lucinda to confess—to stay and face the consequences. But instead, Lucinda ran. And Dosia was left to bear the blame."

Richard scoffed. "That is the most ludicrous tale I've ever heard."

"It's the truth," Olivia said, stepping towards him. "And deep down, I think you know it, too. Besides, what reason would Theodosia have to lie? What would she possibly gain from it?"

He opened his mouth to respond, but was interrupted by a sharp knock at the door. A moment later, Sterling entered and crossed to the entry, admitting a familiar figure.

"Mr. Crosby," the butler announced.

The Bow Street Runner stepped into the hall and bowed crisply. "My lord. I bring news."

Richard's voice was clipped. "Well? Speak."

"I followed Mr. Smith after he departed your home last

night. He went to a coaching inn on the edge of Town. I gained access to his room, only to discover a woman there. Upon interrogation, she confessed to impersonating Mr. Smith. You will never guess who it was."

Richard's heart sank. "Miss Lucinda Smith."

Mr. Crosby's brows lifted. "So you're aware."

"I've only just learned the truth," Richard said.

"Well," Crosby continued, "she admitted to everything. The idea came to her when she read *The Female Husband* by Henry Fielding. Furthermore, she said she acted alone and insisted that Miss Theodosia had no knowledge of her schemes."

"And you believed her?" Richard asked skeptically.

"I did," Crosby said with a decisive nod. "I've dealt with liars and criminals for over a decade, and I can usually tell when someone's hiding something. Miss Smith was adamant and she had nothing to gain by exonerating her sister."

Richard raked a hand through his hair, making it terribly disheveled. "Botheration," he muttered under his breath. How could he have been so blind?

Mr. Crosby shifted his stance. "There is some good news. Lady Olivia will be able to pursue an annulment now."

Olivia gave a small nod. "I am grateful for that."

Crosby turned to her with a bow. "My apologies, my lady. I've not had the pleasure. I am Mr. Crosby and I was hired by Lord Wilton to investigate your husband's whereabouts."

Olivia offered a composed smile. "Thank you for what you did, Mr. Crosby."

Turning back to Richard, the Bow Street Runner said, "Miss Smith will remain in Newgate until her trial. She is being charged with vagrancy. You may wish to speak to the magistrate to see if you can influence the outcome and contain the scandal."

"I shall," Richard said tightly.

Crosby bowed once more. "If there is nothing further, I'll take my leave."

Richard gave no protest. There was nothing more to say.

When the door shut behind the Bow Street Runner, silence settled once again in the hall. A silence broken only by Olivia's voice. "Now do you see the error of your ways?"

Richard's shoulders sagged. "I may have... misjudged her."

"'May have'?" Olivia repeated incredulously. "You accused her, shouted at her, and called her a liar. Yet she did nothing wrong. You didn't just misjudge her—you wronged her."

He turned back towards the window, his voice hollow. "Yes. I was wrong. Is that what you want to hear?"

"No," Olivia said. "What I want is for you to go after her. To apologize. To tell her the truth and to beg for her forgiveness."

"I don't beg."

"Then it's a good thing she left," Olivia said flatly. "Because you don't deserve her."

He turned to her. "You think it's as simple as saying I'm sorry? That I can undo everything with one conversation?"

"No," she responded. "But you can try. Because you care for her, Richard. You can pretend you don't, but I see it. Everyone sees it."

He looked away, unable to meet his sister's gaze. "I ruined everything. She gave me her trust and I destroyed it."

Olivia stepped forward and touched his sleeve. "It's never too late to make amends. There is nothing more beautiful than finding someone who wants your all. Even if your all is a mess. And trust me, you are a mess, Richard."

"It is too late."

"Perhaps, but do you not owe it to yourself to at least try?"

He let out a bitter laugh. "I can't offer for her now. My name is already teetering on the edge of ruin. I need a bride with a spotless reputation."

Olivia's brow arched. "And you think a young lady with a

spotless reputation would want you? Titles may carry weight, but so do scandals—and let us not forget, I was the one who dragged our family's name through the mud."

"I have to try to restore it," he said stubbornly.

She gave him a long, searching look. "Not if it costs you your happiness. Don't fix one mistake by making another."

"But I have to try."

"Just for a moment, set aside your duty and ask yourself one question. Who made you feel alive again? Who made you smile when you thought you couldn't?" Olivia asked.

Richard stared past her, out the window again—though the drive was empty now. "Even if I went after her, do you think she would forgive me?"

"I think," Olivia said softly, "that if you find the courage to speak from your heart... she might just let you try."

Their mother's voice came from the stairs, drawing his attention. "Olivia is right," she started, "but only you can decide if Miss Theodosia is worth fighting for."

He swallowed. "What would Father say?"

As she descended the stairs, their mother replied, "He would have told you not to let duty stand in the way of happiness. He understood what it meant to love someone so fiercely that it eclipses everything else."

Richard exhaled, his resistance faltering. "But my duty—"

His mother raised a hand and interrupted him. "Is to your heart, Richard. Do something selfish—for once. Choose love, not obligation."

His voice cracked slightly. "When I look at her... I know. I know I've found what the world spends its whole life searching for."

"Then go," his mother encouraged. "Go to her and tell her. You hide your feelings well, but I'm your mother. I see more than you think."

He looked down, guilt washing over him. "But I treated her so poorly. I accused her and humiliated her."

"Then spend the rest of your life making amends," she responded. "She's worth it."

Olivia stepped forward. "I agree with Mother. If you let her go now, I promise you'll regret it every day for the rest of your life."

Richard's eyes flicked back to the window. "Even if I wanted to go after her, there are countless roads she could have taken. By now, the coach could be halfway to Kent or turned towards the coast—"

His mother smiled, just the faintest arch of amusement at the corners of her mouth. "This is why I instructed the driver to take the exact same route you took when you collected Dosia. I thought you might come to your senses."

"That was brilliant," he remarked.

"And because I know you far too well," she added, "I also had your horse brought around to the front. You'll want to ride hard, I imagine."

He was already moving towards the door. "I won't waste this."

As he opened the door, Olivia called after him. "Tell her she made you believe in love again. Tell her you were a fool. And then, for heaven's sake, don't mess it up this time."

He paused. "What if..." he began, his voice lower now, uncertain. "What if she doesn't feel the same? What if she doesn't care for me the way I care for her?"

Olivia smirked. "You are a marquess, remember. Don't ladies fall at your feet to vie for your attention?"

"But Theodosia is different. She had never seemed to care for my title," he said. "With her, I never know quite where I stand. It is maddening."

Olivia's expression grew thoughtful. "Then let her see the man beneath the title. Not the marquess. Just you. Speak to her as a man who has fallen in love—completely, imperfectly, and honestly," she advised. "That will make all the difference."

Richard merely nodded, though his mind was already racing. Olivia's words echoed in his ears, heavy with truth and impossible to ignore. He departed from the townhouse with a purposeful stride. At the bottom of the steps, the groom stood waiting beside his horse, already saddled and restless, as though it sensed its task's urgency.

"Thank you," Richard said, grasping the reins. With practiced ease, he mounted his horse and adjusted his grip.

Then he urged the horse forward, heels pressing firmly into its sides.

As they turned onto the main road, his thoughts spun with words he might say—*I was wrong. Forgive me. I never should have doubted you. I never should have let you go.*

But nothing sounded worthy enough. Nothing could undo what he had said or how he had made her feel.

And still, he had to try.

He had given speeches in Parliament, but this... this would be the most important speech of his life.

Because this one might mean the difference between winning back the woman he loved—or losing her forever.

───────────～───────────

Theodosia sat in the coach, her hands clasped tightly in her lap, though they trembled despite her best efforts to still them. A solitary tear traced a slow, silent path down her cheek, and she made no effort to brush it away. Now that she was finally alone, she was allowing herself to cry.

This was the right choice. It had to be. She told herself that returning to her village, to the quiet rhythm of estate life, would bring her peace. It was all she had ever aspired to. A safe, orderly existence. Predictable. Respectable.

But she was no longer the same woman who had arrived in London. That woman had been content with obscurity and responsibility. This one—this broken, heartsick version—had tasted something far more dangerous.

Love.

And all because of him.

Richard.

She pressed her lips together, trying not to think of the way his eyes crinkled when he smiled, or the warmth of his hand on her waist as they'd danced. When he had looked at her—*truly* looked at her—it had felt as though she'd finally been seen. And for one impossible moment, she had believed she could belong somewhere other than where duty had placed her.

But none of that mattered now.

She was going home.

So why did it feel as though her home was no longer a place, but a person?

She let out a choked laugh at the absurdity of it. Madness. She was being utterly mad. He had insulted her, cast her aside, and sent her away without even granting her the courtesy to tell him the whole truth. She should be grateful to be rid of him. She should feel relieved.

But instead, she felt as if she were making a huge mistake for not staying and fighting for him.

A sudden shout outside startled her from her reverie. The coach jolted, slowing down. She leaned forward, frowning. What on earth—

The coach came to a halt.

Before she could draw the curtain back to peer out, the door was flung open, and there he stood—*Richard*—his hair windswept, his cravat slightly askew, and his expression far too earnest to be anything but real.

He stepped up and slid into the seat across hers without invitation, his chest rising and falling with unsteady breaths.

Theodosia blinked, stunned. "What are you doing here?"

"I came to talk to you," he said, his voice rough with emotion.

Her brow arched. "Why? I do believe we said all that needed to be said at your townhouse."

He winced. "I disagree. Since then, I've learned the truth about your sister, and I have come to offer my apology."

Her arms crossed instinctively. "Let me guess. Olivia told you to come."

His lips twisted. "No... Yes. She may have encouraged me. But that is not why I'm here." He leaned forward, his gaze imploring. "I came because I behaved shamefully, and I need you to know that I regret every moment of it. I was wrong not to listen. Wrong to doubt you. And I am sorry."

She studied him, suspicion and sadness warring within her. "You were more than just wrong. You were cruel. You never gave me the chance to explain. You chose anger over trust."

He nodded solemnly. "I won't argue. I was arrogant. Foolish. And I know I don't deserve your forgiveness. But I am asking for it all the same."

"And what of my sister?" she asked. "What is to become of her?"

"She was arrested," he admitted. "But I will speak to the magistrate on her behalf. If she cooperates with the annulment proceedings, I will ask for leniency."

"That is fair."

He hesitated. "Does that mean you accept my apology?"

Theodosia was silent for a long moment. He looked sincere. Remorseful. And she was not a woman who carried grudges. At last, she replied, "It does, my lord."

A flicker of hope lit his eyes. "The name is Richard, if you don't mind."

"I do not wish to be too familiar with you."

A smile tugged at the corners of his mouth. "I wish you would."

"I appreciate you coming all this way," she said. "But a letter would have sufficed."

"Perhaps," he said. "But a letter would not have allowed me to say what I truly need to say."

She tilted her head. "Then say it."

Richard shifted in his seat, visibly struggling. "As you are well aware, I am a marquess. But beneath that title, I am still just a man." He exhaled and dragged a hand through his hair. "This isn't coming out the way I rehearsed it."

"What is it that you intend to say?"

Running a hand again through his already disheveled hair, he replied, "I know I have no right to ask you this, but is there a part of you that sees a future with me?"

Now that was the last thing she had expected him to say. "I beg your pardon?" she asked, fearing she had misheard him. Or at least misunderstood him.

"I don't know when, but somewhere along the way, I fell in love with you," he said. "I look at you and I feel as though I've found something I didn't even know I was searching for. And it terrifies me. Because now that I've found it, I can't bear the thought of losing it."

She was quiet, stunned by the raw honesty in his words.

He reached across the space and took her gloved hand. "I know this is all so sudden, but I don't want to face life without you. I love you for the part of me that you bring out."

She swallowed. "Why me?"

"Because you don't care about what I can offer you. You care about who I am. And that... that is everything."

She looked down at their joined hands. "You realize I'm only the daughter of a baronet. I am hardly a match for a marquess."

"I know there are other women, but I don't want anyone else," he replied. "I've spent my whole life doing what was expected of me. Fulfilling duty after duty. But for once, I want something for myself. And what I want is you."

She gave him a pointed look. "But I seem to annoy you to no end."

"I was never irritated," he said. "Merely confused by how thoroughly you unsettled me."

"And your mother and sister?" she asked. "They are well aware of your intentions?"

He chuckled. "Who do you think sent me after you?"

Her heart swelled with disbelief and cautious hope. "This feels like a dream."

He leaned in, eyes never leaving hers. "If there is one thing I know for certain, it is that you have always belonged with me," he said. "Marry me, Dosia. Be my marchioness. Be mine."

She laughed softly, her lips trembling. "I would make a terrible marchioness."

"I disagree," he said. "And besides, I hope you'll take over managing the estate accounts. You'd do a far better job than I ever could."

She perked up. "Truly?"

"Truly." He moved to sit beside her on the bench, never letting go of her hand. "I know my limitations. And you, my dear, are not one of them."

Feeling as if she were about to burst with happiness, she replied, "Then I suppose I have no choice but to say yes."

His brow quirked. "Is it the accounts that convinced you?"

"No," she said, turning fully to face him. "I'm saying yes because I love you. I think I have for some time."

"Are you certain?"

"I am," she said, her voice steady. "I realized it during the waltz. I felt safe when I was in your arms and realized I never wanted you to let me go."

He lifted her hand and pressed a kiss to her knuckles. "And I think I first fell for you when you dared to dismiss me so soundly in your drawing room. No one had ever spoken to me that way. It was... exhilarating."

"You didn't appear exhilarated at the time," she teased. "In fact, you looked downright bothered."

"Promise me you'll always speak your mind," he said. "I want all of you. Your thoughts. Your opinions. Your fire."

She smiled. "I warn you, you may regret it."

He leaned closer, eyes locked with hers. "I don't know what tomorrow holds. But I know who I want to face it with." He paused. "May I kiss you now?"

She nodded, her voice caught in her throat.

And then he kissed her—gently at first, reverently, then with deep, unmistakable certainty. And as his lips moved over hers, Theodosia felt her world shift once more.

But this time, it was not falling apart.

It was falling into place.

Their moment was cut short as the coach suddenly lurched forward, the wheels groaning and the horses' hooves clattering on the road as the carriage resumed its course.

Richard broke the kiss, his breath warm and uneven against her cheek. He didn't pull away entirely but leaned in until his forehead rested gently against hers.

"I told the driver to turn the coach around if I didn't emerge straightaway," he murmured. "I wasn't entirely certain how this conversation would end."

Theodosia's lips curved with quiet amusement, her heart still pounding. "I think it went rather splendidly, all things considered."

He pulled back just enough to look at her, his eyes dancing with mischief and something far more tender. "That it did," he agreed. "But now I find I am not particularly inclined to continue talking."

"I quite agree. Words, at the moment, feel terribly tiresome."

Her reply had barely passed her lips when he captured her mouth again, this time with less hesitation and far more certainty. His hands gently framed her face, his thumb brushing the curve of her jaw as he deepened the kiss. It was a kiss that spoke of promises and passion, of things that could not be adequately expressed with mere conversation.

And as the coach rocked gently along the road, Theodosia melted into him, her fingers curling into the fabric of his coat, no longer doubting that her place—her *home*—was here, in his arms.

EPILOGUE

Eight years later...

Theodosia sat at the large desk in the study of their country estate, the morning sun casting a golden glow through the tall windows. Beside her, perched on a cushioned chair with her small feet dangling above the carpet, sat her seven-year-old daughter, Tessa. The child leaned forward with eager concentration, her brows knit as she examined the neatly folded account sheet in front of her.

Theodosia pointed to a particular line. "Can you tell me what the amount is due on that account?"

Tessa's eyes lit up as she located the figure. "Four pounds," she announced proudly.

"Four pounds," Theodosia echoed with a nod of approval, dipping her quill into the inkwell. "Very good. Now, we shall enter that into the ledger together."

She carefully wrote the amount in her tidy script, the scratching of the quill filling the momentary hush. When she had finished, Tessa clapped her hands lightly.

"This is so much fun, Mother!" she declared, her face full of delight.

Theodosia smiled at her daughter's enthusiasm. "Isn't it, though? I daresay you shall be running this estate yourself one day."

A soft chuckle from the doorway caused them both to glance up. Richard stood leaning against the doorframe, his arms folded loosely across his chest.

"I had a feeling I'd find you both in here," he said.

Theodosia grinned. "Tessa has been helping me with the household accounts. She shows considerable promise."

"I have no doubt of it," he replied as he stepped into the room. "She is, after all, your daughter. But as it happens, she is also quite late for her riding lesson."

Tessa gasped and slid off the chair. "Goodbye, Mother!" she called over her shoulder as she dashed out of the room, her dark-haired curls bouncing behind her like a ribbon unfurling.

Theodosia laughed, her hand resting over her increasing belly. "I just adore that girl."

Richard strolled over to her and raised a brow. "And what of our sons, Timothy and Michael? Are they so easily forgotten?"

"Never. I love them all with every part of my heart." Her hand caressed the gentle swell of her belly. "Just as I love this little one already."

He extended his hand towards her. "May I assist you, my lady?"

With an amused smile, she placed her hand in his and allowed him to help her to her feet, though the motion was more graceful in theory than in execution. "Thank you, my love. This little one is making every movement an adventure."

Just then, the butler appeared in the doorway, holding a polished silver tray. "A letter has arrived for you, my lady."

"Thank you, Adkins," she said, reaching for the envelope.

Her eyes brightened as she saw the familiar handwriting. "It's from Penelope."

"And what does your dear friend have to say?"

She broke the seal and read quickly, her smile softening before it faded slightly. "Penelope and her family will be arriving in a fortnight for a long overdue visit."

"That is excellent news."

"Yes, though she also writes that Lucinda has gone missing again. Apparently, matters between her and Mr. Pritchett are... strained."

Richard groaned. "I still can't believe she married that man after her brief time in prison."

"It was a practical arrangement," Theodosia replied with a sigh. "Lucinda had no desire to manage the estate on her own. And Mr. Pritchett was—well, convenient."

"If by convenient you mean dull and disagreeable, then yes," Richard muttered. "Last time she disappeared, didn't she go to Bath for the Season?"

"For three months," Theodosia confirmed. "And not a single letter during the entire stay."

He shook his head. "I doubt Mr. Pritchett minded. He likely appreciated the peace and quiet."

She gave him a look of mock reproach. "That may be true, but it is still rather sad. If you were to vanish for months on end, I should be thoroughly cross with you."

Richard stepped closer and wrapped his arms gently around her waist, careful of her rounded belly. "And why would I ever wish to leave you, even for a moment?"

"Perhaps you might seek refuge from my swollen ankles and irritable moods?"

He leaned down and kissed her lightly. "Your ankles are a delight to rub. And you forget, I find you beautiful. Always and forever."

A grin tugged at her lips. "You say that now. But wait until the final month when I resemble a waddling hippopotamus."

"A most elegant hippopotamus," he murmured with a twinkle in his eyes.

Before she could reply, Lady Wilton appeared at the threshold, looking pleasantly flustered. "I've just come from the nursery. Your boys are requesting your presence most urgently. Apparently, there's been a disagreement over a toy elephant and who shall be its rightful keeper."

Richard let out a chuckle and stepped back. "Then we must intervene at once. Come, my dear. We'll settle the great elephant dispute before your well-earned nap."

Theodosia arched a brow. "And how, pray tell, did you know I needed a nap?"

Richard offered his hand again, his smile mischievous. "Because you always need a nap. Or two. Or three."

"I make no apologies," she said with a shrug as they walked out together, her hand tucked safely in his. "Growing your children is exhausting work."

As they made their way down the corridor, Theodosia's arm rested lightly in the crook of Richard's, their pace unhurried as they strolled side by side.

"I must say," Richard remarked, "I'm rather relieved that Tessa didn't inherit my woeful grasp of numbers. I can only hope our sons are equally fortunate."

"It hardly matters to me whether they have a talent for arithmetic or not. All I wish is that we raise them to be kind, honorable gentlemen." She turned to glance up at him. "Men like their father."

He looked down at her. "You're very generous with your praise, my love."

"It's not praise if it's true."

They walked a few more steps before Richard came to a halt, drawing her to a gentle stop beside him. He turned to face her fully, his gaze warm and steady. "You know," he said, his voice lower, more thoughtful, "abducting you all those years ago may have been the only truly brilliant decision I've ever made."

A smile tugged at her lips. "And here I thought it was the beginning of your descent into madness."

He chuckled. "I'm not sure what my life would be without you. I don't care to imagine it."

"I feel the same," she murmured, her hand slipping into his.

He studied her for a long moment. "What did I ever do to deserve you?"

"Well," she teased, lifting her chin playfully, "I've always had a soft spot for brooding lords with strong jaws and far too much pride."

Laughing, Richard slid his arms around her waist, drawing her closer. "You don't just love me—you see me. You've always seen past the title, the responsibilities, the façade. With you, I've never had to pretend. You make me feel safe, Dosia. You make me feel like I matter."

Her heart gave a soft lurch at the raw honesty in his tone. "Then I am glad you finally came to your senses and offered for me."

"I would propose to you a hundred times over," he said, brushing his lips across hers. "Today, tomorrow, and every day after that."

A laugh escaped her lips. "I daresay one marriage is sufficient, don't you think?"

But Richard only shook his head, his eyes fixed on hers. "Loving you has been the most beautiful adventure of my life. You've taught me that love isn't something to fear or avoid—it's something to build a life on. You are my home. You always have been. And I will love you—fiercely and forever."

Her breath caught at the reverence in his voice. "I daresay it is you who is being generous with your praise this morning."

"And why shouldn't I be?" he asked. "You've brought more joy into my life than I ever imagined possible. I'll never stop being grateful for you."

Rising on her toes, she kissed him softly before murmuring, "Would you care to join me for my nap?"

"As tempting as that sounds, I have a stack of correspondence taller than Tessa waiting in the study. I can't very well sleep away the afternoon."

A slow, mischievous smile curved her lips. "Who said anything about sleeping?"

His brows shot upward. "Ah. I see."

"I mean, truly," she added with feigned innocence, "it isn't as though I can become more pregnant."

A slow grin broke across Richard's face, his mood suddenly bright. "Well, in that case, let us go visit the boys with all due haste."

With a determined stride, he began to lead her down the corridor, and Theodosia's laughter rang out. "I do love you, Richard."

"And I, you," he replied without looking back.

Her heart was full. No matter what trials lay ahead—no matter the storms that might one day shake their world—she knew this much to be true: their love was a constant, an anchor. It had been forged in adversity, strengthened by time, and made resilient by trust.

And with that thought, she followed after the man who had become her whole world.

The End

AUTHOR'S NOTES:

To the modern reader, the idea of a woman dressing as a man to trick another into marriage might seem unbelievable. However, this occurred more often than one might think in the past. A valid marriage in England was legally defined as being between a man and a woman. Yet, there were a surprising number of weddings where it was later discovered that the husband was, in fact, female. In some cases, the bridegroom's true sex was not discovered until after death.

One notable example is that of Mary Hamilton, who presented herself as a man named Charles and married Mary Price in 1746. Hamilton's case was documented in legal records, and she had reportedly married multiple women over the years. Henry Fielding even wrote a book titled *The Female Husband*, which was based on Hamilton's story.

NEXT BOOK IN SERIES:

When duty collides with desire, can love rewrite their fate?

Mr. Evander Addington had his life carefully mapped out—a quiet, predictable future as a Fellow at Oxford. But everything changed when his older brother unexpectedly passed away, making Evander the reluctant heir to an earldom. Suddenly thrust into the spotlight of the *ton*, Evander finds himself in a world he never wanted to be a part of. The only decision still within his control? Whom he would marry. And for that, he chooses the one woman he's always loved—Lady Olivia Kendall.

After a scandal ruined her reputation, Olivia never dreamed of marriage. Branded by Society, she had resigned herself to a quiet life as a spinster. So when Evander—her dearest friend—proposes a marriage of convenience, she is torn. The union could restore her standing, but what would it cost him? And would he come to resent the very offer that could save her?

As they embark on their new life together, the tension around them grows undeniable. Someone is determined to force Evander's hand, and Olivia may soon find herself in the scheme. With each mounting threat, a single, unexpected kiss breaks through her carefully built defenses and changes everything. Now Olivia must decide: will she risk their friendship—and her heart—for a chance at true love?

ABOUT THE AUTHOR

Laura Beers is an award-winning author. She attended Brigham Young University, earning a Bachelor of Science degree in Construction Management. She can't sing, doesn't dance and loves naps.

Laura lives in Utah with her husband, three kids and her dysfunctional dog. When not writing regency romance, she loves skiing, hiking and drinking Dr Pepper.

You can connect with Laura on Facebook, Instagram or on her site at www.authorlaurabeers.com.